Charging

Gold Hockey #10

Elise Faber

CHARGING
BY ELISE FABER
Newsletter sign-up

CHARGING
Copyright © 2020 Elise Faber
Print ISBN-13: 978-1-946140-92-0
Ebook ISBN-13: 978-1-946140-91-3
Cover Art by Jena Brignola

GOLD HOCKEY SERIES

GOLD CAST OF CHARACTERS

Heroes and Heroines:

Brit Plantain (Blocked) — first female goalie in the NHL, loves boy bands

Stefan Barie (Blocked) — captain of the Gold

Sara Jetty (Backhand) — artist and figure skater

Mike Stewart (Backhand) —defenseman for the Gold, romance guru

Blane Hart (Boarding) — center for the Gold, number 22

Mandy Shallows (Boarding) — trainer and physical therapist

Max Montgomery (Benched) — defensemen for the Gold, giant nerd

Angelica Shallows (Benched) — engineer at RoboTech, also a giant nerd

Blue Anderson (Breakaway) — top forward in the league and for the Gold

Anna Hayes (Breakaway) — Max's former nanny, no relation to Kevin Hayes

Rebecca Stravokraus (Breakout) — Gold publicist, makes killer brownies, known at PR-Rebecca

Kevin Hayes (Breakout) — forward for the Gold, no relation to Anna Hayes

Rebecca Hallbright (Checked) — nutritionist for the Gold, plethora of delicious vegan recipes, known as Nutrionist-Rebecca

Gabe Carter (Checked) — doctor, head trainer for the Gold

Calle Stevens (Coasting) — assistant coach for the Gold, former national team member

Coop Armstrong (Coasting) — talented forward on the Gold, addicted to historical romance audiobooks

Mia Caldwell (Centered) — 5th degree black belt, brings the snark

Liam Williamson (Centered) — Gold forward finding his love for the game, charming and pushy in equal measures

Charlotte Harris (Charging) — new Gold GM, hates losing and the game Chubby Bunny

Logan Walker (Charging) — defensemen for the Gold, skills include: cockiness and being able to buy presents that make Charlotte squirm

Devon Scott (Block & Tackle) — former player, current owner Prestige Media group

Becca Scott (Block & Tackle) — Devon's assistant

Additional Characters:

Bernard — head coach

Richie — equipment manager

Dan Plantain — Brit's brother

Diane Barie — Stefan's mom

Pierre Barie — Stefan's dad, owner of the Gold

Spence — former goalie, married to Monique, daughter Mirabel

Monique — married to Spence, former model

Mirabel — daughter of Spence and Monique

Mitch — Sara's boss

Allison and Sean — Blane's parents

Pascal — Devon Scott's security lead

Roger Shallows — Mandy's dad

Grant and Megan — Devon's parents

ONE

CHARLOTTE

"D amn," she muttered, sitting down at her computer and slipping off her heels.

They'd lost.

Her first year as General Manager, and she hadn't been able to get the job done.

She made a show of checking her emails, of sending a few notes to their big sponsors and to the board, thanking them for their support of the team and for a good season, but in reality, all she could think was that she'd lost.

Fuck, she hated losing.

Had hated it from the first time she'd lost the Chubby Bunny contest when she'd been a Daisy at Girl Scout camp.

She *still* hated it.

Hell, she'd picked a career whose main focus was building an organization that could win as much as possible, *that's* how much she hated losing.

What she hated even more?

Being the only female GM in the league and losing in the second round of the playoffs.

God, was it too much to ask for the Cup, just one more time? Probably.

She sighed. The Gold had won the previous season, and again two years before that. Two championships in four years was still a hell of a record.

It just . . . wasn't *her* record.

"Fuck," she muttered, shutting down her computer. She'd left the locker room long ago, after thanking the players for their hard work, letting them know she was so proud of them. It would take some time for the sting of the loss to fade, but they were a good group. They would be fine. After seeing to the team, she had stopped to see the training staff and the support team, reiterating their importance to the organization. Then she'd stayed in her office, the door open for hours, open and available for anyone who had needed a quick word.

And there had been a lot of them.

But that was her job. To keep all the moving pieces moving, to make sure no balls were dropped. To ensure that everyone felt valued and supported, even during the tough times.

Though emotionally taxing, she loved her job, even on nights like tonight.

Still, she was tired, and the revolving door of players and staff had trickled off. The arena had grown quiet, its halls empty.

Time to go.

Sighing, she shoved her feet back into her heels. Since that was basically akin to torture after wearing them all day, she was not thrilled when the knock came at the door, but she still called, "Come in," while continuing to pack her bag.

If only she'd known who was on the other side.

Unfortunately, her superpowers didn't extend to X-ray vision and seeing through walls—which meant when the man opened the door and pushed inside her office, Charlotte didn't have the chance to gird her loins.

Like she'd been doing all season.

Because—also unfortunately—she'd made the decision early

on in her tenure to bring Logan Walker to the Gold. He was ferociously talented at defense. Big and strong and fast, he'd made an excellent replacement for Stefan Barie this season.

He was also her ex.

And just being in the same room with him had her body remembering *exactly* why he'd become her ex.

Cocky smile.

Sexy body.

Flaming chemistry.

But not ready to settle down.

As one might expect, take a young Charlotte Harris, add in one cocky, sexy, scorching Logan Walker, and the result had been a broken heart.

Not just broken. Shattered.

The pieces scattered to the four corners of the earth.

In case anyone was wondering, young intern meets rookie hockey player did not make for a happy ending.

But that was fine. It was *better*. She'd gotten tougher and stronger, and she'd promised herself that she would never let anyone in that deeply again, never allow herself to be as vulnerable.

"I knew you'd be like this," he said. And fuck if that gruff voice didn't send a shiver down her spine.

She ignored him, continued packing her computer bag. He'd get to the point, or he wouldn't, and she'd keep doing what she did best. Putting her head down and charging forward.

"Always hate losing."

His voice was closer now, but she still didn't look up, even though the spicy scent of his aftershave was drifting through the air, tickling her nose, making her fingers clench on her bag.

No.

Ignoring him and his sexy body, his sexy voice, his sexy scent, she packed a bunch of shit she didn't need, all so she didn't have to look at him.

She reached for a pad of sticky notes—

Warm, calloused hands on hers.

"You don't need a sixth pad," he said, that voice curling over her shoulders, sending heat between her thighs.

She jerked away. "You don't know *what* I need," she snapped.

A sigh. A hip resting on her desk. "Why did you pick me up, Char?"

Charlotte swallowed, zipped her bag closed—*with* the sixth pad of sticky notes, thank her very much—and forced herself to meet his gaze. "You were the best man for the position. We needed solid D. You brought it."

Green eyes, such a rich emerald they almost looked black, locked on hers. "That's it?"

"That's it." She picked up her bag. "I'm tired, so I'm sure you're doubly so." She started to round the desk but stopped, knowing she needed to be professional. Not only was she the first female GM, but she'd set a standard for herself when she'd joined the organization. "You played well this season and especially during the playoffs."

A nod. "Thanks."

That confused her. Before, his cocky would have taken over. Today, he seemed . . . modest? Come to think of it, she hadn't seen a lot of cocky this season, at least not when it came to his game play. But it had been eight years since they'd been alone in a room together, she supposed things had to have changed.

Not that it mattered.

Things had changed on her front, too.

She wasn't the naïve little girl anymore.

She was strong and powerful and had a whole lot of people depending on her.

"If you'll excuse me." Charlotte pointed to the door. "We should be going."

"Your feet hurt."

Her brows drew together. "What?"

Logan nodded at her feet, clad in a lovely pair of heels that, while beautiful, were also the equivalent of bear traps—and if that wasn't the perfect metaphor for the man in front of her, she didn't know what was.

"Those heels hurt you." His head tilted to the side. "Why do you wear them?"

She scoffed. "None of your fucking business, Walker."

A smile—slow and hot and sliding like silk over her breasts, her stomach, between her legs. "I knew you'd say that."

"I—"

He held up a box she hadn't noticed, pushed it into her hands when she stepped back. "Open it," he said, voice dropping and joining that silk of his smile to dip between her legs. "If you think you can handle it."

And then he was gone, the door closing behind him, leaving her with a heavy ass bag packed with who knew what, aching feet, and a box in her hands.

A box given on a challenge.

A box he knew she'd open.

Because Charlotte Harris didn't give in or back down. She liked that even less than she liked losing.

So, she opened the lid.

And instantly knew she was in trouble.

Two

Charlotte

S lippers. The fucking man had given her slippers.

Lavender and fuzzy with embroidered stars and moons all over.

"Fucking hell," she muttered, and for one second, she was right back there. Lying in the bed of the pickup truck that had been his first purchase when he'd made it to the big leagues, her head pillowed on his shoulder, his body surrounding her, warming her more effectively than the blankets above and below them.

Dark skies all around. The crisp air of late fall and early winter.

When he'd still been interested in her.

Before she'd slept with him and he'd moved on to the next woman whom he'd cuddled close.

In those few glorious months, they'd spent so much time together.

She'd been an intern moving up the ranks, handpicked by the GM to learn the different facets of the team.

He'd been the new rookie, not knowing the guys well, a bit of an outcast on an established team where most of the other players had wives and families.

And she'd traveled with the team.

It was unusual for an intern, but her position, and the reason she'd gotten involved with the organization in the first place, made a lot of things about her first paying gig after college unusual.

But all that unusualness meant that she'd spent a lot of time with the players.

A lot of time with Logan.

With Logan sneaking down corridors and kissing in empty rooms.

With Logan slipping into her hotel room so they could order room service and watch bad TV.

With Logan in the back of his truck, staring up at the stars—

Her finger brushed one of the embroidered stars. It was made of sparkly gold thread, tucked neatly near a crescent moon, and it brought those memories that had once been so safely stowed away to the forefront of her mind.

Painful longing. Such painful longing after he'd broken things off.

Because, God, she had *loved* Logan.

She used to wish—

"No," she hissed, shoving the slippers back into the box and slamming on the lid. Char picked up her bag and slung it over her shoulder, teetering for a second before regaining her balance. It had been a long day—cough, a long *year*—so she was ready to go back to her house and not wear a suit or heels.

For at least a weekend.

Because although there would be a short break, pretty soon, the meetings would start up again. Scouts would need to be sent out, positions would need to be filled as the normal turnover from support staff and players occurred—different job offers taking her staff, contract issues changing the roster. There would be endless marketing meetings about the direction of the team, its social media and public image, practice facilities and all the issues that came from having to coordinate what the team needed in two separate spaces, planning ahead for travel, checking in with the analytics crew, making sure the team stayed on budget.

Luckily, she had plenty of people under her.

Luckily, she'd interned in most of those departments and knew some of the pitfalls.

But it was a big job.

And she enjoyed every part. Loved that she could put her degrees—bachelor's in business, master's in sports management—to good use. Loved that she'd been able to make her way from intern all the way up to GM through perseverance, hard work, and sheer dint of character.

The team might not have won, but she'd achieved something special this year.

And just like that Chubby Bunny contest, she was going to come back for a second chance, only the next time she'd win the whole damned thing.

Purse in her other hand. Jacket over her arm.

She almost left the box, but in the end, she picked it up, started walking to the door. It was as she struggled, arms thoroughly full, to turn the knob that she realized what she was doing.

Carrying the box when her hands were already full.

Letting Logan into her head.

Allowing him to make her feel things she didn't want to.

"Ugh."

Despite that, she didn't put the box down. Because she wasn't going to lose to anything, not even gravity, dammit. No fucking way. She got that freaking knob turned and the door opened and made her way down the hall on aching feet.

But the heels stayed on, and the slippers stayed in that damn box . . . at least until she saw the trash can.

Then both the box *and* the slippers went *kerplunk*.

The *thunk* as they hit the bottom of the plastic was beyond satisfying.

Char smiled, feeling better already. Then she hiked her bag

higher and turned the corner to head out to her car, her mind on a long, hot bath, on comfy pajamas, and a large glass of rum punch. Though . . . if she knew then what happened to those slippers after she'd gone, she wouldn't have been nearly as sanguine.

It wasn't until later that she understood her downfall had been born the moment she'd allowed Logan Walker into her office that night.

Logan *Fucking* Walker.

His specialty was devastating her life.

THREE

LOGAN FUCKING WALKER

He sighed as Char turned the corner after dumping his gift in the trash.

It wasn't unexpected.

But he hated the idea of her walking around in those torture contraptions, hated with a fucking passion the thought of *anything* hurting her.

Of course, that overlooked the fact that *he'd* hurt her.

"Fuck," he muttered, walking over to the trash can and retrieving the slightly battered box. Thankfully, it had been the sole thing in this receptacle, the Gold staff being scarily efficient at their jobs.

And that included the newest addition of Char.

GM.

Fuck, he'd been so excited to hear the news over the previous summer. So damned proud of her. They'd met during their lowly rookie/new intern years, and to see her climb high, to fulfill the dream she'd once talked about had filled Logan with a pride he knew he had no right to feel.

Because he'd broken any connection between them.

Not just broke but utterly decimated it. Threw it down the fucking garbage disposal and flipped the switch.

Shredded the tie connecting them in order to set her free.

But he was done letting her fly.

They weren't what they once were—untried, in an insecure position. They had long-term contracts, money in the bank, credibility in the league.

And they were part of the Gold.

Relationships ran rampant through the ranks.

Coach and player. Trainer and player. *Player* and player—though in fairness, Stefan Barie, the former captain of the team, had retired a full year before.

So, what difference did one more relationship mean?

And GM and player didn't sound so unusual amongst the mix.

It would probably be unexpected at this one. Which member of the Gold would manage to tame the seemingly untouchable Charlotte Harris? Or just as likely, when would the impervious Charlotte Harris drink the water and steal the heart of one of her players?

Hell, there was probably an ongoing bet on both of those scenarios right at this moment.

The only difference was that Logan had already touched her, had already wriggled his way into her heart.

He'd just had to break it in the process of letting her go.

What was the saying? *If you love someone, let them go?*

Well, he'd done that, and it fucking sucked. Worse was when his life had lived out the second part of the saying. The *if they don't come back, you never had them* part. Because he'd made sure Char would never come back, made sure she was firmly pointed on the trail to fulfill her own dreams.

Fun times.

Sighing, he tucked the box under his arm, forced himself to focus on the present. He wished he'd handled Char a different way, wished he'd been gentler, had coaxed her down the path she needed to be on.

But he hadn't.

And yes, he was fully aware that he sounded like an overbearing ass.

But the Char he'd fallen for eight years before wasn't the Char of today. She'd been soft, with stars in her eyes that were covered by rose-colored glasses, and . . . she would have done anything for him.

Logan had seen what happened when a woman gave up everything for the man she loved.

He'd lived it.

Going on almost thirty-five years of resentment (of course, he'd only been alive to bear witness to twenty-nine of them; his older sister was lucky enough to have been involved in thirty-four of them, his older brother just thirty-one). But as an adult, Logan understood a little better. His mom had left a promising career to move across the country, to marry a man she loved, to pop out several kids, and all that time, she'd gotten little to no appreciation.

His father certainly hadn't provided it, nor bred it into his kids.

He'd been of the dinner-on-the-table, wife's-job-is-the-housework sect, and for his mom, who'd been the regional manager of a national chain of banks, that hadn't gone over well.

Of course, it wasn't like his parents had talked about their problems.

That would have been too easy.

Instead, they'd set about making each other and everyone around them miserable.

Fun.

His childhood had been a blast.

At least he'd had hockey. As far as escapes went, that was one of the best.

He slipped out of the rink, moved across the parking lot in a quick clip, then got in and set the box in the passenger's seat as he considered his next move. Breaking up with Char had been a necessity as had been pushing her away so forcefully that she wouldn't try to get back together with him.

But years had gone by.

The present was different than the past.

And it had taken him all of one glance of eight-years-older Charlotte to know that his feelings for her were the same.

He loved her.

He didn't want to hurt her.

He didn't want to compromise her dreams.

So, he'd watched and waited. Planned and puzzled it out. Then *he* drank the Gold Kool-Aid, realized they had the skeleton of other successful relationships in the organization to model theirs after, and he'd decided that he was going to win the girl.

Well, win the *woman.*

For the second time.

Though really, who was counting?

FOUR

CHAR

Her bath was drawn.

The candles were lit.

It was after two in the morning, and she hadn't gone to bed yet.

But such was the nature of hockey, of being a GM. Games started in the evening, they went late, and there were always things to be done afterward.

When she'd originally come to the Gold, she'd made it a point to be the last one in the arena, the last one at the practice facility, but that wasn't always a realistic life strategy for her, especially on game days.

Most other days, she did end up locking down the place.

But on game days, the arena belonged to the players.

She stayed until the final buzzer rang, ran down her post-game checklist, and then got out of the way.

Micromanaging was not her style.

Char liked to have systems in place that could run efficiently without her, capable people at the helm. She'd learned this from her mentor, Luc, the GM for the Baltimore Breakers.

The man was a former player and a great manager, who'd double-dared her into an internship with that team after they'd had a debate over management styles in a coffee shop of all places.

She didn't even remember how it started.

Just that they'd both been standing in an obscenely long line, at an obscenely early hour, and he'd mouthed off about the incompetent staff.

She'd whipped around, terse rebuke on her tongue about it being a management issue, as they clearly hadn't enough baristas on that shift.

And they'd had an argument in the middle of the shop, the people in line behind them bypassing them, the line eventually disappearing altogether.

Until he'd sighed and raised his hands palm out, saying, "I know when I've been bested."

"Damn right," she'd said smugly, turning for the counter.

"But I'm right about *this*," he'd said, coming up after she'd told the barista the drink she wanted, giving his own order, and paying for both drinks before she could protest. "Come and work with me. I need someone like you to pick fights with me."

Char hadn't agreed then and there.

But she had eventually accepted the job offer.

And learned so freaking much.

She hadn't even been a sports fan before then, let alone knew the difference between a blue line and a red line or what constituted boarding. But she loved learning new things, loved handling all the moving pieces, loved jumping into dealing with a crisis. It hadn't taken long to fall for the game, to give her heart over to the passion and speed, the amazing skills of the huge players so graceful on a quarter-inch-thick piece of steel.

The game and community had been a Cupid's arrow.

Then she'd seen Logan.

And fallen in love all over again.

Stupid, stupid girl.

Well, at least she hadn't quit her internship. That had been her first instinct after Logan had been traded.

He'd ended things before jumping a plane to L.A., and the next week, minutes after she'd walked out of Luc's office, offering her resignation letter—one he'd refused to accept—she'd seen the tabloid pictures.

Logan cuddled up to an actress.

Logan hauling said actress into his lap as he'd kissed her in the middle of a club, one big hand on her waist, the other in her hair.

Char had torn up the letter then and there.

But she hadn't been able to shore up her heart.

That had been torn out of her chest, thrown onto a crowded L.A. freeway during rush hour, run over again and again and *again*. Because she'd known the feel of Logan's mouth, of his hand gripping her waist, of his fingers tangling in her hair.

She'd been acutely aware of what she had lost.

Also, she'd been acutely aware of what she had almost lost. Her career, her livelihood, her pride in her work.

All almost thrown away for a man.

And as the years went by, as she saw him appear in the tabloids over and over again, each time with a different woman on his arm, Char had let go of the kernel of hope in her heart.

The one that she'd been holding on to that said Logan had broken things off because, while she loved her job, she'd loved him more. That he'd known she would have followed him to the ends of the earth and back and didn't want her to sacrifice her life's dream for his.

She'd held on to that kernel, that hope, that desperation for him to come waltzing back to Baltimore for longer than she cared to admit, even to herself.

Then she'd finally let it go.

And she'd soared.

Three years as an intern—the final two because she'd gone back to school to get her master's in sports management. After she'd spent a year as Luc's executive assistant, she'd taken on the official role as an assistant GM. And that was what she'd done for three years, where she'd been happy and content, knowing that Luc was grooming her to take over his role.

In fact, when Pierre Barie had initially offered her the GM position at the Gold, she'd turned him down.

Her team was a known quantity, and she'd worked her ass *off* for seven years, getting to know every facet and system, building a family, working under Luc and loving every minute of the challenge.

She'd gone to her mentor and told him about the offer, thinking they'd share a laugh about Barie trying to poach her.

But Luc had encouraged her to go.

To take the job.

God, she'd been so freaking hurt at first. Thankfully, she'd gotten good at containing her emotions, listening to the facts, carefully crafting her side of the argument . . . so she'd let him say his spiel and had just waited to take a turn to convince him that *he* was the wrong one.

Except, he hadn't been.

So, off she'd gone.

To the opposite coast, to beautiful California, land of the ocean fog and unpredictable earthquakes. And the Gold.

Who had a fucking incredible system in place.

A family. A great support staff. A roster that was on point— albeit lacking a strong, established defensive leader after Stefan Barie's retirement.

Great bones but lacking a bit of hands-on managing.

Pierre Barie was Stefan's dad and had stepped in after the previous board and GM had been involved in a few too many scandals. He'd taken a distanced approach to the team, in part because Stefan was the captain and his son, and the conflict of interest was acute. But also because Pierre wasn't a hockey lifer. He had other more lucrative businesses that took up his time, and the Gold were clearly doing fine.

But Stefan's retirement meant that Pierre was reevaluating his investment.

And his time spent on something that was no longer benefitting his son.

Not that there had been favoritism, but Pierre had flat-out told her he wouldn't have bought the team if his son hadn't been playing, wouldn't have spent so much time digging the organization out of the fucking mess it had landed in if Stefan wasn't playing.

Now, he wasn't going to do anything to jeopardize Brit, Stefan's wife and the current Gold goalie, or her career—especially not when doing so would fuck up his relationship with his son.

How did Char know this?

Because he'd told her. And because she was good at her job and had investigated the shit out of the Gold before accepting Pierre's offer.

No longer dumb.

No longer letting a man make her decisions for her.

When Luc had made the argument for her to go, she'd researched and spoken to her contacts in the league. She'd looked into Pierre's other businesses, even into the tabloids that seemed to love the Gold and their plethora of happily ever afters that evolved from within the organization.

Something that was typically a no-no at best, or at least a conflict of interest, or, at its worst, a symptom of an unhealthy power dynamic between the women in the organization and the players.

Except . . . it had taken her exactly one evening of researching to realize that those men would crawl over broken glass for their women.

And that Pierre had been very careful in the writing of contracts, as well as encouraging those in relationships to document everything through HR.

Kosher.

Smart.

She'd wrinkled her nose at that, wanting the ammunition to tell Luc he'd been wrong, that the Gold job wasn't a good bet.

Instead, she'd ended up with a bigger salary offer and a house south of San Francisco.

"An empty house," she whispered, closing her laptop with a sigh.

Enough with the emails, enough with the reminiscing.

She needed to plan for next year.

She grabbed her glass, the open bottle of rum punch. So, it was nearly empty. This was a no-judgment zone. If she wanted to drink her two thousand calories, then she would damn well drink those calories. And if she wanted to have more than those calories, then she'd have more than those calories—

Char blinked, cutting off the rambling in her mind. That was a lot of calorie talk. A lot of rambling calorie talk that gave her a clue into the other reason she was blinking.

The booze.

Too much after too long of a day. Too much on a mostly empty stomach. She'd been so nervous, it had been impossible to eat.

And now she was doing her best to pickle her liver.

"Probably enough, Char," she whispered, heading for the kitchen and stowing the bottle away—after refilling her glass just once more because . . . they'd been eliminated from the playoffs, because Logan had brought her slippers, because she remembered all too much.

She pushed the fridge closed, took her glass and her tired self in the direction of the bathroom.

Her phone rang.

Two in the morning.

And her phone was buzzing on the counter.

Which meant it was either an emergency or her mother.

Char knew which without even thinking about it. She reached for her cell and answered the call. "Hi, Mom," she said.

"Hi, baby," her mom replied. "I'm sorry about the game."

She grunted. "It's fine."

Her mom laughed, way too chipper for five in the morning Baltimore time. "Definitely not fine, but you'll get them next season. Oh, your dad wants to talk to you. Let me put you on speakerphone."

There was some fumbling then her dad came on the line. "You did a fabulous job, honey. Sometimes things just don't fall into place."

They were trying to make her feel better, but she was slightly buzzed.

And had just lost the biggest game of her life.

And Logan had given her slippers.

Slippers!

"Yeah," she managed.

"You sure you're all right?" her mom asked.

"I'm fine."

Silence.

"Do you think you'll make it home to visit soon?"

"Umm . . ." she waffled. She wanted to visit, missed the time spent with her family, but part of her had felt a bit left out over the last few years. Her brother and sister were always together or hanging with her parents, and she was on the opposite coast, no longer fully party to all of the inside jokes and funny anecdotes. "I—"

"Will and Amelia want to see you. We thought we could all have a family dinner, maybe do a day trip or go somewhere for a weekend."

"I'll look at my calendar," she said. "See how soon I can free up some time."

"But the season's over," her mom protested.

"Isla," her dad warned.

And guilt. *That* punctuated the buzz. "I'll come home soon," she promised. "I just don't know exactly when. I have to wrap up some things here."

A beat. "Okay," her mom said. "We love you, honey, and are so proud of you."

"Thank you," Char whispered. "I love you, too. Can I call you back in a few days? I was just heading to bed."

Her mom's voice gentled. "Of course. Get some sleep, baby."

"Don't work too hard," her dad added.

She said goodbye and hung up, missing her family and what their relationship had been like several years ago. She wanted that closeness back but didn't know how to get there, probably because she didn't understand exactly what had changed.

Was it the move?

Her job?

Or just her? Maybe there was something wrong with her inside.

"Ugh, Char," she muttered, plunking her cell onto the counter and glancing up at the ceiling. She took a long, slow breath. "It's late. You're slightly buzzed and disappointed and a terrible loser. That's *it*."

Feeling marginally better, she reached for her phone.

The doorbell rang.

Her eyes flicked to her smartwatch, saw it was nearing three.

"What the fuck?"

She snatched her cell, shifted so she had eyes on the hall leading to the front door, and, feeling suddenly stone-cold sober, pulled up the app on her phone that controlled the cameras on the porch.

As usual, it seemed to take forever to load.

Then when it finally did, all the air left her lungs.

The bell went again, and Logan stared right into the camera, somehow seeming to be able to see her right through the technology. The night vision made his eyes seem black, but she knew those deep pools of emerald would be able to look right through flesh and bone and see the vulnerable woman she was beneath.

Walls. Good God, she needed all of them.

Needed them quickly.

Her fingers spasmed on her cell and thank fuck, but a wave of anger washed over her. "He threw you aside like garbage," she whispered. "Like you didn't mean a damned thing and then went on to spend the last eight years fucking everything in sight." A deep breath released slowly. "And he's just a player."

That was it.

Calm washed over her, and she glanced down. She was still in her suit. She'd sobered up, all signs of calorie talk gone.

And one of her players was on her porch.

She had an open-door policy, had told them they could show up at any hour, for any reason, had made sure her address was readily available.

But they rarely needed to see her here.

And Logan had, for obvious reasons, never come.

The bell went again.

He was here now, and she had to deal with this. Put the past to bed once and for all. Simple as that.

Char turned off the kitchen light, hit the switch in the hall, filling the space with a soft, yellow glow, and pocketed her cell as she strode to the front door. One quick flick had the lock open. Another had the knob turned. The last had the heavy wooden panel tugged open.

He stood there, all casual for all it was three in the morning, his legs spread loosely, his thumbs in his pockets, but his gaze arrowed to hers, froze her in place.

Her chin came up, and she spoke through the pounding of her pulse.

"What can I do for you?"

He kissed her.

One second he was two feet away, the next his mouth was on hers, his lips soft and yet demanding, his tongue sliding in to dance with hers when she gasped. It was hot and searing, but it was a reminder—of how they used to be, of *what* they used to be.

And as she was still grasping that—and the fact that she was kissing him back, that her hands were gripping his shoulders and pulling him closer when she should be pushing him away—he broke the contact, cupped her cheek for a split second, then stepped back and shoved a box into her hands.

"You forgot those," he said.

A nudge had her back into the house, teetering on wobbly legs.

This time, it wasn't from the booze.

Oh no, this time, it was all Logan Walker.

The door closed, his voice came muffled through the wood. "Lock up."

She dropped the box on the floor, slammed the bolt home, and stormed off to the kitchen.

She didn't bother with the glass, just grabbed the whole damned bottle of rum.

Logan *Fucking* Walker.

FIVE

LOGAN

He sat in his car for long minutes, watching the light show taking place inside Char's house.

Off and then on. Rinse. Repeat. And repeat some more.

First, in the front of the house. Then in the hall he'd glimpsed before Char had slammed the front door in his face. Next, upstairs in what he assumed was her bedroom. This educated guess was based on the two large windows with only a faint outline of light peeking around the edges of what he assumed were blackout shades, considering the large number of late nights and necessary sleeping in after games. Then those rectangles of light disappeared before another square, this time not just a border, but a full one, albeit slightly softened through frosted glass in what he would bet his slapshot on was her bathroom.

Because Char and her baths.

When they'd been together before, she'd taken more baths than showers, bringing a glass of rum and a book and soaking until she resembled a prune.

Bubbles clinging to deep russet skin. Strawberry and bourbon scented body wash. Hot water sluicing over his body when he gave in to the temptation of sliding in behind her. The tub would always overflow, and neither of them ever gave a damn.

Fuck, he'd done so many loads of sopping wet towels.

Grinning, he waited in his car, watching that window like a pathetic version of Romeo, sitting there when he should, without doubt, be sitting in his apartment, drowning his disappointment in losing the Cup with a beer.

Instead, he sat in the dark and plotted.

He was twenty-nine years old.

He had a five-year, multimillion-dollar contract with the Gold. A contract that had a trade approval clause, one that had been written very effectively by Devon Scott of Prestige Media Group and ensured that if he didn't approve the trade, he would be paid out his contract.

In the professional sports world, he had it all.

In the having-some-semblance-of-a-personal-life world, he had nothing.

Which sounded completely melodramatic; he knew that. Logan had his family, and he was one of the lucky ones with decent parents who lived their own lives and didn't butt into his, and a pair of siblings he got along with extremely well.

Mostly because they had all survived their parents' volatile relationship.

His mom and dad were kind and caring to the people around them, had been wonderful, supportive parents in many ways; he couldn't deny that.

But . . . they weren't great with each other.

Communication was lacking. His mom harbored understandable resentment about being the one forced to leave the job she loved, to put everything on hold for her family, her kids, all for little to no thanks and zero chance of reentry into her former business circles once the kids were old enough for her to go back to work.

Plus, it was tough to hold a consistent position when a

woman had a husband who traveled frequently, who didn't leave his office early *ever*—not for doctors' appointments or school plays or hockey practices.

He'd pick up slack on the weekends by spending all day with Logan at the rink or taking Cecily to her volleyball tournaments, but he'd missed a lot.

And as far as he knew, they'd never sat down and discussed the disparity, talked through what they both wanted and made compromises. He didn't know whose fault that was—if one or the other of them had attempted or rebuffed—but he had watched the resentment grow over the years.

Grow large enough that he knew he couldn't risk doing that to Char.

Or any other woman for that matter. Which was why he was twenty-nine and, aside from the whirlwind of him and Charlotte, had never been in a serious relationship.

Never.

He'd slept around a bit, but those days were long gone, and frankly had been long gone for years. First, he'd been so excited to have anyone of the opposite sex somewhat interested in him. Then, he'd been trying to forget Char. *Then* he'd realized there was no forgetting Char, not when she was quietly and persistently making her way through the ranks of management, making her mark on a sport that was still male dominated. Not when her rise had become less quiet, more noticeable to the press.

Along with everyone she dated.

Athletes—but not hockey players.

Two movie stars—one that had been on the A-list circuit.

A governor.

And Logan had scoured the news, her social media, the gossip sheets for any and all details of who Char had been seeing because . . . he'd been jealous as hell.

Because even though he'd blown up their relationship, felt he'd had to in order to secure both their futures, he'd never gotten over Char.

He knew he'd done the right thing.

But in many ways, missing Char was the gift that kept on giving.

That was going to change. He was done scouring the gossip columns for news of Char's love life. He was done trying to lose himself in work—and definitely done with losing himself in women who could never live up to her.

And . . . he was way fucking done with spending almost every day in the same building, the same plane, the same room as her and not being able to show her how much he cared.

The only problem was how to get back through to Char.

She was different now.

Harder. Tougher. Nearly impossible to read.

Logan had some insights because they'd once been so close, but when he'd signed with the Gold, he'd hardly recognized her. Not because she'd aged or physically changed, but because she had walls of steel and rebar four-feet thick that surrounded her.

Not cold.

Just . . . separate.

So, he'd watched and waited, plotted and planned, and . . . frankly, he had no fucking clue how to win Charlotte back. He hadn't known when he signed. He didn't know after nine months of working with her.

Hell, the only thing he *did* know was that he'd been lost.

And the only thing that made him feel found was Char.

The light in the bathroom flicked off, the one in her bedroom came back on a moment later, but it only stayed on for a few minutes. Then the house went dark and stayed dark.

In bed. She'd be asleep soon.

He'd always been jealous of that, of her ability to slip into sleep the moment her head hit the pillow. Logan was awake. Char was out.

Logan was alone.

Char was . . . alone, too.

She worked into the wee hours. She was always at the rink,

always preparing for the next game, the next battle. Meetings with different members of the organization from sun up to sun down, never missing a game or a road trip.

Beyond committed.

But just as alone as him.

Well, Logan was tired of being alone, and he was betting that Char was, too. That bet was risky, might cost him his job, his career.

But he'd seen the slice of lonely in Char's expression.

And he was going to make it disappear.

Six

Char

Stop pouting and go back to the drawing board.

She glared at her cell, and by default, the message from Luc. Sighing, she pushed out of bed and stumbled to the bathroom, eyes bleary but fingers working in tandem.

I'm not pouting. And I don't need a drawing board. I just need to tweak the one I already have.

Mint toothpaste was on her tongue when her phone buzzed again.

That's the spirit.

A beat.

So, who are you going to let go that I can pick up?

Spitting out the foam and rinsing, she glared at her cell for the second time in as many minutes.

Stop trying to piss me off.

A buzz.

Sometimes that's the only way to get through to you.

She grinned.

You're just saying that as someone who benefitted from pissing me off.

His response came a second later.

Damn right.

Char sent a rolling eyes emoji.

Also, before I let you go. I'm proud of you, kid. I know you didn't win, but you did really good.

Maybe it was Luc or Logan or talking with her parents. Maybe it was the loss or just being so close to something she'd worked so hard on but missing out at the last moment. Maybe it was just realizing that her life wasn't quite as great as she'd been pretending.

She presumably had it all. Parents who were happily married. Siblings she adored. A good friend and a great mentor in Luc. A job that fulfilled her.

And yet . . . there was a hole inside her.

One that had once been easy to ignore but now was growing, a sinkhole gaining speed as it pulled her slowly in.

Her phone vibrated again.

Accept the compliment gracefully.

She snorted.

Just like you accepted being knocked out of the first round of the playoffs gracefully?

A buzz.

Exactly.

Char chuckled and shook her head, remembering how it had taken her a solid fifteen minutes to talk him down from the edge.

Luc?

Yeah?

Thanks.

Anytime. Come home to Baltimore at some point soon so we can have a beer.

Two conversations. Two requests to head East. Even putting aside missing her family and the work she'd had to do before she left, she knew her trip would have to come sooner rather than later. Either that, or she'd be hosting her family and Luc before long.

And her house was not big enough for the Harris family *and* her former mentor, whose personality filled up all available space, Luc.

Planning on it, already.

Plan faster.

Another grin.

You're not my boss anymore.

Remind me why I allowed that to happen again?

Char giggled as she turned on the shower.

Because you love me.

That I do, kid. That I do. Talk soon.

After typing out a goodbye, she stepped into the shower and let the water sluice over her. Maybe she was imagining that hole. She could just be tired and worn out from the season, under-standably on an emotional edge.

Right?

Her eyes drifted to the slippers Logan had bought for her. Sometime in her rum-fueled buzz earlier that morning, she'd gone back for the box and brought it upstairs. Now the offending cube of cardboard sat just to the side of the sink and was taunting her.

A sliver of longing wove through her. She could open the box, open *herself* up—

Fuck.

No, she wasn't imagining it.

———

"How are you doing?" she asked Liam when he paused on the threshold of the office.

She'd gone to the arena, purposely leaving her door open in case anyone wanted to talk. Most of the consoling had happened the night before, and the back offices were mostly empty today, except for a few players trickling in and cleaning out their lockers in preparation for summer.

"Bummed," he said. "But looking forward to next season."

"I feel you," she told him. "The team is lucky to have you. That tear of points you had at the end of the series almost snagged us the win."

"Almost." He made a face.

She patted his arm. "We'll get them next season."

"That we will." A nod. "Anyway, I just wanted to stop by because Mia wanted me to let you know that she's running a self-defense clinic this weekend." He shrugged. "She does one every couple of months for free for the women who work for the Gold and I wasn't sure if you knew about it." Liam extended a flier. "The info is there if it's something you're interested in and available."

Char gripped the paper, that strange longing feeling filling her again. Pride and warmth in his voice when he spoke of Mia. Love in his eyes. Her heart squeezed. "Thanks, Liam. I'll try to make it."

He grinned. "I'm the dummy that night, so if you have some beef with me about my gameplay, now would be the time to knock me onto my ass."

"Don't get that ass injured," she teased. "I paid a pretty penny for it."

They both laughed and then spent a few more minutes discussing Liam's summer plans before his phone buzzed. He glanced at the screen. "Mia," he said. "Reminding me that I need to talk to you about the class."

"Well, that mission's accomplished."

"Exactly." He shook her hand. "Thanks again for a great season. I've enjoyed playing for you."

After that they said their goodbyes, and Char returned to her desk, carefully tucking the flyer where she'd remember to check the dates, and then she did her best to clear her decks for the moment.

A knock had her glancing up.

"Mandy," she said, "how are you doing?"

One of their most talented trainers for the Gold, Mandy was married to Blane, their veteran defenseman. She was also heavily pregnant.

"I'm great. Fat and exhausted, but great." She leaned against the doorjamb. "I wanted to invite you to my last-hurrah-before-I-push-out-a-kid dinner next week." She lifted her hands. "It's not a baby shower—I don't need gifts. I just need some adult conversation before it's all breastfeeding and dirty diapers."

"I thought Blane was on dirty diaper duty."

Mandy grinned. "I can neither confirm nor deny that statement."

"Certainly not when it would take away one of the pillars supporting your last hurrah dinner."

A wink. "Exactly."

Char's desk phone started ringing. "Thank you for the invite. I'm going home to visit my parents in Baltimore, but I'll try to make it."

"Great! Brit says I'm required to tell you that I won't cook or bake anything."

"I'll look forward to hearing that story at the party, I mean, dinner," she said as the phone kept ringing. Mandy waved her goodbye as Char snagged the receiver, disappearing down the hall, and it took Char a few seconds to realize that the longing was back. This time it was intertwined with warmth.

Liam and his invite.

Mandy and the pseudo-baby shower.

The Gold were a family, and they were doing their best to include her. They'd done it all season, she realized, offered up the invites and stopped by to visit and chat. But she hadn't recognized the gestures for what they were, not when she'd been obsessing over every aspect of the team and season.

Some GM, she was.

But even as she answered her phone, she knew this realization was less about her ability to do her job and more about her tendency to keep people at a distance.

Something to ponder.

Something to consider if she had the courage to change.

Because . . . Logan.

SEVEN

LOGAN

"Cheers, man," Blue said, tapping his glass against Logan's.

They were all sharing a pitcher of beer, Logan excluded. He'd stuck with water for the impromptu meal Blue, Coop, and Kevin had invited him to join in.

Lunch overlooking the water before Blue and Anna, his wife, took off for a much-needed vacation. The young parents were looking forward to some time together, especially as Anna had been earning her degree.

Their son, Aiden, would be staying with Max and his son, Brayden.

"I really hope Aiden sleeps for them," Blue was saying. He'd been talking about the recent transition from crib to bed and how he and Anna had failed to stick with the change a few times before. Now their three-year-old was older and more stubborn . . . and much better at opening doorknobs.

Logan grinned and sipped his water.

"Why are you hoping for sleep?" Coop asked. "Don't you want them to feel the lack of sleep pain?" Coop being a newer dad himself. His daughter was almost one and firmly entrenched in babyhood.

"I *want* them to watch him again, so I have some chance of sweeping my wife off on vacation again."

Kevin met Logan's eyes and they shared a look.

That look saying *Good Thinking.*

Coop got on the same wavelength, too, extending his fist for a bump before picking up the menu. They spent the next few minutes choosing food and ordering then talking about anything but hockey.

They'd all lived and breathed it, now they wanted to talk about family vacations and being lazy on a beach.

His cell vibrated in his pocket.

He glanced at the message and stifled a sigh.

Your mother is impossible.

Logan shoved it into his pocket, but the buzz that came a minute later was to be expected.

Your father says that I should quit my job and spend all day cooking and cleaning. Well, I did that enough while you three were growing up! No more!

Kevin scooped up a bite of pasta. "And then Rebecca—"

Logan typed out a message to each of them.

It said basically the same thing. Or a variation of it, anyway.

I'll talk to him.

I'll talk to her.

Thirty-five years and they still couldn't hash out their own arguments.

"You good?" Coop asked.

Logan shoved down the knot in his gut, focused on this time with friends. "I'm good. Family stuff."

"—then Rebecca said, 'I'll never make brownies for you again,'" Kevin finished.

They all sucked in a breath.

PR-Rebecca's brownies were legendary.

"What'd you do?" Blue asked.

"I said I'd go rake the leaves."

"At midnight?" Logan asked, having obliquely followed the conversation, about a "damn" tree Kevin had insisted on keeping when they'd moved into their new house, and the noise the deer living in the woods around them made while crunching through the leaves it dropped.

"Yup." He shrugged. "In my underwear, with a flashlight clenched in my teeth."

They all busted out laughing.

"Hey! Those brownies are the best thing I've ever had in my mouth," Kevin said. "You know you'd do the same."

"Never in doubt, man," Blue said. "Never. In. Doubt."

"How long did you rake before she took pity on you?" Coop asked, displaying the insight that made him such a great player on the ice.

"Maybe ten minutes," Kevin replied, grinning.

"Damn," Coop said. "She must really love you."

"Don't know what she sees in you," Logan teased.

"Hey!" Kevin tossed a napkin at him.

"I don't know," Blue said. "Log has a point."

They started laughing again, chuckling through the waitress dropping off their food and refilling glasses.

"Assholes," Kevin muttered, though he was laughing, too. He picked up his fork and narrowed his eyes at Logan. "You're the only single one here. What's the worst thing you've ever done that's pissed off a significant other?"

Logan froze, gut twisting again as he scrambled for an answer.

Scrambled to say anything other than he broke her heart.

EIGHT

CHAR

She was wearing those fucking slippers when the doorbell rang.

Char knew it had been stupid to put them on, but she'd crawled out of bed that morning and had seen the box. Then she . . . well, once the lid had been opened, her fingers stroking across the soft-as-silk liner, she hadn't been able to stop herself from slipping them on.

Glorious.

Like walking on clouds.

Either that or she'd spent way too much fucking time of late in heels.

Probably both.

But now she was in her rattiest pajamas, with the slippers on her feet, her hair pulled up into a haphazard bun, and in no way prepared to be answering the door.

She was a woman in an industry dominated by men.

She was a *black* woman in an industry dominated by white men.

In too many ways she was the sole representation of her

gender, her race, oftentimes both, but she'd long ago accepted that fact, accepted that she needed to always be perfect.

A hole in her black graphic tee emblazoned with "This shirt is the color of my soul"—a hole that showed off a fair amount of side boob, was nowhere near perfect.

Neither were lavender and fuzzy slippers.

And her cause was certainly not helped with the embroidered stars and moons.

The bell went off again.

She weighed her options and decided to ignore whoever was at the door, whether it was a salesman trying to sell her pest control or a player who came needing counsel. The season was over. Char could give herself one day off, for God's sake.

Plus, she reminded herself, as guilt crept in because she was the one who'd created the whole open-door policy at her house for players and staff in the first place, if it were a serious problem, they'd call her. Everyone had her number. So, if it was important, her cell would ring, and she'd deal with it.

For now, she was going to make herself breakfast—*er,* lunch.

Except . . . maybe she should check the camera?

Just to be sure.

"No, Char," she growled. "Take this day."

Nodding to herself, she pushed off the stool where she'd been checking her emails, because her inbox didn't take a day off, even if she was planning on doing so, and headed to her fridge.

The doorbell didn't ring again, so she was safe from that disruption, at least. But as she surveyed the contents of her refrigerator, Char knew another was headed her way. She'd either need to put on suitable clothing—read: not a T-shirt with a near-guaranteed nip slip—or order in. The choice took her all of two seconds.

Order in.

After closing the fridge door with her hip, she moved back to the kitchen island and her stool where she did most of her work, even though she had a perfectly nice office.

But the truth was that she never felt comfortable in that room of mahogany wood, with the big desk she'd felt obliged to fill the space with.

Maybe she'd redo it over the break.

Go with white walls. A glass-topped desk. Pale blue accents. Maybe a soft, cushy chair she could curl up in.

Yeah, that would be nice.

It would give her the same vibes as her kitchen—soothing and flowy. Though, she knew the real likelihood of her feeling comfortable in her office, even post-remodel would be unlikely. Or maybe not unlikely so much as she knew she would always be drawn to the kitchen.

Because it was the center of the house.

Where she'd sat with whatever mix of her family was around, siblings, aunts and uncles, her sassy grandmother, all talking over one another and teasing incessantly as they'd cooked dinner. What some would have called the proverbial Girl's Zone, had been thoroughly invaded, her dad crossing battle lines when he'd cooked his special chicken or pasta or red velvet cake recipe, or when Char's mom had been watching the Super Bowl but her father couldn't have cared less about the big game.

On those instances, her dad had made snacks while her mom had yelled at the TV.

But on Oscars Night?

The roles had been reversed.

Fluid lines of quote-unquote gender responsibilities. Both taking turns, and both recognizing when something was important to the other so they could support and care for each other.

Perfection.

That was her parents. They were still married after thirty-seven years and still sickeningly happy.

Char couldn't be jealous or resentful. Not when they'd given her a childhood filled with so much laughter and love, not when she had learned so much from them.

But when she'd learned so much, had so much, it was hard to

picture a relationship that wasn't *everything* they'd had, and Char had enough insight into herself to know that she couldn't ever settle for anything less than what her parents had.

And enough to know that she may never find it.

Anywho, she digressed.

This wasn't the time to think of her love life—or lack thereof lately—nor the time to remember with painful clarity that the one time in her life she'd felt some semblance of peace and happiness that mirrored her parents' own was when she'd been with Logan. This was time to regroup, recharge.

To prepare for next season.

Nodding to herself, she reached for her cell.

But as she unlocked it, opened the app to DoorDash in some lunch from *Molly's*, a flicker out of the corner of her gaze drew her focus.

She spun, and a shriek caught in the back of her throat.

Char clamped a hand to her chest, heart racing. "Motherfucker," she snapped at the man—*the man!*—who was leaning casually against the opening that led into her kitchen. "What the hell are you doing in my house?"

Logan shrugged, a tiny smile curving the edges of his mouth.

She lifted her brows. "A shrug," she said. "*That's* your response?"

"You didn't answer the door." Another fucking shrug. "The back slider was unlocked."

Patience. She was striving for it. Striving and not finding it. "There was a reason I didn't answer the door," she growled.

"Oh?" Affecting innocence. "There was?"

She stomped her foot.

Which was the complete wrong move because it drew his focus . . . to her feet.

To those fucking slippers.

Char braced herself, waited for him to comment on the fact she was wearing the gift she'd deliberately thrown in the trash two nights before. Instead, his lips curved farther as his gaze slid upward, gliding over her flannel rainbow-printed pajamas, then higher still to her T-shirt. Stopping there. Pausing to take in the saying screened on the front, and maybe it was just her, or maybe the man just never missed a detail, because she felt the hot weight of his stare settle on the hole.

The hole. The *hole.*

Lurching, she reached for a hoodie lying crumpled on the counter next to her laptop and slid it on, zipping it to her chin.

Which she lifted and paired with the order, "Get out."

The man crossed his ankles, made himself more comfortable against the wall. "What happened to your *open-door* policy?"

She resisted the urge to find another hoodie to put on, or better yet, one of her business suits. Royal blue with a crisp white shirt. No pencil skirts for her. They just made her five-foot-two frame seem even smaller. She was wide-leg trousers and fitted jackets. Starched, collared shirts with neat rows of buttons. Classic, put-together.

Not hole-riddled rainbow pajamas.

But . . . she was also a professional, and this was her job.

"What did you need, Logan?" she asked. "Is there an issue with someone on staff? A concern about your contract?" His face didn't change, except . . . she thought she detected a glimmer of pain in his emerald eyes, prompting her to ask, "Your family? Are your folks okay?"

He pushed off the wall, walked toward her. "They're fine."

"Good." She held her ground as he closed the distance between them, as he came close enough for her to smell the spicy, masculine scent. It took precisely one second for her to be back in the bed of his truck, his body pressed to hers, the cool nip of the evening air on her skin. He was so fucking handsome it took her breath away.

And he'd broken her.

A fact that was very hard to remember when he was so close, when he was brushing back a loose curl of her hair that had escaped her slipshod efforts at a bun, and when that simple touch felt incredible.

She stepped back.

Tactical retreat. A necessary retreat, because as hard as she'd made her heart, as effectively as she'd been able to keep the men she'd dated safely away from the inner sanctum of her emotions, *this* man had always been able to waltz right through those barriers.

"You asked what I needed," he said, taking a step toward her, making her retreat all but ineffective.

Char glued her feet in place, held her ground.

She would only retreat so far.

Which Logan seemed to know because his smile grew, because he took another step closer.

"What do you need?" she asked.

Closer again. Logan moved until his boots brushed against the toes of the slippers, until his scent surrounded her again, until she could feel the heat of his body wafting through the thin layers of her clothing.

Scorching emerald eyes.

A calloused palm smoothing back her hair.

The man who'd always been her weakness coming so, so close.

He lowered his hand, the back of his knuckles brushing her temple, trailing over her cheek, down her throat.

She shivered.

"You."

The word was laced with heat and made her gaze dart to his, where she felt her pulse speed for a second time in as many minutes, her heart thumping against her lungs. Need had darkened those emerald eyes, a need she recognized from their time together, a need her body felt acutely.

Her nipples went hard. Her mouth watered. Her thighs trembled.

Her pussy throbbed.

God, had she ever wanted another man as she always wanted Logan?

"No," she said, not sure if she was answering herself or telling him to back off. Not sure if she could honestly say she did want him to back off.

Either way, Logan retreated, stepping away from her, walking with loose-limbed grace over to where he'd been standing when she'd first noticed him in her kitchen and stooping to pick up two canvas tote bags.

"What are you doing?" she asked when he headed over to her fridge.

"Putting these away."

These presumably being the groceries he was stocking her refrigerator with. Milk. Eggs. Several blocks of cheese. A jar of jelly. Mayonnaise, mustard, ketchup. A bag of apples, a container of spinach, a loaf of bread. He closed the door, went back over and retrieved two more bags. Rice. Bananas. Bread. Cereal.

And more.

Charlotte finally got over her shock, started toward him.

Logan was just stashing the box of cereal in her sadly empty pantry when she reached him.

"What the fuck are you doing, Logan?" she snapped, grabbing the box from the shelf and shoving it against his chest. "I don't need groceries." He glanced down at her, and she didn't need to be a mind reader to hear his thoughts. Or frankly, the single thought that was present in his expression. *You don't need groceries?* One look at the empty fridge, the scarce pantry would disabuse that notion.

But what she'd really meant was that she didn't need groceries from him.

She didn't need anything from this man.

Logan put the box of cereal on the shelf, well, on a higher shelf, one she wouldn't be able to reach without a stool, and Char knew the move was deliberate, same as his stacking several cans of soup and other nonperishables on that same shelf. Presumably out of reach, but she'd been short her whole damned life. She had plenty of stools.

In fact, she reached for the one propped in the corner of the pantry.

She'd shove those cans of soup so far up his—

"I'm trying to feed you," he said, snagging the stool from her grip and shoving it into the opposite corner.

She'd have to go through him in order to reach it. Ugh. Fine. She had another stool in the hall closet. She'd go grab that and—

"Don't be difficult."

Char's feet skidded to a stop and she halted mid-turn to rotate and face him, fury erupting through her. "Difficult?" she asked, almost tripping over the word she was so fucking pissed. "*Difficult?*"

He didn't know *anything* about difficult—or rather, anything about how difficult *she* could be.

She'd honed those skills over the years.

She could show him precisely how *difficult* she could be.

She *would* show him—

He bent—a long way down since he was a foot taller than her, and a foot was a long fucking way when she was just wearing slippers instead of spiked heels. He was going to kiss her. *Fuck*, she wanted him to, wanted his lips on hers, his tongue in her mouth, his large hands stroking and cupping and pulling her flush against all of his hard.

Her lips parted.

Her body drifted forward.

He scooped her up and carried her from the pantry.

"What are you doing?"

Logan set her on the counter. Not the one with her laptop, but instead the one that was adjacent to the stove. He placed a hand on her belly when she would have hopped down. "Stay."

"Stay?" she asked, incredulous. "*Stay?*"

His lips curved. "You repeat yourself around me a lot."

"Maybe that's because you *don't listen*," she gritted out.

"Nope." He kept his hand on her belly, the heat drifting through her skin, sinking down, warming her from the inside out. "That's not it."

"That's not—"

Now, he kissed her.

One brief touch of his mouth to hers.

She lifted her hands, every thought in her brain encouraging her to shove him away. Instead, her limbs seemed to take on a mind of their own, her arms wrapping around his shoulders, her legs around his waist.

And she kissed him back.

He groaned against her lips, the rough, masculine sound vibrating through her, tightening her nipples, making her pussy clench with longing.

God, it had been so good between them.

The best.

He rested a hand on her arm, wrapped his fingers around her wrist, tried to tug her off him. But she didn't want to let go of Logan, not when he was kissing her, not when desire was pooling in her center, need coiling through her body.

She wanted more kissing. More touching.

It was her day off. She could—

He set her away from him, chest rising and falling rapidly. "You," he growled, "are dangerous."

Char's lips parted, a protest on the tip of her tongue.

Logan kissed her again, swallowing that protest as effectively as Brit swallowed up the puck in the goal crease. Brit. *Brit.* Hockey. The Gold. Her job. The fact the man who was kissing her within an inch of her life worked for her.

Oh, God.

Oh, God.

She shoved at his chest. Not lightly, but rather desperately. Desperate with a tinge of panic.

Hell, who was she kidding?

It was *all* panic.

She couldn't do this. She. Couldn't. Do. This.

Logan pulled back, crouching a little to meet her eyes, but for as strong as Char considered herself, for all that she had giant brass balls when it came to work, she couldn't find the strength in this instant to force her gaze to his.

He saw too much.

He meant too much.

She didn't want that to be the case, but she also wasn't a liar. Not to the world, not to the people who worked for her, and certainly not to herself.

"Don't panic," he said.

"I'm not." Her throat had to work hard to swallow said panic she wasn't having.

He grinned, cupped her cheek. "Welcome back."

Narrowing her eyes, she pointed to the door. "Don't let it hit you on the ass on your way out."

The bastard kept grinning, even as he stepped back.

But not toward the door.

Or at least not toward the door she wanted him to exit through. Instead, he moved around her and opened the fridge, grabbing the eggs and one of the blocks of cheese.

"What are you doing?"

He carried the supplies to the counter, pulled out a pan from the drawer beneath her stove. "Making you breakfast."

It was said so matter-of-factly that it took her a minute to process.

"What?"

He opened cabinets until he apparently found what he wanted, pausing to pull out a medium-sized bowl. Then he began opening more drawers, stopping when he'd located a cheese grater. "Breakfast," he said with a smirk. "That's the meal you usually consume in the morning."

"It's not the morning."

Realizing she was still sitting on the counter, she went to jump down.

Logan appeared in front of her before she barely shifted more than an inch, his palm on her tummy again, the heat making her pulse pound.

He could pound something else—

Get. A. Grip.

"Stay," he said, for the second time.

And for the umpteenth time since he'd appeared in her kitchen, Char got her hackles up.

"Stay. *Stay?*"

"On repeat, Starlight," he said, pressing a kiss to her temple after freezing her in place with the old nickname. His lips moved to the spot behind her ear, touching the sensitive skin there, sending a shiver down her spine. "Don't you know I love how those chocolate eyes look when they're sparking with fire?"

She'd begun to melt, to lean into him.

Then his words processed.

"You have some fucking nerve."

A cocky grin. "Newsflash, baby, I also like it when you yell at me."

Sighing, she shoved at his chest. He backed up all of six inches, so when she slipped off the counter, the front of her brushed the front of him. Her braless, pantyless front, rubbed all along his hard, *hard* front.

She'd had a plan or at least a purpose for getting off the counter.

But hell if she could remember it.

Not when her nipples were acting extra perky from the sensation of rubbing against his yummy chest. Not when he was so close, so big, so strong, so . . . fucking tempting.

Tempting.

He'd been tempting before. So fucking tempting just before he shattered her heart. So tempting before she'd nearly given up everything for him.

Enough.

Just enough.

"Leave," she said, no hint of soft, of heat in her tone now. She slipped between the counter and his body, ignoring the way her body reacted to his this time, ignoring that draw as she strode out of the kitchen.

Ice in her tone.

In her veins.

Desire muted by reality.

This man had broken her. She wasn't going to let that happen again.

"You'd better be gone by the time I come back down."

She hurried up the stairs.

Not a retreat.

It was, quite simply, the only survival mechanism she had at her disposal.

NINE

LOGAN

He was creeping on Char through her windows again, only this time he'd upped the ante by remaining in her back yard.

He'd just plated the omelet, had been intending on washing the pan, but then he'd heard her footsteps at the top of the stairs, so he'd only been able to fill it with water then scoot out the back door.

He'd pushed her enough today.

Now, he needed to feed the beast.

Grinning to himself, he kept his gaze on the kitchen, on the plate with the steaming hot omelet. She'd come down and see it, smell the deliciousness of that cheese, her mouth watering.

Or maybe that was just him.

Because he was starving.

"Focus," he muttered, waiting for her to appear. He had a plan. Fill her belly, keep her thinking of him—

"You're fucking unbelievable, you know that?"

Logan jumped like a cat that had seen a cucumber.

That was, multiple feet and scrabbling through the air.

And thanks to Max and his copious amount of YouTube scrolling for bringing that particular viral video to his attention.

But that wasn't the point.

The important part of the situation was that Charlotte was standing in the open door, her arms crossed, smirk teasing up the edges of that luscious mouth.

Fuck, she was beautiful.

"Not so funny when you're on the receiving end, is it?"

He snorted. "You know you can't say shit like that around me, Starlight."

Her brows drew together. "What—" She halted her question after the one word, shaking her head and sighing. "*Really?*"

Logan shrugged. "You've been around plenty of locker rooms. What do you think?"

Brown eyes on his, holding him in place.

Then she sighed again, turned back for the door.

She disappeared inside.

He should go. Really, she'd told him to leave. He'd pushed. He'd kissed and touched and gotten under her skin. If his whole end goal was to win the girl—excuse him, the *woman*, because Char would like him calling her a girl about as much as she had liked him telling her to stay—then he should leave her to her day off.

Slow and steady.

Rebuild her trust in him.

She popped her head out of the opening. "Are you coming or what?"

Coming how exactly? he thought before he firmly shook his head. Not the point. "Coming where?" he asked out loud, and that was also not the point, especially when the talk of coming how and where had him thinking of *what* he wanted to be doing when he came.

Namely, Char.

"Inside," she said.

That had him blinking. "You told me to go."

She smiled—the huge, wide grin that was tinged with mischief and was one of the main reasons the press loved to photograph her. Charlotte was gorgeous any time of the day or night, beautiful inside and out, but when she smiled, Logan swore the Earth stopped revolving around the sun.

Instead, it spun around this woman.

"Did you *see* the size of that omelet you left on my plate?"

He walked toward her. "It's a perfectly respectable-sized omelet."

"For a behemoth such as yourself," she said, still smiling, though it was softer now. "Come inside, Log. Let's figure this out. We need to work together, not be at odds."

He followed her in, ignoring the whole *come inside* thing.

"We have been working together, Starlight," he said, closing and locking the door behind him. "That's not exactly at odds."

"It hasn't exactly been comfortable," she pointed out.

No, it hadn't.

Because he'd been longing for this woman, dreaming about her, wishing things had turned out differently, even while knowing he still wouldn't have changed how he'd ended their relationship. He'd known what he would be missing back then, just as he knew now.

"I want us to be able to be friends."

Logan stopped.

The urge to bust out laughing was strong, so strong, in fact, that his mirth nearly burst free.

Thankfully, he managed to pause, to breathe.

Because friends.

Friends hung out together. Friends ate and hugged and touched and spent time at each other's places. Friends was slow and steady. Friends gave him a chance to convince this woman to trust him.

"Yeah?" he asked, studying her closely now.

She crossed her arms, lifted her chin. "Yes. Friends."

He hesitated. Because he knew that while friends gave him

an in, it also gave Char an out. She could use it to keep her distance more easily. Friends may spend time together, but they also didn't kiss, didn't hold or caress one another like he wanted to touch this woman who held his heart in the palm of her hand.

She gave him a look he recognized.

One that told him he could accept her offer, or . . . that he could go fuck himself.

Since he'd prefer to fuck *her*, Logan said the only thing he could. "I'd love to be friends with you, Starlight."

Her brows drew together. "No kissing?"

He considered that. "Does on the cheek count?"

She sighed. "Logan."

Lifting his hands in surrender, he said, "No kissing." And so, maybe he'd crossed his toes inside his boots before he headed over to the plate he'd made for her.

"Promise?"

"Mmm-hmm," he said, opening the drawer to pull out a second fork.

"Logan," she said on another sigh.

More toe-crossing. "I promise." He brought the plate over, closing her laptop and shoving it to the side before setting a fork on either side of it.

"You're a fucking liar," she grumbled, sitting on the stool and picking up a utensil.

"How do you figure?" he asked innocently.

"Because I know you and your tricks," she said, nodding at the empty stool. "Your little toes are probably crossed right in those boots of yours."

"What about yours?" he asked, not admitting to anything. "How are they feeling in your slippers?"

Her breath caught.

He took the opportunity to scoop up a bite of omelet and offer it to her.

She allowed her mouth to open, for him to slide the fork

inside. She closed her lips around the tines, chewed and swallowed.

Then moaned.

And he was back to thinking about coming.

"This is delicious," she said.

He scooped up another bite, brought it to her mouth. "Good," he said, feeding her again. "Because it's the single thing I know how to cook."

She was mid-chew, her eyes having slid closed, but at his admission, they flew open. "Logan," she said. "Please, tell me you're joking. You cannot almost be thirty and the only thing you know how to cook is an omelet."

He shrugged. "It's food."

Char paused then shook her head. "That's it?" she asked. "*It's food* is the only explanation you're going to give me?"

"I'm really good at ordering salads on Doo-Dash?" he said, and yes, it was more of a question than a statement.

She huffed out a breath.

"Will you teach me?"

Brown eyes warmed as they held his gaze. "You want *me* to teach *you*?" She chuckled. "I think you'd be better off watching a cooking show. My parents didn't pass many of their foodie skills to me, no matter how hard I try." A shrug tinged with self-consciousness. "And much to their chagrin."

He fed her another bite. "I seem to remember some very delicious cookies," he said.

Maybe it wasn't wise to remind her of the past, of their time together, not when it had ended so explosively. But . . . he wanted her to remember the good times, wanted to build them up, to peel away the veneer that buried them.

She studied him closely.

"I seem to remember that I baked three batches in order to get a dozen decent cookies."

He couldn't hold back his grin. "You did?"

"I did." Char made a face. "I don't even quite know how I

managed to get twelve good ones. My apartment smelled like charred sugar for weeks."

"That's why you stayed over?" he teased. "To get away from the smell?"

Her lips twitched. "I traded burnt cookies for hockey funk. I don't know which was worse."

Another bite. "I'll have you know that I haven't had hockey funk in years."

"How many years?" she asked after she'd finished chewing. "One? Two? Because I've smelled that locker room after games, and let me tell you, it's certainly not peaches and cream."

He had a sudden image of a ripe peach, juice dripping down its skin, sliding over lush curves. He wanted to taste the sweetness, to lick and kiss until the stickiness was gone, until it was just his tongue tracing every inch of her, until he was just tasting the woman beneath. Just Charlotte.

The image and its subsequent longing was why it took him too long to reply.

"I figured you'd be immune to it by now."

She shuddered. "I don't think anyone can ever get immune to hockey funk." A chuckle. "That sounds like a bad genre of music."

He laughed and she joined in, but after a few minutes they both stopped, a sudden seriousness entering their conversation. "Fuck, Char," he whispered. "I didn't want to hurt you. I—"

"I know," she said. "We were too young. We needed the distance so we could both grow." A nod, her expression turning rueful. "I-I just wanted to impress you so badly, and I loved you so fucking much."

I loved you.

Past tense.

That shouldn't hurt. That was the bed he'd made up, the same one he'd rested in for over eight years.

But it still did.

But . . . this wasn't just about him and his decisions, his regrets, his love for this woman that had never *ever* waned.

This was about Char and the pain he'd caused. He set down the fork, reached over and covered her hand with his. "You did impress me, Starlight. Probably more than you can ever know."

Her eyes skittered away, and she picked up her own fork, scooped up a bite, and fed herself, all while not looking at him.

"I didn't want to break up with you," he said.

She sniffed, spine going ramrod straight. "It's okay, Logan, you don't have to feed me a line of bullshit. We were both in our early twenties—an intern and a rookie—it was always a recipe for disaster."

"No."

"And if Luc had found out?" she asked, naming the GM that had taken her under his wing, the one who he'd gone to for a trade when it became clear that for as strong and smart as Char was, she would have given up everything for him. "We would have been in serious deep shit," she said and scooped up a bite. "It was just as well you were the smart one and ended us before things got bad."

Logan could deal with a lot of things.

Eight years apart from the woman he loved, watching her love other people, live her life and fulfill her dream, unable to be at her side.

Having her hate him because he'd broken her heart.

Ending a relationship that had meant more to him than his own career.

Those were all things he'd knowingly shouldered, things he'd been able to cope with.

Because Char had been happy and working for her dream.

Maybe not right at first. They'd both been wounded deeply.

But she'd gotten over him. Moved on.

Because Logan had drawn the line at watching her love for him die a slow, incremental death, seeing it rot by inches, until nothing was left, not even fond memories.

"I don't know how smart it was," he told her, picking up his fork again since it seemed as though she'd taken up the task of feeding herself, "but I'm so proud of you." Her eyes flew to his, and he couldn't resist brushing his fingers over the shell of her ear, along her jaw, down her throat. Her skin like silk. "You've done so much, Starlight," he said. "Accomplished all you hoped. So yeah, proud doesn't even begin to describe it, not when it's been a privilege to watch you thrive."

"Logan."

He shoved a bite into his mouth before he admitted to the privilege of loving her.

"Can't you see that you've done great things, too?"

He snorted. "I won the Cup with L.A., and yeah, that was incredible. I shot some commercials, secured some endorsements." A shrug. "But none of that is extraordinary. You, baby. You broke barriers. You dreamed big dreams and managed to hold on tight to them."

She nibbled the corner of her mouth. "I don't feel like I did much. I mean, I'm proud of myself, of course, but I only did what lots of other people have done. Keep my head down and work hard, and I had several lucky breaks."

"Maybe," he said. "But Luc saw your value, and you chose to leap. And you didn't squander your chance." Brown eyes met his and though they were still warm, Logan detected a trace of discomfort in their depths. "I'm guessing this is where you tell me that you've had enough talking about you and your greatness?"

She snorted. "I'm confident that you've fawned over me long enough."

He waggled his brows. "So, is this where you fawn over *me?*"

Another snort. "I think you've had far too many people fawn over you." She nudged the plate toward him. "Finish it off, behemoth. I've had my fill."

Since she'd eaten more than half of the omelet and he'd barely had a few bites, Logan took Char at her word, though not before admitting, "My family is good at making sure I don't take all the fawning seriously."

Her expression gentled. "How is your family?"

"Great. Cecily is married now."

"No!"

"Yeah." He grinned. "And much to my parents' disappointment, she has no plans of settling down further. She and her new husband sacrificed a wedding and an expensive honeymoon in favor of an elopement in Vegas and six months of backpacking around the world."

"That sounds like Cecily."

His sister was an adventurer, a woman who always kept the world on its toes, so it certainly wasn't a surprise that she'd forgone the white dress and big shindig, even though his mother had been desperate for a chance to throw a big party.

"We all flew out and watched her take her vows in front of Elvis."

Char grinned. "When in Vegas."

"Exactly," he said. "And then my new brother-in-law plied my mom with many a strawberry daiquiri and an all-expense-paid trip to Neiman Marcus to soothe her disappointment."

"Smart," Char said. "What did she get?"

Logan scooped up some omelet. "I think the better question might be, what *didn't* she get?"

Charlotte laughed.

The sound was the warm breeze on a summer day, the gentle swoosh of a lake's waves in the evening twilight, a thick coat when the cold was seeping through his clothing. It was beautiful and comforting and meant so much.

But what meant more was Char squeezing his hand, sharing in his happiness over his sister and mother.

What meant more was her letting him in—even just as friends, even just the smallest bit.

What meant *everything* was the absence of hatred in her eyes.

Ten

CHAR

Logan had taken her booting him from her house with good humor.

And he didn't even reappear at her back door or teleport himself into her kitchen.

But though he'd gone, she couldn't deny that his presence was still heavy in the air. His spicy scent, the two forks in the sink—dishes that were only there because she'd had to argue with him about doing them in the first place.

Sighing, she finished drying the pan, stuck it back in the drawer, and then set about loading the dishwasher with everything else.

What the fuck was she doing?

Her eyes went to the plate she was stowing in the bottom rack of the dishwasher. She wasn't a moron, didn't take shit from anyone, least of all herself.

The *what the fuck* didn't have a thing to do with dishes.

It was directed to herself, to her interactions with the man who'd broken her, the man she'd just invited into her house for breakfast.

"Idiot," she hissed.

And yet, she couldn't deny that she felt more settled right then, after sharing a meal and some conversation with Logan than she had in years. In . . . eight years.

"Why Logan?" she asked, closing the dishwasher and avoiding the temptation of her laptop. She was going to take the day off, dammit. She could deal with whatever crises were hurtling toward her tomorrow.

The trouble was that Char didn't have a ton of hobbies.

She lived and breathed work.

She took baths and drank rum to unwind.

And returned emails and looked at stat sheets and negotiated contracts. That was her happy place, and one she'd gladly spent the majority of her time in. But the season was over. The team had lost—fucking hell—but there wouldn't be much left for her to do until draft day came around.

There might even be weeks and weeks without much for her to do.

The thought made her shudder.

It also made her reach for her bottle of rum.

So, she'd just had breakfast. It was nearly two in the afternoon, and she was *taking the day off*. Pouring a fingerful, she stowed the bottle away then carried her glass out into her small back yard.

She lived in one of those typical California suburbs, large houses on small lots, all cloistered together, all with tiny slivers of a back yard.

Char wasn't much for nature, didn't like to go hiking or stick her toes in the sand—though there was plenty of both of those things within driving distance. She much preferred her bubble baths, her books, and bingeing on shows and movies.

Or cuddling in the back of a pickup truck with plenty of blankets and a sexy hockey player to keep her warm.

So, the small yard didn't bother her.

Especially when she didn't have too many plants in it to worry about killing.

She'd hired a gardener soon after moving in, along with a landscaper to redesign the yard to be drought tolerant, but cozy. The effect was a green and colorful space filled with native trees and bushes, with very few flowers. An umbrella shaded the deck. A lounger with a bright floral cushion was positioned beneath it to get just the right amount of afternoon sun, and she crossed over to that chair and set her drink on the table.

It only took a few more steps to retrieve a blanket from the storage box, and while she considered returning inside for her E-reader, Char ultimately decided she was too lazy.

She wanted to sit and drink and enjoy the sunshine.

Soon it would be summer, and the fog would cling to the hillside, the sun only peeking out on days that were uncomfortably hot.

She much preferred the cool late spring days.

Yet, none of this thinking about weather or loving her back yard got her any closer to the reason why she'd invited Logan into her house.

For all intents and purposes, she should hate him.

But . . . she couldn't.

Then she'd stopped at the top of the stairs, had seen him hurry for the back door, smelled that he'd cooked something delicious for her, and part of the ice around her heart had simply melted. And that ice had melted more when she descended a few more steps and had seen him looking through the back windows, longing on his face.

Longing that resonated deeply.

Loneliness she could never get rid of.

A well of emptiness that had been inside her from the moment Logan had left her.

Fucking hell.

She lifted the glass to her lips, took a long swallow. "You're getting soft, Harris," she muttered. "You live for the business, for the team. Nothing more."

And . . . she still couldn't lie to herself.

The bottom line was that Char wasn't as content as she liked to pretend. Something was missing, and she had the sneaking suspicion that the something missing was a some*one* missing.

"Damn," she muttered, shaking her head at herself. "You're a mess, girlfriend."

Yeah, she was.

But she also wasn't going to let it ruin her afternoon.

So, instead of moping, she shoved the heavy feelings away, stopped the arguing and recriminations, and just *sat* in the sunshine, watching the clouds float by. A moment of still and quiet when her life had been the opposite of late.

She wasn't about to upend her life for a man.

Not even one as tempting as Logan.

ELEVEN

LOGAN

He'd left Char's house determined and with a glimmer of hope that he could salvage things between them.

And he'd driven over the brown hills, through the twisting road, all the way to the ocean. Not the warm water of the Caribbean or Florida, nor the white sand beaches. This one was filled with substrate of an ordinary brown and had a severe drop-off halfway down.

But beyond that drop-off was a gorgeous stretch of flat beach.

He could drop to the sun-warmed ground, sink his toes and fingers into the shifting sand, and just be.

The crash of the waves.

The blue sky punctuated with curls of fog.

The . . . ringing of his cell phone.

He silenced it, collapsed back onto the sand and stared up at the sky. For all of two seconds. Because then his phone began to ring again.

With a sigh, he extracted it from his pocket.

One glance at the screen had him sighing again.

"Hi, Mom," he said, after swiping a finger to answer the call and putting his cell up to his ear.

"Hi, honey," she said. "I'm sorry about the game."

"Thanks, Mom," he told her. "There will be more games."

"Still sucks."

She chuckled and he grinned.

"You trying to revamp my high school years?" Logan had complained to her about losing too many times to remember, and her response had always been *there will be more games*. His response had always been *still sucks*.

"I've decided to reverse the rules," she said.

"Oh how the tables have turned."

"Exactly." A beat. "I'm sorry we didn't make it out for the game."

"It's fine, Mom," he said. "Things happen."

"No," she said. "Your *father* happened. He didn't like that you paid for the tickets and wouldn't use them, and then there were no flights and—" She broke off. "I'm sorry," she murmured. "I shouldn't complain about him. He's your father. I just . . . God, sometimes he drives me . . ."

Logan closed his eyes and waited until she got it out of her system.

This was a fine skill he'd honed over many years—the whole waiting-until-one-of-his-parents-had-finished-complaining-about-the-other ability. He'd perfected the proper moment to hmm and ha, the right time to chime in with a sympathetic noise.

Finally, she wound down, and he said, "I'll be home in a few weeks. We'll spend a lot of time together, get our fill."

"I love you, baby," she said. "I'm looking forward to that. Did you have your flight scheduled yet?"

"I love you, too." He sat up. "And I haven't booked it yet. I have a few things to wrap up here first. But I'll let you know the dates soon."

"Okay, because you know I'm working at the skilled nursing home now."

"I know," he said. "If my visit conflicts with your job, that's on me. Your clients count on you, and you know I would never hold you working against you."

Right sentiment.

Wrong thing to say.

Case in point—

"Your father feels differently," she grumbled. "He got so mad when I wasn't home to cook dinner. But did it ever occur to him that *he* could cook dinner?"

No. Logan could confidently say that it wouldn't have occurred to his father.

"You know you could talk to him—"

"Talk!" she cried. "He won't listen—shoot, honey. I'm sorry, I'm doing it again. I won't complain about your father anymore. I—"

"Oh, hey, you know what? My other line is ringing," he said. "I need to get that. I'll call you soon, okay?"

"Okay, honey. Love you. Bye!"

She hung up, and Logan, his other line *not* ringing, but also an effective skill he'd honed in order to get his mom off the phone, collapsed back into the sand again and sighed.

Talking.

God, he wished his parents would do more of it with each other than with him.

His phone buzzed, and he knew without looking who it would be.

"Hi, Dad," he said, after answering the call.

"Your mother—"

Logan sank back down onto the sand, stifling a sigh, and waiting for a moment where he could get a word in edgewise so he could get off the phone.

But that moment was long in coming.

Eventually, however, he managed to end the call, to sit back and try to unknot his twisted gut. He would never tell his mom this, but part of him had been relieved when she'd told him they wouldn't be able to make it out to the final game. He hadn't needed to wade through the bitter comments and underlying passive aggressiveness.

His phone vibrated, and he would be lying if he said he didn't glance at the screen through half-closed lids.

Relief poured through him.

It was a text. Just a simple text from his sister.

I just got the one-two punch of voicemails from our parents complaining about each other. You okay?

He made a face.

Just peachy.

A buzz.

Sure, you are. Ignore the calls. Your life would be infinitely better.

He was starting to understand his sister's point of view in this aspect.

I'm thinking you're right.

Her response came through a minute later.

Of course, I am. Sorry about the game.

It's fine, Cec. How's backpacking?

Another vibration.

Nice deflecting. But I am sorry you lost. Also, Austria is

*beautiful, Spain is amazing, and I wish I could travel for
the rest of my life.*

Logan's heart squeezed.

I'm glad you're happy.

Me, too. But, Log, what about you being happy?

This was a text conversation. She shouldn't be able to be so
insightful with just letters and cell phone screens.

*I love you, sis. Now go back to your regularly scheduled
program of honeymooning and having the time of your life.*

He could picture her sighing, but her message didn't push—
or not much anyway.

Love you, too, little bro. Also, you deserve to find your happy.

Yeah, he was working on that.

For now, that happy was listening to the waves and feeling the
sun on his skin.

Later, he hoped it would be because Char had found it in her
heart to give him another chance.

TWELVE

CHAR

The sun had just begun its descent, the temperature began to drop, and she'd finished her glass, was pondering either a refill or an early bath and an evening spent in bed with her book, when she heard the ringing peels of her doorbell. "Good grief," she muttered, not moving but keeping her eyes trained on the side of the house, half-expecting Logan to appear from around the corner.

When he didn't, Char wasn't disappointed.

She wasn't.

Don't look at her like that.

"Don't look at who?" she muttered, standing up. "Yourself?"

Maybe. But also . . . look she *was* disappointed. Stupidly or not, there was something about Logan that drew her, even after all these years.

Hence *friends*.

Except, now she was wondering if she'd just signed her own death warrant by pushing Logan to be friends. She'd wanted to categorize him in that way in order to keep her heart safe, but the truth was that her heart had never been safe from him. He'd always been able to wriggle in and make himself at home.

It was why the rest of her relationships hadn't ever worked out.

She'd loved him. She'd thought they had that special magic of her parents—caring for each other, seeing all the flaws and good things, but loving each other more because of them. Instead . . . he'd gotten in, implanted himself, and left.

"And now he's back," she murmured.

Or perhaps more accurately, he'd decided to waltz back into her personal life, not content to stay solely in her business world.

"So, shove him back into his lane."

Char froze, the protest already welling up in her throat.

"That's your answer, dumb ass."

"I happen to like your ass." A beat, as she gasped and turned to face the man who she'd apparently conjured up just by thinking of him. "Don't talk down to it," Logan said, lips quirking, pretty green eyes dancing. He had a flush of pink on the tops of his cheekbones, as though his olive skin had been out in the sun for just a little too long.

She plunked her hands on her hips. "Is there a reason you keep breaking into my back yard?"

He shrugged. "Is there a reason you don't answer your doorbell, except at three A.M.?"

She would not be amused.

She would not smile.

But damned if the man wasn't right.

The only time she'd answered her door for him was the one occasion she should have been most wary. Though, in fairness, she'd gotten considerably *more* wary after the man standing a few feet away from her had shown up on her front porch.

"I was comfortable," she said. "And I figured that anyone important would call or text."

"And what if someone important *did* call *and* text?"

She lifted her brows. "Did you?"

An unrepentant grin. "No."

She sighed and shook her head. "What are you doing back here?"

"Don't friends hang out?"

"Friends usually have boundaries, and they don't hang out every minute."

Guileless green eyes on hers. "Is that so?" He nodded to her house. "Why don't you teach me more of these mysterious friend rules?"

Char pressed her lips together, fighting once more against the urge to smile. "Why are you really here, Log?"

His chest rose and fell on a large exhale. He took a step closer, gaze serious now. "Do you really want to know?" he asked, moving closer still, until he was near enough for her to see the streaks of brown hidden in the depths of his emerald eyes.

Did she want to know?

It took her less time than it should have to admit, "Yes." She did.

Fingers down her cheek, a soft touch smoothing back her hair. "There's no one else I want to spend time with," he said.

Her breath caught.

Then she frowned.

"No one?"

Logan snorted, the puff of air disturbing the curl he'd just tucked away. "Why do you sound so incredulous?"

"Really?"

Lips close and yet so far. Temptation mere millimeters away. She wanted. *God* how she wanted.

No.

Char stepped back, paced away. "I'm mean, come on, really? You're confused that I sound incredulous?" She spun around, met his stare, and found it clouded with what was definitely confusion. "You've decided to flip the script on something I thought I knew for eight years, Logan. I was hurt. Devastated. And you were in the tabloids with an actress." She sucked in a breath. "Then I didn't hear from you, didn't see you anywhere except on the ice, not even when you were playing in my building." Another breath, this one a struggle against that old, jagged pain. "Then you agree to sign with the Gold, and I spent the first half of the season expecting something. An explanation. Derision. For you to make a pass."

"Char—"

She turned away again, continued her pacing. "Instead, I get the consummate professional. A leader on the ice. An asset off. The perfect fit."

Heat at her spine.

She didn't turn around, couldn't bear to look into his eyes.

"Then the season's over," she said when he didn't speak. "And you show up with a present, with groceries. You tell me you want me. But I haven't seen one fucking bit of that *want* for eight years." Char's hand shook as she absently went to push back her hair, but then Logan was in front of her, doing it for her, his hand lingering as it cupped the side of her throat.

And fuck, his touch was everything.

Her body was alive. Her nerves fired with pulses of pleasure. Need burned hot through her center.

"I had to wait until the season was over," he said, carefully wrapping his arms around her.

"Log—"

"Friends hug," he said, moving slowly enough that she could stop him, could step back or push him away. But all of those depended on her having one ounce of self-control when it came to this man.

And—case in point as her body pressed flush to his, as her arms wrapped around his waist, as she inhaled that spicy scent directly into her lungs—she had none.

Not with Logan.

Never with Logan.

Gorgeous, handsome Logan. Sweet, caring Logan. Heart-breaking, shattering—

His palms slid up and down her back, a slow and steady rhythm that calmed and made her yearn more than ever. "I had to wait until the job was done, Starlight," he said.

"Why?"

"Because I will never get between you and your dream."

One sentence that undid her.

One sentence that broke her heart all over again.

That made anger and hurt and terror and *so fucking much* hurt well up inside her. She pushed against his chest, shoving hard enough to make him stumble back a step. "You already did," she said, eyes burning with tears she would not let fall. "You shoved yourself into my dream and then casually set it aflame. Then you danced on the ashes before they had even cooled."

"Char—"

"No," she said, throwing her hands up. "Don't push me on this, Logan. When I said friends, I didn't mean that as an avenue to something else. I meant fucking *friends,* and that was it."

"Star—"

"Either take it or leave it," she said, leaving the blanket, abandoning the glass, and shoving past him to move toward the slider. "Because the one thing I know for certain is that when you ended us eight years ago, you ended everything—our future, our present, our possibilities."

She yanked open the door, slammed—and locked it— behind her.

Then, heart aching, eyes stinging, throat clogged with tears, she went upstairs to take a fucking bath.

Thirteen

Logan

He'd fucked up.

And he hadn't even had the opportunity to give Char the *why* of why he'd ended things between them. He'd known he shouldn't have gone back to her house.

It hadn't been in his plans to see her again, the ones made in the dark much earlier that morning, but after he'd gone to the beach, after the phone calls and sitting on the sand, counting the minutes that passed by, he hadn't been able to stop himself. Hadn't been able to find his patience when all he wanted to do was go back to her place and kiss and touch, coax and love his way back into her heart. As the waves had crested on the shore, their ever-pounding rhythm had wound him tighter and tighter.

Until the ocean was no longer calming.

Until he'd been unable to sit still.

Still, Logan had planned on driving back to his place, to work out until oblivion found him.

Then he'd seen the exit for Char's house.

And he hadn't been able to resist.

Just as he hadn't been able to resist going into her back yard when she hadn't answered the doorbell.

Stupid.

So fucking stupid.

But she'd been beautiful in her cut-off jeans, her legs on display, the curves of her ass tempting him even from ten feet away. She'd smiled when she'd first seen him, the impact of that initial reaction filling him with so much fucking joy that he'd blown it.

He should have led with *I deliberately broke up with you, in a way that ensured you'd move on, so you didn't give up your life for me.*

Or perhaps, *I still love you and I've never stopped.*

Or better yet, *I'm so fucking sorry and I'm getting on my knees —even the bad one that sometimes still aches from ACL surgery—to beg you to give me just one more chance.*

He hadn't said any of those things.

Instead, he'd given a half-explanation that only hurt her further.

Fucking hell.

"Shit," he muttered, jabbing at the button on his garage door opener to close the heavy metal panel after he'd put his car into park. He turned off the ignition, slammed out of the door, kicking it shut with enough force that he'd probably dinged it.

Or broken his toe.

Well, what did he need his toes for?

Hockey was done for the moment.

He was alone.

He was . . . fucking moping.

Sighing, he dropped his chin to his chest, inhaled deeply, and tried to quell the anger. All season, all *fucking* season he'd been striving for patience, slowly trying to prove to her—hell, to *himself*—that he deserved another chance, so when he'd finally pulled the trigger, he'd found it nearly impossible to go slow.

If that wasn't a fucking pattern in his life, Logan didn't know what was.

Slow down, you'll crack your head open! his mom had regularly bellowed when he'd barreled down the road on hand-me-down rollerblades.

Slow down with the puck, you'll make fewer mistakes had been his travel coach's favorite mantra.

Slow down. Think. from Luc before he'd asked for the trade.

Even this season, Calle, the assistant coach in charge of offense had told him to move *slower and more deliberately* when funneling the puck up to his forwards on the board.

Slow down.

So easy in retrospect, so fucking difficult in the moment.

He'd always wanted everything as quickly as possible. First place in every tournament he played growing up, first on the ice during travel hockey, first game in the NHL, first goal, first full-season league. First . . . woman he'd loved.

Speed had been great for his career—granted, he was able to temper it.

Which he had.

He'd made it an asset instead of a detriment.

But speed wasn't great necessarily when it came to relationships, not when it meant first love had turned into first heartbreak in the span of several months. And speed really wasn't fucking great when he was trying to show the woman he'd never stopped loving that she could trust him to take care with her.

Fucking barreling right through on those rollerblades again.

Another sigh had him lifting his chin.

He punched the alarm code and pushed into the house, closing and locking the door behind him. It wasn't that he was obsessed with safety or saw a threat behind every corner, but he'd lived in big cities for years now.

This wasn't the small town he'd grown up in, nor the small suburbia Char had spent her last years in.

This was San Francisco, and that meant there were some inherent dangers.

So, locking her doors was definitely an item he planned to address on his plan to take care of her, but it had been shuffled down a few spots because . . . well, first he needed to figure out how to get her to not kick him out of her house.

Or back yard.

Or maybe, he should just start with getting her to talk to him.

He crossed to his fridge on another sigh, knowing that the contents were much sparser than what he'd filled Char's with that morning but happy that at least she had food to eat for dinner while she was probably plotting ways to happily dismember him.

Or dull his skate blades so he'd eat it on the ice—

No. She wouldn't mess with the team.

She'd just mentally voodoo doll him in ways that wouldn't affect his play. His cock twitched, and not in a good way because he knew that *she* knew that he didn't need his dick to play hockey.

That would be the first to go.

Cupping himself and shuddering, he acknowledged his ridiculousness then moved on to more important things than his cock.

Dinner.

He had a mind to eat dessert, but since that wouldn't be happening for the foreseeable future, he focused on food by pulling out the fixings for a salad—spinach, crumbled tofu, quinoa, precut slivers of pepper—and ate with the deliberate focus of fueling his body rather than taste. Not that it tasted bad, but it wasn't a giant steak and a loaded baked potato, and strictly speaking, he didn't need to continue Nutritionist Rebecca's meal plan, but he was going to. He'd never felt better, but more than that, it had been really fucking difficult to transition into her plan. It wasn't like he wanted to eat junk food all summer, but he also really liked to indulge in his food and beer and didn't want a repeat the struggle of cutting out extra carbs and sugar and meat.

He couldn't even do cheat days.

No self-control.

Diet plan day in and out. Limiting the animal products—odd omelet with organic cheese aside. The blueprint for his diet was to predominantly focus on plant-based proteins, to avoid processed foods and refined sugars, and not often indulging in his prescheduled Cheat Days that Rebecca built into the plan.

Because . . . circling back to not having any self-control. To moving too fast and—

His phone buzzed.

Frowning, he put down the fork, wondering who would be texting and why. The season was over, the Cup awarded to someone else. The guys would be returning to their families and, in some cases, to their own countries. They had two months off before team activities would be scheduled, and even then, the time commitment would be light until the season ramped up.

Most guys had their own rest and training schedule. Healing up, securing some ice time, hanging with their families, fishing— there was a lot of fishing.

Not Logan's cup of tea.

But he did have a cabin in the woods. It backed up to a river some *could* fish in. He just preferred to watch the water flow by, to hang out and do nothing, to be with no one.

Well, he wanted to be with *some*one.

She just—rightfully—wanted to light his dick on fire.

Cool.

His phone buzzed again, reminding him of the message, and he picked up his cell, glanced at the screen.

Then immediately shook his head and sighed.

Because Brit had fired up the team's group text chain.

His phone vibrated rapid fire in his hand, moving almost faster than he could as he unlocked the screen and began to scroll up through the newest messages to ferret out what the hell had gotten the boys—and girl—so worked up.

Brit had sent:

Housewarming party at Kevin and Rebecca's house tonight.

This Rebecca wasn't Nutritionist Rebecca, but rather PR Rebecca, and while she hadn't used PR in front of this Rebecca's name, Logan knew which one she was talking about based on the spouse.

Kevin—forward on the Gold—with PR Rebecca.

Gabe—head trainer—with Nutritionist Rebecca.

See what he meant about the Gold being a family? There were so many crisscrossing relationships that his head had practically spun when he'd come to the team and had been trying to keep track of them all.

That tactic he'd given up on.

Eventually, he'd just gone along for the ride, and pretty soon he'd grown to understand the various dynamics.

Which was why he kept reading.

Max: Last minute much?

Brit: As if any of us losers have anything better to do.

Coop: I resent that term.

Blane: Even if it fits? *rolling eyes emoji*

Brit: I'm declaring this an honorary Cheat Day.

Max: I'll bring the pizza. Players only, or everyone?

Kevin: Everyone is invited. We've got the food covered. Molly's is delivering.

Blue: Cool. I'll bring an IPA.

Brit: I've got the shitty beer covered.

Liam: We know you do. I'll bring something good to make up for Brit's bad taste.

The messages went on, escalating the teasing for several minutes before everyone began to sign off and gather up kids who were around or good beer that would be too refined for what Brit had termed her college-aged palate. Logan squeezed in a reply, saying he'd be there, too.

Because, what else did he have to do?

Sit around and think about how he'd blown it with Char?

Pack his shit and drive up to the Sierras and hide out in his tiny cabin?

He'd save that for next week.

Rolling his eyes at himself, Logan washed his plate then headed upstairs to change into party clothes.

And yes, he knew full-well that if one of his teammates heard him refer to what he was wearing as party clothes that he'd be served up a heaping pile of shit-giving with no end in sight.

But . . . that was also why he was going to the impromptu gathering.

Because they gave him shit. Because he'd give it back—to Brit and her beer, to Max and his nerdiness, to Blane and his inability to father boys, despite really wanting to. His wife, Mandy, also a trainer for the team, was pregnant with another girl, and so his future of pink hair bows was secure. Though Brit had bought little Madeline skates for her first birthday, so there was certain to be plenty of hockey in the girl's future.

Plus, with women like Brit and Charlotte in her circle, not to mention the fact that much of the staff and management were female, Madeline had no shortage of role models to look up to.

Hockey was for everyone.

Not just a slogan for the league any longer, it had been whole-heartedly embraced by the Gold organization.

More than words.

Actions.

And—

He froze in the middle of buttoning a fresh pair of jeans as the puzzle pieces in his mind settled into perfect arrangement. He'd given Char some words, knew she deserved more, but . . . more than anything he might *say*, she needed actions.

Show her.

Not tell her.

He'd taken a creative writing class in college, a long torturous semester where he'd felt completely over his head, but one in which the instructor said one thing on repeat.

Stop telling and start showing.

Words didn't mean shit if they weren't paired with actions.

Then add in his tendency to move too fast and . . . well, disaster was the first word that came to mind.

He'd given Char a thoughtful present, he'd done a little groveling, and just because she'd let him kiss and touch her, had offered up friendship, he'd assumed—

Fuck. He was an ass.

Because he'd stopped by her house that evening thinking that he just needed to wear her down a little more, that by Char extending the hand of friendship, she'd then given him the green-light and it was only a matter of time before he would worm his way back into her heart.

But the truth was that *nothing* was guaranteed.

Least of all her accepting or forgiving him or even coming to an understanding of why he'd done what he'd done.

He needed to show her what she meant to him.

He needed to prove he was worth her taking a chance on him again.

Because he'd helped build those walls around her heart, had effectively handed her the bricks, the mortar. Maybe he didn't regret the decision he made, knew it had to be done, but also . . . fuck, he'd been so young, so stupid.

So fast.

Always moving too fast.

He caught a glimpse of his reflection in the mirror, saw the war within himself—the knowledge of what he needed to do fighting against his instincts to barrel in and get her back.

But there was only one outcome in that scenario that resulted in winning back Char's trust.

So, Logan knew exactly what he had to do.

He needed to slow *way* down.

In fact, he thought he was going to slow down so much that he'd be late to the party.

FOURTEEN

CHAR

She didn't normally get to sit around with the team like this.

No barriers.

No necessary professional distance.

Just some adults and kids hanging out, eating way too many baked goods from Molly's—something even Nutritionist Rebecca couldn't get too mad about, considering the season was over.

Well, that and the fact that someone had bought Rebecca's favorites—a gluten and sugar-free pastry filled with eco-friendly chocolate.

Char personally thought it tasted like sand.

But she had dutifully taken the bite Rebecca had offered, and clearly the nutritionist liked it, so she kept her opinions to herself.

Plus, she was too busy filling her stomach with Triple-Chocolate Orgasm cookies to be focused on much else. Brit had plunked a bottle of dark lager into her hand and told her to prepare to have her mind blown.

She had *something* blown.

Stifling a snort because that might have been funny if she'd had *something* to blow or if *someone* had blown her—which, side note, was maybe not possible, or perhaps more accurately, wasn't something she particularly wanted. Lips and teeth and a tongue, yeah that was more her speed—

Logan walked into the room, head bent slightly as Max stood next to him, chatting his ear off.

Probably about the latest fantasy show that had taken Netflix by storm.

God, he looked good. He was tall and lean, with a thick black beard that she wanted to feel against her skin, especially if he paired it with his teeth and lips and tongue. Because . . . God, they'd been good together. After they'd broken up, she'd never had sex with one iota of the intensity as it had been with Logan. Their chemistry had been off the charts.

And based on the kiss the other morning, it was still that way.

As though he knew she was staring at him, he turned his head and those gorgeous emerald eyes met hers.

Even from across the room, she felt the intensity, felt what he wanted to do to her. Char's breath caught and she shifted, an ache between her legs, heat dripping down her spine like honey.

Eight years and she still wanted him like it was the first time.

She knew she should look away.

But she was held captive.

"Is your tongue having an orgasm?"

No, but something else is desperate to have one.

Brit dropped onto the cushion next to her to punctuate that question, or maybe the thought—fuck, she hoped it had remained just a thought.

"What?"

"I've seen the way you look at—"

Char inhaled, fear gripping her when she realized how transparent she'd been by staring at Logan, by basically eye-fucking him from across the room when she was supposed to be a fucking professional.

And because the world was the way it was—read: a cruel

motherfucker—Brit got a full glimpse of Char nearly choking on her last bite of orgasm—she meant *cookie*.

Cookie, dammit.

Not sex.

Brit patted her on the back. "Easy," she said. "Sorry, I didn't mean to startle you."

"All"—*cough*—"good"—*cough*—"it's"—*cough*—"my fault."

Char inhaled, this time managing to not choke on her cookie, and then took a long sip of beer. "I'm fine," she said when she'd finished. "I should have been paying closer attention instead of woolgathering."

Brit's blue eyes locked onto hers and Char had to resist the urge to fidget.

"I've never"—Char braced herself for Brit to call her out, to say something like *I've never seen a GM who wants to fuck one of his players*—"heard someone use the term *woolgathering* in actual conversation before."

Char snorted, gaze darting to the side. Logan had moved farther in the room but hadn't come over to her, wasn't even looking at her, even though she'd just nearly choked to death giving that double chocolate orgasm cookie a blowjob. "Oh, no, don't give me that nonsense. It's not *that* uncommon."

"You sure you weren't born in 1950?"

Char smacked her lightly on the arm.

"Goaltender abuse!" Brit joked. "I need that shoulder." She grinned. "And so do you."

"Maybe my plan is to devalue the price of you and that shoulder."

Brit froze for a heartbeat before a grin broke out on her face. "You're devious, and I, for one, love it."

"Because I want to injure you so I can pay less when I renew your contract?"

"Yup." Brit took a sip of her beer. "Well, that and the fact that you've got a sense of humor and don't take yourself too seriously."

Char shrugged. "It's part of the job, part of the needle we women find ourselves having to constantly thread. We can be tough, but not too tough. We can be outspoken, but only so long as we don't hurt some man's feelings. We can assert ourselves, but only so far, otherwise we're a bitch."

Brit's eyes went sad. "Are you feeling that way here? With us?"

Shit.

"God, no." She reached over and squeezed Brit's hand. "This organization is incredible, and I think that's not only because of the focus on gender and racial equity but also because of the men here. We've got allies, not barriers." Straightening, she smiled at the goaltender, who was older than her, but also seemed very young in many ways. Maybe it was the fact Brit was a goalie and goalies were weird, or maybe it was just that Brit was young at heart and had an innocence to her that no one had managed to dim. "I was thrilled to be offered the job, and my experience has been incredible. It's just all the rest of it—the media, the blogs, the nasty headlines. You've been there, done that."

Brit made a face. "Yeah, I know a bit about how rough the media circus can be." She leaned back. "My advice is to avoid looking at the sports blogs. It's a brutal world of misogyny. Hell, they're still saying I'm a publicity stunt, and I've won the fucking Cup. Twice."

"You're my first choice in goalie, any day of the week," Char told her, and she meant it. Brit was smaller than male goalies, but she was beyond talented and a critical part of the Gold roster.

"Yes!" Brit fist-pumped.

"What?" Char asked.

"My contract offer just went up."

Char lifted her gaze to the ceiling and sighed, her eyes flicking to the side when she felt Logan come closer. But the man was apparently engrossed in his conversation with Max, and he didn't once look at her. Shaking herself, she forced herself to pay attention to Brit. "Didn't my invite tonight come with the promise that we were forgetting I'm technically everyone in this room's boss?"

When the other woman had texted and invited her to the team party, Char had been conflicted—and not just because Logan would come (though he'd just shown up, so if he really wanted her and her *friendship*, wouldn't he have arrived earlier?). Instead, she'd struggled with the urge to refuse on principle, because she should keep distance between herself and the rest of the world.

But how could she keep her distance and also encourage the organization to be a family?

Families didn't keep their distance.

Or good ones didn't.

Brit shrugged, teased lightly, "You're the one who brought up contracts." But she didn't belabor the point. Instead, she changed the subject.

To one that Char was trying and failing to ignore.

"Did you need to discuss something with Logan?"

"What?" Char tore her gaze away from the beautiful man who made her thighs clench together and her pussy ache.

"Logan. Did you need me to get him for you?"

Yes. Yes, she did. She wanted Brit to go over there and bring Logan to her, to offer him up like some sexual gift where there would be no consequences for her heart or her job.

But there were always consequences.

"No." She blinked, dispelling the memory of how good Logan had been at giving her orgasms and how much better he might be with eight more years of practice. Char turned to the woman next to her and lifted a brow. "Why do you ask?"

"Because you look like you either want to fuck or kill him."

What had Char been thinking about this woman being innocent? Because clearly Brit wasn't, or at least she saw too fucking much.

"You're wrong."

Brit patted her shoulder, shook her head slightly. "Why does it sound like you're trying to convince yourself?"

Because she was?

Char tipped her beer bottle and took a long swallow, buying time, but also rocked to the core. If Brit noticed, then who else would?

Would Logan?

And if he *did* realize how much she wanted him and he pushed or began pursuing her in earnest, how in the fuck was she going to be able to resist him?

She wouldn't be able to.

Her pulse sped, heart thudding in her chest. Maybe it was because she was the boss and trying to interject some distance between herself and this woman who saw too much. Or maybe because the thought of Logan recognizing too much and realizing she had no defense against him, made her panic. Either way, Char knew in that moment that coming to the party had been a horrible idea.

She had to go, and she had to go now.

"You know what—" She started to stand.

Brit dropped her hand to Char's wrist. "I was like you."

Saw too much. Brit saw too much.

Char forced a smile. "We women in a men's world have to stick together."

"That's not—" Brit stood, dropped her voice. "Look, I know I'm overstepping"—a chagrined smile—"but that's my M.O., so I'm just going to say it. I almost let the best thing in my life go because I was too scared to step outside myself, because I was too worried what the world would think." A light squeeze of those fingers. "Logan is a good guy. He—"

"He broke my heart."

It just slipped out.

The admission was critically embarrassing. Char should be way over a young love gone wrong, some hurt feelings from nearly a decade before.

But the door had been pushed open, and she remembered.

How hopeful she'd been.

How much it had hurt when he'd gone.

Her eyes burned, and it took her a moment to realize that Brit hadn't said anything back. She turned to Brit, words tumbling out. "It was a long time ago, way before either of us were here—" A sharp shake of her head. "It doesn't matter anymore. He is a good man, and I wish him a good future. I just—"

"I understand," Brit said softly, after Char struggled to find out exactly what she *just.*

Just what?

Couldn't? Shouldn't? Was too scared to? Was too furious to?

Take her pick.

They all fit her churning emotions.

"I shouldn't have said anything. I'm sorry."

Pulse still pounding, cheeks scorching hot, Char knew she had to keep it together. She reached over and gave Brit a quick hug. "No," she murmured. "Thank you for caring." She pulled back. "But I think I've had enough tonight."

Brit nodded then glanced over Char's shoulder, eyes widening. "He's coming this way. Do you want me to run interference?"

"No." What Char *wanted* to do was to turn around and run into Logan's arms, to pretend nothing bad had happened between them, and to trust him like she once had. That he was her other half, that he was a good man who would treat her like her dad did her mother.

But that trust was gone.

"I have to do this."

"You don't," Brit whispered. "You really don't." Respect in her pale blue eyes. "But I get why you feel like you have to." She stepped back and scooped up her beer from the side table, voice raising in volume and chipperness. "Well, I'll just go grab another one of my crappy beers."

Then she was gone.

And Logan was at Char's back.

FIFTEEN

LOGAN

She turned slowly to face him, and the weariness in her eyes killed him.

But . . . actions.

Show not tell.

He shoved down how much that hurt him and extended the bottle of water he'd grabbed for her after watching her almost choke to death while talking to Brit. He'd wanted to storm over, to cradle her in her arms, but he'd promised to show, promised friendship, promised to go slow.

So, he'd extracted himself from Max's inane conversation about whether druids was the proper term for some magical being in the show he was currently bingeing then had made his way to the cooler.

Now, he struggled to contain his body's reaction when her fingers brushed his.

"What's this?" she asked when the damp exterior of the bottle met her skin.

Which got him thinking about damp things he *shouldn't* be

thinking of, especially when he was trying to firmly friend zone himself.

"I'm guessing your throat hurts," he said, then mentally kicked himself.

Throat. Damp. Next he'd be discussing how *hard* things were.

And speaking of which—

Focus.

"You were coughing," he said lamely. "I figured you might need something to drink."

Her gaze moved from the bottle up to his, those chocolate depths indecipherable as they held his stare for long moments. Then she dropped her eyes back to the beer bottle she already held.

"O-oh, I-I—" he stammered. "I'll—"

"Thanks, Log." She took the water from him and he had a difficult time looking away from the slender fingers, their nails tipped in pale pink polish. Somehow, it suited her, though it made part of him crave how she'd used to sport all sorts of shades.

Bright green and red for Christmas.

A plethora of autumn tints when the leaves began changing.

Team colors when they'd been on a winning streak.

Now they were pretty but subdued.

He'd done that.

Or maybe it had been a combination that he'd kicked off, but that life and professionalism had required.

Or maybe he shouldn't be thinking about her fucking nail polish when he had so much to make up for.

"Did you get some food?"

She glanced up at him, brows drawn together, and Logan was so twisted up by his longing for this woman that it took him far too long to connect the pieces. Fucking hell, of course she got some food. She'd just been choking on it.

He'd brought her the water bottle *because* of it.

Good grief.

Logan closed his eyes, clenched his jaw. He needed to stop fucking this up. The stakes were too high and—

Fingers on his hand. "Are you okay?"

He swallowed, cleared his throat. "I'm fine. I—"

Fuck.

He what? Had thought himself into such a circle that he was absolutely terrified in this moment of saying or doing the wrong thing. All he could think was *show not tell, slow down, actions not words* on repeat through his brain.

And funny story, that made it incredibly difficult to think of anything reasonable to say, to do.

"Log—"

Get a grip.

"Char, I—"

"*I'm pregnant!*"

The room went absolutely silent, everyone turning to PR Rebecca.

"What?" Brit asked into the quiet. "I thought you couldn't have—" She broke off, shook her head. "Oh, my God! Rebecca, are you serious?"

The slender brunette nodded, and it was the first time that Logan had ever seen her appear the least bit uncertain. "It was a surprise," she said, teeth nibbling into her bottom lip as she glanced up at Kevin.

Logan's teammate's face was soft, gentler than he'd ever seen. "A great surprise," he said, brushing a tear that escaped Rebecca's eye.

Someone sniffed.

The sound seemed to propel everyone into motion.

Mandy, heavily pregnant with Blane's second daughter, rushed over to Rebecca, hugging her as tightly as her belly would allow. "Honey! I'm so happy for you. That's amazing!"

Brit was only a step behind. "Congratulations! I'm thrilled for you both."

Sara—a quiet brunette and former international figure skating champion, who was married to Max Stewart, a defenseman who'd retired from the Gold last season at the same time as Stefan, their former captain—joined the huddle, followed by Max's and Blue's wives, Angie and Anna, respectively. Nutritionist Rebecca was there a heartbeat later, her soft voice nearly inaudible. Soon everyone was talking, excitement filling the room.

Logan didn't know the whole story, but he could pick up enough to understand that Rebecca being pregnant was happy, amazing news.

"I should—" Char's fingers were still on his arm, and he briefly covered them with his own when she jumped and blinked. "I'll just go congratulate Kevin and Rebecca."

Her lips parted. A breath shuddered out.

"Char?"

"Yes?" she said and visibly shook herself. "You're right. We should go offer our congratulations."

She tugged, making to extract his hand, and instinctively, his own hand tightened, not wanting to break the contact, not wanting to let her go. That mantra was ramping up again, spinning through his mind. *Slow, show. Words, trust. Actions—*

He forced his fingers to open, to release her.

Another shuddering breath.

And he remembered the other thing he'd grabbed for her. He extended the napkin-wrapped cookie, the same variety she'd nearly offed herself on. "Here," he said, pushing it into her now free hand. "It was the last one."

She peeled back the corner, glanced between the cookie and him. "I—"

He allowed himself the smallest bit of contact. "Just enjoy it, Starlight."

Then he stepped back, turned away, and forced himself to walk away from the woman he loved.

It made every nerve in his body burn with regret.

But he kept walking anyway.

He'd done it once for her own good, had crawled away from her inch by inch in order to save her dream.

Today, what propelled him was the knowledge that if he did it correctly this time around, then perhaps he would manage to save both of their hopes for the future.

SIXTEEN

CHAR

He'd walked away.

He'd shoved a cookie in her hand and just strode away.

Well, a cookie *and* a water bottle, but still.

He'd just gone.

A beat of annoyance trailed her confusion, but before she could work up any ill-will, she focused back on her surroundings, on what had just been announced. She was new to the team and didn't understand everything that had gone into Rebecca's announcement, but Char knew enough to get that it was a huge deal.

Even without everyone else's reactions, seeing Rebecca with tears in her eyes, her typical shark-like and calculating expression softened with love as she stared at her husband, Kevin, would have told Char enough.

This was life-changing news for the Gold's often cynical publicist.

This wasn't a shot staged to garner likes or positive press. This wasn't a setup in order to frame the announcement in the best possible light.

This was . . . Rebecca wanting her family around when she made the announcement.

And fuck if that didn't bring tears to Char's own eyes.

Eyes that dropped to the cookie in her hand and had her remembering that she'd once hoped to have kids with Logan, then that she'd once hoped to have them with someone, anyone. But life had changed that. *She* had changed that.

Unwilling to open up, to open the gate to the walls surrounding her heart.

It was easy to put blame on Logan for crushing that dream.

But the truth was that she'd crushed it just as effectively over the last eight years by avoiding any real connections with the men she dated.

The moment—and she meant the *moment*—they wanted to get serious, Char had bolted.

To get too close was dangerous.

Plus, she was the first black woman, the first *any* woman in the assistant GM position. Then the first in the GM role itself. That was too important to slow down.

So clearly, she couldn't open up fully.

Work was important.

Work was *more* important.

And if the men in her life weren't satisfied with the piecemeal bits and morsels she tossed their way, then the door was there and they could walk right through it.

She needed to keep her head down and keep pressing forward.

Because . . . she'd prove everyone wrong.

She, a black female, could do it all, and fuck anyone who told her differently. That made her a BAMF and badass motherfuckers didn't take names. They kicked asses and demanded people get out of her way.

Barriers? What barriers?

Resistance? She'd wear it down.

Walls? Well, she sure as hell had built thick-assed ones herself.

But . . . what did any of it mean?

Her family was proud of her, no doubt. *She* was proud of her, proud of how relentless she'd been in pursuing what had once seemed like a far-fetched reality and doing it in a way that didn't crush the people beneath her.

Oh, she'd fought like hell for her dream, but she'd never been battling enemies or the people who said she couldn't do it.

She'd been battling herself.

She was *that* enemy. Her biggest enemy.

Because in thinking she had to close off everything around her, she hadn't really been living her full dream.

She'd merely been ticking off boxes.

Intern. Check.

Master's. Check.

Assistant GM. Check.

GM. Check.

Alone? Also check.

Too scared to let anyone really in? Too terrified of being hurt again that she'd let her childhood and college friends wane under the guise of too much work? Check. Check.

And as she stood, separate from these people who'd built an amazing family, one she'd been taking credit for all season, thinking it was she who'd put the final pieces together, *she* who'd made it special, Char realized that she was the least important part. These people trusted each other; they loved without fear.

It was plain as day to see.

Coop cupping Calle's cheek and pressing a kiss to their daughter's head.

Stefan lacing an arm around Brit's waist and pulling her back against his chest so that someone else would get a chance with Rebecca.

Liam, his arm around Mia's shoulders, enthusiastically congratulating Kevin.

Gabe stroking Nutritionist Rebecca's back, lightly reassuring her when she seemed overwhelmed by the noise and women surrounding her.

Kevin never letting go of PR Rebecca's hand.

Blue holding his and Anna's daughter while Anna pressed a kiss to the publicist's cheek.

Blane steadying Mandy when she teetered off-balance with her large belly.

Sara smiling over at Mike, her hand on her stomach hinting at a secret, her gaze saying they wouldn't share with the room at large and take away from Rebecca and Kevin's news.

Angie crouching beside Max's son, Brayden, clearly relaying the news because the little boy smiled hugely then wove his way through the women to hug Rebecca.

Love.

It was in this room. It was clear as day.

And the absence of it in Char's heart, in her life was just as clear.

Fuck, how that hurt.

Her eyes met Logan's.

And fuck how *that* hurt.

Her breath caught. Her heart felt like it had been tossed into a blender. Her insides churned and roiled and . . . she felt like she might be sick.

She stumbled back a step, nearly colliding with the coffee table before catching herself. She couldn't do this. She couldn't be here. It hurt so fucking much, and she didn't want that hurt filling the room, dampening the joy.

Char needed to go.

The back of her throat burning with bile, she sidestepped the crowd and got the fuck out of the house.

Later, she'd make up an excuse for leaving, congratulate them properly.

She'd send a gift or flowers or—her fingers crumpled the double-chocolate orgasm in her hand—*cookies*.

Tonight . . .
Tonight, she just needed to go.

Seventeen

Logan

Not following after Charlotte went against every single one of his instincts.

But slow, steady, patience—

He caught a glimpse of her through the window of the front door, saw her stop on the porch, her chin falling forward and her shoulders shuddering.

Fuck slow and steady.

She was hurting, and he wasn't just going to stand there like a moron, watching her suffer.

He slipped away from the conversation, not that anyone was paying him much attention. They were all too thrilled for Rebecca and Kevin, and he was happy for them, too. He just . . .

His heart was on that porch, hurting and alone.

He grabbed his jacket from the table by the door and went outside, dropping it onto Char's shoulders. It had been warm earlier, but night had fallen, become enshrouded with fog and a chill. The thin sweater she was wearing could hardly protect her.

"Log—"

Sad brown eyes on his, damp with tears.

He bundled her close to his side and walked her around to the side of the house. Then he did something that was probably inappropriate, but something that he couldn't stop himself from doing.

He hugged her.

Just pulled her against his chest, rested his chin on her head, and wrapped his arms around her.

Char didn't go stiff.

Instead, she melted, sank against him, turning her head so her cheek was against his chest, her shuddering breaths soaking through his T-shirt.

Logan held her, knowing that this strong, capable, *wonderful* woman leaning on him for a few minutes was a gift, perhaps the greatest of his life. He rubbed slow circles up and down her spine, took long, slow breaths, hoping that her breathing would steady to match his.

And when it eventually did, when the barest hint of stiffness entered her frame, he released her.

Wide, damp brown eyes on his, but there were no tear tracks on her cheeks, no pain in her expression. There was plenty of confusion, he could easily see in the moon's glow, but the hurt was banked, and for that, he was beyond thankful.

"Why?"

He touched her cheek. "You were hurting," he whispered. "I hate it when you hurt."

Weariness crept in. Her lips pressed flat. "You didn't then."

"Char, sweetheart," he whispered. "I'm sorry."

"Why, Log? Why did you break my heart?"

Quiet words, but the pain had floated in on the coattails of weary, and though he hated the sight of it with a passion, didn't want to say or do anything to increase that emotion, or to push her farther from him, Logan knew that the time was now. He had to tell her why he'd done what he'd done. He needed her to know.

"I asked to be traded."

Her eyes went wide. *"What?"*

"Back then," he said, "I knew we were moving too fast, too quickly. I knew that you were going to give more than me, going to give up too much, and I knew I couldn't let you put your dreams on hold for me." He held her gaze. "So, I went to Luc and told him that we were together, but that I knew it wasn't the best for you . . . and I asked him for a trade."

More hurt. More fury.

More . . . understanding.

"I could never fathom why he took that hit on the trade. You were a rising star, and who we got in return couldn't compare."

"Coleman did well for the team."

A beat, then, "But he wasn't you."

Logan sucked in a breath, although he didn't have the opportunity to form that air into words because she went on. "And furthermore, who made you the person who got to decide what was best for me? Huh?" She poked a finger into his chest, the small bite of her nail poking into him the tiniest pinprick of pain. But it was enough to remind him he was here, telling Char the truth of what happened after all this time, and that if he bungled it, then he might be able to muster all of the *slow down, patience, move steadily* bullshit in the world, but he'd never get her back.

Logan opened his mouth, readying the list of reasons why, all of the logical motivations he'd had for making sure that Char got to live out her dreams.

But none of that came out.

Instead, he said, "*I* made that decision, and it was the right one, the *only* one to be made."

Her brows lifted. "That's it?"

And dumbass that he was, he said, "That's it."

Eighteen

CHAR

The man had lost his fucking mind.

And maybe so had she, because she jabbed her finger into his chest, repeated, "That's why? *That's why? That's. Why?*" When he nodded, she scoffed and started to turn away, disgust in her every pore. What in the fuck was wrong with him?

He covered her hand, held it against his chest.

"That's not what—"

She turned back just in time to see him break off with a firm shake of his head.

"I'm— I didn't want us to turn into my parents, Starlight," he said.

That stopped her, brows drawn together. Their parents still being married after many decades when everyone in their circle seemed to be the product of divorce was something that had connected them, something that had brought them closer. Family dinners and events, holidays spent with each other, celebrating and teasing and loving each other in a way the rest of the world might not understand.

Except . . . she still talked to her family, still loved and saw them as often as possible, but she didn't have what the people inside Rebecca's house had.

She didn't have *that* type of family.

Because she'd pulled back, erected walls.

Because of the man in front of her, she thought, fury boiling within her. Up and up, bubbling to the top of the pot, threatening to cascade over the top and scald everything around her.

Just in time, logic prevailed.

Because this man might have hurt her, but *she* was the one who'd pulled back from everything else.

At first, because she didn't want to keep hurting. Instead, she had wanted to get lost in something that wasn't Logan.

Then because it was safer to be the deserted island in the middle of the ocean.

Crystal clear, blue water surrounding her on all sides, isolated, untouched—except perhaps from a visit from a passing ship or flock of birds or—

Logan shifted, dropping her hand and pacing away from her, thrusting his fingers into his hair and mussing the locks. He groaned. "This isn't—" Another shake of his head as he spun back toward her, all of that long, lean gorgeousness stalking toward her. "This isn't how I wanted to explain it." He ground his teeth together, glanced up at the dark sky, and she watched his shoulders flex as he inhaled and exhaled deeply.

She was wrong.

She might be that isolated island in the middle of the ocean.

But it wasn't just birds or ships visiting.

It was a hurricane.

And his name was Logan.

He stopped in front of her, green eyes nearly black in the evening's light, chest rising and falling rapidly. He was so much bigger than her, stronger physically in a way that made part of her question whether she had any hope in hell of keeping him at bay, or if perhaps, she didn't want to keep him at bay, and instead launch herself into his arms and ask him to keep her safe from the winds threatening to tear her to shreds.

Stay insulated and safe?

Or hop into the churning waves for what might possibly be the best surf of her life?

Char didn't surf.

But she wasn't an idiot. She was in the eye of the storm, Logan was there, he was troubled, and clearly more had happened behind the scenes of their breakup than she understood.

So, waves or not, she wanted to know.

She snagged his hand when he paced close enough, weaving their fingers together and tugging him to a halt. "Start at the beginning."

Startled emerald eyes on hers, a chiseled jaw clenching. "This goes way back," he said. "I—" He thrust his free hand through his hair, mussing it further, making Char's fingers itch with the need to fix it. "It's a long story."

"We lost the big game. The season's over. No meetings, no practices, no media." She shrugged. "Just tell me everything, Log, because seriously, what else have we got to do that could possibly be more important than this?"

His gaze held hers, even as his fingers convulsed. "Nothing," he murmured. "Nothing is more important than this, than you."

She couldn't deny that his words, the way he looked at her, the firm grip of his hand around hers . . . she had absolutely no hope of denying that they soothed a ragged tear in her heart, that they made her feel as though she could take her first full breath in years.

Perhaps since the moment he'd gone.

"My parents are unhappy."

Char blinked. That was pretty much the last thing she'd imagined him saying. He'd panicked because his feelings were too big or they'd moved too fast or they were too young or—

Except, she'd known it was more than that, hadn't she?

That was why it had hurt so much when he broke things off.

Because one moment they'd had absolutely everything—love, companionship, passion, friendship—and the next it had been snatched away, torn asunder by the person she'd trusted most in the world.

"Okay," she said softly, when it seemed like he was struggling with how to go on.

Green eyes on hers. "I know we talked about our families a lot when we were together, how our parents were still married, how cool it was that we got along with our siblings—"

She inhaled quickly. Had something happened with his family, with his brother and sister?

No. She'd *know*.

If something serious had gone down during the season, she would have known. Although, if it had happened before—

"But your parents actually like each other," he said, stopping the panicked spiral in her mind. "Mine . . . well, I guess tolerate one another would be the most apt word, but the reality is that they've been together so long, I think it's simply a case of convenience, as in, it's more convenient for them to stay together than to separate."

"I'm sorry," she whispered.

He made a face. "I'm not telling you this for sympathy or because I'm still hung up on the fact that things always have been tense between them. That's just life and the way it was."

Logan paused again, and she found herself stepping closer, reaching up to cup his cheek. "So, why *are* you telling me?"

"Right." He took a breath. "Okay, so—"

A burst of noise around the front of the house had them both freezing in place. She waited for the sounds to quiet, for the players and kids to depart, but they seemed to be congregating on the porch, talking over each other. Voices were lifted in excitement, a baby was screaming, a young male voice was singing the last pop song a cappella—and not particularly on key.

"I—" Logan broke off on a wince as the volume rose.

And even though they were around the corner, Char could

barely hear herself think, let alone focus on what Logan was trying to tell her, and it seemed as though the noise was making something hard for him to verbalize even more difficult.

Instinct took over.

"Come on," she said, tugging him through a row of trees and away from the cacophony. The yard wasn't fenced, and they were able to slip out the side of the property and onto the long driveway that led down to the main road. Her car was parked just a little ways down. "Did you drive?"

"Yes," he said. "I'm parked almost near the bottom."

A nod, the plan forming in her head. "I'll drop you at your car," she said. "Then you can meet me at my place."

"Char," he said, expression tentative. "I'm not trying to manipulate you or—"

"I know."

"And you still want me to go back to your place—" He halted, free hand coming up to cup her cheek. "As friends?"

She hesitated then admitted what should have been the truth in her heart from the beginning. Being just friends was impossible. She could be his boss—and only his boss—or she could be . . . more.

"No."

It was the barest whisper, but she knew that he'd heard because his fingers convulsed around hers, his breath hitched, and his body came very close.

She'd had his mouth on hers less than forty-eight hours before.

Recently enough that she knew exactly what she was missing, so much so that she nearly turned around and claimed it for herself, because he was a fucking incredible kisser.

But . . . passion wasn't their problem.

She owed herself the opportunity for closure, and maybe she also owed him the chance to explain himself.

Reaching forward, she grabbed onto the handle and tugged open the driver's side door, the locks automatically disengaging as she did so. Fancy—or at least that was what her mom had deemed the system when she'd come to visit a few months ago, and Char couldn't exactly blame her. There had been plenty of food on the table growing up. They'd had power and electricity and a place to live. But there hadn't been brand new cars or expensive vacations or electronics for Christmas.

So, locks opening at the touch of her hand *was* fancy.

She sat down, started to close the door, but Logan caught it. "Wh—"

He reached over her and buckled her belt, tracing his thumb lightly over her cheekbone as he began to straighten. Her breath caught, her pulse thundered. His mouth . . . *God*, it was right there.

He backed up, softly closed her door, and rounded the hood, eyes on hers the entire way.

It would have been an impressive display of peripheral vision if she hadn't seen him carry the puck up the ice hundreds of times without ever looking down, and anyway, her thoughts weren't much on hockey, not when he was opening the door and sliding into the passenger's seat.

His spiced scent filled the interior of her car, washing over her in waves.

Or maybe that was her attraction to him. Or maybe it was the waves of his scent and her attraction to him, and also her yearning . . . for an explanation, for a family like the one inside Rebecca's house, for one person to love her more than anything else in the world.

He pressed the button to start the ignition, and because she'd instinctively rested her foot on the brake, the engine fired up.

More fancy.

More—

"Less thinking, Starlight," he whispered, those emerald depths unfathomable. "More driving."

Her breath shuddered out. She moved her gaze to the windshield.

There was a part of her that wanted to continue to delay, that worried this big explanation and long story of Logan's wouldn't be enough. That she wouldn't be able to forgive him. *Ever.*

And she liked this respite.

This cautious bond between a man who knew her in a way no one else in the world did.

She liked how he looked at her—like she'd hung the moon and stars they'd so often loved to stare at while bundled up in the back of his pickup. She loved how he touched her, made her feel desirable and vulnerable and strong, all at the same time. And she really loved how he listened to everything she said, that he didn't discount or dismiss, that he listened, but that he didn't just give in. Maybe sometimes he pushed back, and even though that could sometimes irritate her, she respected that he challenged her.

He paid attention. He wasn't scared off by walls.

He'd . . . brought her slippers and groceries and cooked for her and—

She didn't want to lose that.

She'd had it all for one day, and she didn't want it to disappear.

Her pulse pounded, her hands tightened on the steering wheel. Fear sat heavy in her gut, and yearning for a family like the team's inside had a thick thread forming in her heart. She longed for Logan. Knew deep down that his explanation made sense. If she was able to forgive him—and she couldn't deny that a part of her already wanted to—then this *thing* with Logan, whatever the *thing* would become, might have the potential to destroy. It could devastate her career, ruin her reputation, and . . . have her serving her heart up to him on a golden platter.

With fresh herbs.

Or maybe herb butter. Heart with herb butter. Now *that* was a disgusting thought. Char bit back a shudder.

Thankfully, it was disgusting enough that she was able to get out of her head, to check for other cars, and to pull out on the driveway.

Part of her expected Logan to say something.

Instead, they rode in silence for the twenty seconds it took to get down to his car. Probably, she should have had him walk, but Char didn't calculate distance or time into her plan. It was a series of steps.

Get to car.

Get Logan to car.

Get to house.

Get explanation.

Get heart *un*broken. Hopefully. Shit. *Shit.* Was she really hoping that? Did she want all of those things? The heart? The spice? The potential of something big with this man?

The logical part of her brain screamed at her, *No. No! No fucking way.*

But her heart said something else.

War. Down to the very marrow of her bones. It was terrifying. A huge swathe of emotions and memories that threatened to bear down on her. Maybe a few days ago she would have bunkered down into her proverbial cellar, would have braced herself until the tornado passed her by, would have rebuilt the walls, cleaned up the devastation.

Then she would have moved on.

Today, she had seen something wonderful, something she wanted enough to not wish to hide in the basement and lock herself away. She wanted . . . more.

More than what she had in her life currently.

She wanted love and emotions and those fucking tornados, even if they might break her. So, while the thought of swinging that cellar door open was absolutely terrifying, Charlotte Harris had never, *ever* been a coward.

She pushed and battled and never gave up.

Today would *not* be the day she stopped being brave.

Nineteen

Logan

He tried to get his head on straight as he drove, attempted to put his thoughts together in an orderly manner, but Logan didn't make much headway.

His heart was pounding.

His gut was tied into knots.

His will was resolute.

He needed to stop the buildup, to lay out the facts, to get it over with.

"Would have been better if you'd started the conversation in a private place so you wouldn't get interrupted, dipshit," he muttered.

Yeah, well there was that. Which highlghted his whole problem with patience and taking things slow. But . . . Char hadn't turned away from him, even though he'd been traveling forward solely by left and right turns, hardly making sense as he'd taken her down a tangent.

Not a tangent so much as an aside. A necessary aside in order to give her context.

She turned into her driveway, waiting as the garage door slid open. Logan pulled up to the curb, throwing his car into park and getting out. He made it to her as she was just getting out, his jacket still around her shoulders, her purse in her hand.

He held the door for her, closed it after she'd slipped out.

"This way," she told him, hitting the button to close the garage door then leading him into her kitchen and setting her purse on the counter. It was only a quick pitstop because she turned for the slider she'd left unlocked yesterday—and he was glad to see this time it was locked as she flicked open the bolt— and walked onto the back porch.

He followed her out, watched as she completed a ritual he thought she must have done a hundred times before—moving toward the outdoor heater and turning it on, grabbing a thick blanket from a box tucked next to a planter, draping it over the back of one of her loungers.

She'd just started to sit down when her eyes flicked to his, and his heart swelled when she moved back to the chest and snagged another blanket, draping it over the other chair.

Then she settled in, her frame almost dwarfed by his jacket, and doubly so by the thick fleece covering that she pulled up to her chin.

Considering that Logan was almost sweating from the heater itself, he simply snagged the blanket off the lounger and held it close. The fabric was soft, though not as soft as her skin, but it smelled like Char, sweet with the barest hint of spice—as though she'd been bathing in rosewater and then decided to eat something with chilis.

And he was making no sense in his head, pontificating mentally about roses and chilis and still not explaining.

Enough.

"Four months isn't enough time to know a person," he said.

She sucked in a breath. "You're right," she whispered. "Of course, you're right." Soft words, pained words. Fuck, he'd hurt her again without even meaning to.

Logan set the blanket aside and moved toward Char, settling

next to her. "I was so absolutely in love with you that I didn't want to bring in any of the bad stuff, and I deliberately hid it."

Her chin came up. "I didn't need you to do that."

"I didn't do it for you," he admitted. "I did it for me because your family is so great that I didn't want to pollute that with the drama of mine."

"I've met your family—"

"I know," he said. "You met my parents when they were on their best behavior—you as an employee of the organization paying my salary—but that was just it, they were on their best behavior."

"Your sister—"

"My siblings aren't like my parents. We all survived that tension, the always present underlying resentment, and we're closer for it." He shook his head. "But, while my parents are lovely people in many ways, how they treated each other made it really hard going growing up."

"What did they do to each other?"

Logan shoved a hand through his hair and gave her the quick and dirty version. "My mom quit her job and always resented it. My dad didn't understand how hard it was for her to give up her career, to live only for her kids and husband. He wanted his needs met and made sure they were. She was content with playing martyr as hers weren't." He sighed. "Add in a dash of shitty communication skills and plenty of silent treatment on both sides, and you have a lovely thirty-year marriage that is still going strong."

Silence.

Then she shifted on the chair, her shoulder coming to rest against his. "And you saw me as your mom?"

Logan's eyes slid closed. "Yes. No. *Yes*," he admitted. "Partly, but more I saw me as my dad. I had the demanding career with the potential moves that would uproot everything. I had a wonderful woman, who was willing to give it all up and not look back." He peeled open his eyes, turned so he could rest his palm on Char's cheek. "I didn't want you to give up your dreams for me. I had to let you go so you could achieve them for yourself."

Her chest rose and fell on a long, slow inhale and exhale, but she didn't say anything. But because she also didn't push him away, he kept going. "You'd said it in passing at first, mentioned that you would just move with me if I got traded, but then as the rumors swirled and the deadline approached, do you remember what you did?"

She leaned back, expression clearing. "I think it was something along the lines of not wanting the internship in the first place, so obviously, I would quit and become a WAG." Her eyes flashed, but he couldn't decipher if it was because she was mad at him or herself.

The woman he knew today wouldn't give everything up for a man.

The girl she'd been back then might have.

And that had terrified him enough that he'd taken matters into his own hands.

"So, I went to Luc and asked him for that trade," he said, remembering how the GM hadn't wanted to let him go, that he'd pushed back hard until Logan had to admit what was going on with Char, and the only reason he'd been able to get the trade at all was because Luc loved her like a daughter and felt the same way as Logan.

Neither of them wanted any barriers between Char and her dreams.

The big dreams. The ones she'd whispered to him in the dark of night, the stars in the winter sky overhead their only illumination. To go back to school, to work her way up the ranks, to run an organization on her own.

How in the fuck could she have done that trailing around as he made his way through his own career?

The answer was that she wouldn't have been able to.

So, he'd made the decision for them.

Break their hearts now—and do it in one forceful movement

rather than the slow, incremental crack after crack he'd witnessed in his mom.

"Luc knew," she whispered.

"Yeah," he said. "I told him."

Her breath caught, even as clarity danced across her face.

Luc had been absolutely livid. The players weren't supposed to fraternize with the staff, and most especially with the interns, but he'd been able to put that anger aside for Char's own good.

She glared. "So, you two worked together to facilitate the trade, all without talking to me, totally presuming to know everything."

"I did say I take after my dad," he said, attempting a light joke. "Also, this just in, I was a fucking idiot at twenty-one."

"Yeah, you were," she said, gaze dropping to her hands, another breath sliding her shoulders up and down. Then it came back up, locked onto his. "I was an idiot, too." He breathed out a sigh of relief, but then pain crowded back in. "I was immature. I wouldn't have been content just following you around forever, even though I do want to have a family of my own someday."

Logan's heart skipped a beat at the thought of Char's kids. They'd be smart as hell and gorgeous and—

"However," she said, interrupting his thoughts. "You say you did this all for my own good, but what about the girl?"

Logan winced. "What girl?"

A shake of her head. "Nice try, but you know exactly what girl I'm talking about."

He did.

Unfortunately.

"After we broke up, I heard you'd gone to Luc and said you were going to quit anyway," he admitted quietly. The GM had called him, said he needed to find a way to end things permanently with Char so she didn't come after Logan and so she could move on with her life because Luc wasn't losing his best player *and* his best employee. "So, I did what I had to do."

Her brows came up, those chocolate eyes flashed with sparks. "By *doing* someone else days after you'd been inside me?"

"No!" he said. "Absolutely fucking not. I didn't sleep with her. I kissed her once, made sure it got caught on camera—by paparazzi she called herself, by the way," he added when Char's lips parted again. The woman was now a successful actress, but back then she'd been up and coming and had seized any opportunity to make the press. "And, for all that the photographs looked passionate, there wasn't anything pleasant about the kiss. It was acting on both our sides."

"Was there tongue?"

He frowned. "What?"

She shot him a droll look. "You say it was acting, that it was a fake kiss. Well, movie kisses don't have tongue."

Having followed that, somehow, he tugged a strand of her hair. "No, there wasn't any tongue," he said. "From the little I remember of it—and it was about as pleasant as making out with my pillow—I think my dick actually curled up into my body."

"Log!"

"Nor did I enjoy having her that close," he said. "It was like trying to cuddle a garbage bag filled with hangers." Hard when she should have been soft like Char. Add in that she smelled wrong and that he had been longing for a completely different woman. "And more importantly, she wasn't you, Starlight. She wasn't the woman who owned my heart, the one I wanted but had forced myself to let go because I couldn't be the one to stifle her dreams."

Her lips parted.

But he had one more thing to say.

"I regret every single day that I had to hurt you." He cupped her jaw, held her gaze. "But I will *never* regret letting you go. What you've accomplished, the strength and skill you've shown over the years has made me so fucking proud of you." He brushed his thumb over her cheek, capturing the single tear that dripped down her cheek. "And I've never stopped loving you, even though I had to do it from far away.

"Logan." It was a shuddering sound, one that rattled her frame.

Then she was up on her feet, pushing away from him, pacing to the other side of the deck and staring up at the sky.

He'd just poured out his heart.

And she'd walked away.

The silence settled around them, heavy and stifling and . . . unbroken.

She didn't say a single word.

Twenty

CHAR

Twinkling lights in the sky.
Cool air.
The man sitting five feet away.
Eight years, and she felt like she was right back in the past. The cool air surrounding them, the quiet of the night all around, the stars overhead. She'd been transported back in time, the only things missing were Logan's arms around her, the steady thrum of his pulse beneath her ear, his scent in her nose.

He'd told her why.

He'd given her the explanation she wanted, and if she were being entirely truthful with herself, it was also the explanation she was hoping for.

He hadn't wanted to leave her. He hadn't moved right on to someone else. He . . . still loved her.

But—

Char sucked in a breath.

But what?

But . . . did the explanation make any bit of difference? He'd still hurt her, he'd broken her, made her question everything in her heart and mind.

She released the breath, blinked up at the sky, and admitted the truth, if only to herself.

Yes, the explanation made a difference. It made a *big* difference.

It was only—

Char was still scared. She yearned for a family, and if she were being honest, a part of her had never stopped loving Logan either, even when she'd been hurt and heartbroken. But—

Fuck.

All of these *but*s.

She wasn't a woman who second-guessed herself frequently. She used her brain, thought through the pros and cons, weighed those options, and then she made a decision. And stuck with it.

Still, to get confirmation that Logan had been trying to protect her changed the way their breakup was framed in her mind. He wasn't an asshole trying to hold tightly to his bachelor days. He was a man trying to protect the woman he'd loved so she could go out and live her life.

It was the news she wanted to hear.

But—another fucking *but*—it also sliced her to the core.

Because he hadn't discussed it with her. He'd thought he'd known the best course of action, and he'd executed it without once coming and explaining why. Though, and this was part of the reason for all the *but*s, she was now thirty years old. She was stubborn as hell. But her thirty years had garnered her some clarity, some understanding that the world, that people and their emotions didn't work in black and white or right and wrong.

She'd also had thirty years to understand that she could be a stubborn pain in the ass, and that it was very likely that if Logan had told her his worries when she'd been a headstrong twenty-two-year-old, then she would have done her level best to prove them wrong . . . even to her own detriment.

So, had he made the right call?

Another inhale and exhale. Another long, slow breath to center her mind.

Yes. Conservatively, she could say that much.

But did it still hurt? Yes. And did she still hate that he hadn't talked to her about it? *Yes.* And did she *really* fucking hate that he'd seen fit to end any hope of reconciliation by orchestrating a media stunt that had stomped on her already shattered heart? Hell *fucking* yes, she did.

Then add in that Luc had known about their relationship, that he'd conspired with Logan to separate them, and Char's heart felt both healed and a little bruised.

Their intentions had been good.

But they'd still been making decisions about her life without her.

And she couldn't deny that hurt, especially when so many years had passed and neither of them had ever discussed it with her.

Even as she made a mental note to call Luc this week—she needed to hear his side from himself, to ask him why he'd never talked to her about it, especially when she'd clearly been so distraught in the days and weeks after the trade. Of course, she hadn't talked to *him* about it either. She'd gone to him and put in her resignation but wouldn't tell him why, and by the time he'd told her he wouldn't accept it, Logan had been on the gossip sites and she'd wanted something, *anything* to throw herself into.

To work so hard until she forgot.

She *had* worked.

Long and intently and, in many ways, she *had* forgotten—the effect Logan had on her, how her heart always seemed more open when he was around, how he looked at her as though she held the secrets to the universe, and how he touched her like she was a fragile treasure that had to be treated oh so carefully.

"I think that's what hurt the most."

Char was so lost in her own head that she didn't realize she spoke aloud until Logan's voice came from just behind her. "What hurt the most, Starlight?"

She jumped then turned to face him. "That I had pinned all of these hopes and dreams on a relationship with you, one that was gone in an instant." Heart aching, she admitted, "But now what hurts the most is that you thought you knew better about my life than I did. That Luc never mentioned it to me." She sighed heavily. "That I almost gave up *everything* for a boy."

He wasn't a boy now—all long, lean lines and a sparse beard.

He was a man—one who'd grown into his height, who was strong and fierce and . . . whose thick, full beard she wanted to feel between her thighs.

Attraction wasn't the issue.

Rather, she felt as though her weaknesses had been exposed to the sunlight, and she was ashamed and embarrassed. Not to have loved him, but because she was supposed to be strong, and at the end of it all, she'd been a pale approximation of herself.

"I understand why you did it," she said. "And I forgive you for it."

His breath shuddered out, relief flooding his expression.

"But I don't know if I can forgive myself."

"I—" He stopped, studied her closely. "I'm not sure what you mean, Starlight."

"It's just—" Char sighed and slipped between him and the railing, pacing away from him again. "All my life, I've been this strong, powerful woman. Confident in myself, seeing what I wanted and unerringly going after that. And . . . I almost gave up *everything* for a months' long relationship that was unlikely to have survived our Stupid Years."

Logan made a sound that sounded suspiciously like a chuckle, and she whirled around.

"I'm serious!" she exclaimed. "I just don't know how I could have thought I was making the right choice by giving up everything I was working for. It makes—" She cringed, unable to verbalize it.

"It makes you doubt the person you were inside."

Shocked, because that was exactly how she felt, she turned and gaped at him. "How—?"

A sad smile curved the corners of his mouth. "Because that's exactly how I've felt every single day since I left."

"Oh."

One syllable.

A worthless one, at that.

And yet, she couldn't think of anything else to say.

Then she thought of the *only* thing she could say. Because she didn't want to send Logan away. He was in her heart, had always been, would always be. So, maybe she needed to reflect on their relationship and subsequent breakup, needed to have a nice long think about what had happened, what had been kept from her, and how it would apply to the person she thought she was today.

Maybe those doubts would coalesce into clarity.

Maybe they would destroy the strong, infallible person she thought she was.

But she knew that she was too raw inside to search for those answers tonight, not after the stark longing at the party, not after having confirmation that hers and Logan's relationship hadn't ended as she'd once suspected.

Tonight, she wanted to forget. Not about what might be, nor about the past, or well, not *all* of it anyway. She wanted to erase everything that had happened from the time Logan had been traded all the way until he'd shown up at her office two days before.

She wanted to go back and to move forward.

She wanted warm arms and cool evening air and stars overhead.

Which was why she said that one thing aloud. "Come here."

No hesitation from Logan. Not a heartbeat or a moment to

breathe. One second he was five feet away from her and in the next, the toes of his shoes were brushing against hers.

She shuddered and melted and . . . leaned into him.

And when those warm arms found her, when they wrapped around her like they used to, Char knew that everything had altered even as absolutely nothing had changed.

TWENTY-ONE

LOGAN

His back was on fire. His shoulder ached.

The entire right side of his body was asleep.

But he wasn't going to move a muscle.

Char was cuddled up next to him, not gone to the world, but awake and close and allowing him to hold her as she watched the moon and the constellations shift across the sky overhead.

She smelled like roses and spice. Her curvy body fit perfectly against his, as they'd somehow managed to squeeze themselves onto one of the loungers on her deck.

The woman he'd loved for nearly a decade was in his arms.

So, no, he wasn't moving, not one millimeter.

"Do you remember the first time we met?" she asked. Her voice was hushed, even though it wasn't particularly late, but there was something about being outside after dark, the world muted around them, that gave him the same urge to talk quietly as well, to pretend that nothing else existed except the two of them.

"Yeah, Starlight, I do." He smiled. "You told me I smelled."

She snorted. "Well, what else could I have done? I was assaulted from the stench of all those male bodies." A shudder flowed through her, but he didn't mind that it was at his expense, not when the movement brought her closer, all those curves vibrating against him.

"There's a reason we shower," he said.

"That's true," she said. "But it was also a combination of not having the right protocols in place."

"What do you mean?"

"The equipment manager had left. Do you remember that?" she asked, leaning back slightly. Instinctively, he tightened his arms, and he caught the edge of her smile as she rested her head back onto his chest.

He stroked a hand down her hair. "He went to rehab."

"Yeah. He struggled with pain killers after a car accident." She sighed. "He came back toward the end of the season and still works for Luc now, but while he was gone his second in command didn't feel comfortable bringing issues up with management."

"And one of those issues being *our* smelly asses?"

She snorted. "The issue being that the industrial washing machine wasn't working, and so they were trying to handle things by hand."

"By hand?"

There are a lot of players on an NHL team and loads of equipment. Sets for practice, sets for games, extras in case they were damaged. Hell, he knew more than a handful of players who had multiple pairs of skates and gloves just for one game—because they preferred them to be completely dry for each period they were on the ice.

He was a little less picky, though he was finicky about his sticks and the tape and wax he used, as well as his edges—how his skates were sharpened. Oh, and his gloves. He'd been known to take advantage of the dryers in between shifts. And he supposed he really preferred that his laces be waxed and was always sneaking out the earpieces on his helmet, and his visor . . . he preferred that—

Okay, he was a picky mofo.

But the job was his life, and he liked things a certain way.

"Yup," she said, "by hand. Crazy, right?" She shook her head, the riotous brown curls bouncing across his chest. "Not only was it a waste of time and not effective. It was actually a health hazard." He frowned, opened his mouth to ask how, but she nuzzled against his throat, her arm tightening over his middle, and added, "Hockey players get hit with pucks and sticks and punch each other until they bleed."

He snorted. "We're dumbasses."

"Sometimes," she admitted, making him laugh. "But aside from the occasional idiocy, the blood-stained equipment was the real concern. We can't have someone getting a staph infection or worse."

Logan stopped, once again amazed by this woman. "I never would have considered that in a million years," he said, running his fingers over her cheek. "That's why they pay you the big bucks."

She snorted.

"Or the medium bucks," he amended, knowing that his contract was significantly bigger than hers.

"I'm quite satisfied with my medium bucks," she said. "I'm not putting my body on the line like you guys, and truthfully, I only found out about the biohazard issue after I made it my mission to tackle the smell issue."

"You got the industrial washer fixed."

A statement, not a question. Because he knew she wouldn't have stopped until she had sorted it out.

"I got them new washers, sanitation equipment, and an ozone cleaner."

He laughed. "That's why we started smelling so fresh?"

"Damn right," she said. "Couldn't have my nose burning every time I was within three feet of a player."

"Did it burn near me?"

"Fuck, yes, it did." She shifted, crossing her arms over his chest and resting her chin on them. "You were the worst!"

"You wound me," he groaned, tugging on a strand of her hair.

"You know you were."

He smirked. "I do know that. Because you told me. Do you remember that part?"

Chagrin danced on the edges of her expression, and if it had been fully light, he might have seen the barest pink appear on her cheekbones. "I do," she said then bit her lip, her voice softening. "Because it was also the first time I touched you."

"You pushed my hair off my forehead," he said, remembering the feel of her fingers. Such an innocent touch and, "I got hard in my cup."

Her lip popped free, and she gasped. "You didn't!"

"I did," he admitted. "And nearly unmanned myself in the process."

Char giggled and shifted, one leg sliding over the top of his thighs.

Heat arrowed toward his cock, and he placed his hand lightly on the small of her back, resisting the urge to grip both of her hips and seat her more firmly over him. Her breath caught at the contact . . . and truthfully, he was already hard. Again. Just like he had been all those years before.

Which she felt.

That wasn't like before, or at least not how it had been during their first meeting. She'd felt it many times over the months that followed, but that first night, she'd lurched back, her chin lifting even as she'd curled her hand into a fist at her side. He'd seen that glimpse of pink then, made obvious by the bright fluorescent lights overhead, even though he'd been the one to lean close, to bend enough so she could reach him when she'd extended her hand.

Drawn. Bewitched.

Even then.

"I told you to take a shower," she said, rolling her eyes at herself. "I was so upset that I'd touched you, that I'd dared crossed the line between management and player, that I said you smelled."

He snorted. "I didn't take it personally."

"I did." She made a face. "Both the attraction and the insults. Neither were professional." White teeth nibbling into a lush bottom lip. "But I only gave into one."

"Yup." His lips twitched. "The insults."

"Rude!"

"Yup," he said. "You are."

She gasped in outrage, those lips parting, tempting him, and Logan found he couldn't resist any longer. Levering up as he banded his arm around her waist, he kissed her.

And she kissed *him*. Fuck, but she kissed him, gripping his shoulders, her fingernails sharp spikes of pleasure through the fabric of his shirt. She leaned into him, legs straddling his hips, and her pelvis came in contact with his, the heat of her pressing tightly to his cock.

Fuck.

Heat.

Need.

Desire.

It filled every cell in his body, made red haze in on the edges of his vision, had his fingers clenching on her hips, had him parting his lips, tongue darting out to dance with hers.

Nothing was like kissing Char.

Not hoisting the Cup, not scoring a game-winning goal, not getting drafted in the first place. Not holding his nephew for the first time, or how proud his dad had been when he'd scored his first goal.

Char was *everything*.

"Come in the house," she murmured when they broke apart for air. "Come to my bed. Come kiss me and hold me and *touch* me." Her fingers brushed his lips, traced the outline when he might have protested. Because they'd made big progress that night, and he didn't want to fuck it up. "And then when you've done that for long enough, I want you to come inside me."

Twenty-Two

CHAR

She was bordering on brazen.

Which was a characteristic she considered commonplace in her business life but not so much in the bedroom.

Of course, she knew what she wanted, wasn't afraid to ask for it.

But she really enjoyed being able to sit back and not have to be in charge of something, to give and take without considering every angle, to shut off her brain and just *enjoy* herself.

Like she wanted to do with Logan.

"Starlight," he murmured, his tone beyond gentle, and she knew he was trying to be so careful with her, to not hurt her. "I don't think—"

"That's the point," she said, trying to push off him then stopping and glaring when he wouldn't let her go. "Log, *that's* the point, isn't it? Both of us have spent *too* long thinking and considering—me, wondering what I did wrong to make you leave me. You, worrying that we would turn out like your parents. But it's gotten us nowhere. Except, hurt and heartbroken and apart." She sucked in a breath, released it slowly. "I've had a lot of realizations tonight. I've realized I miss my family and hate that I've focused so much on barricading myself in work that I've lost some of our closeness. I hate that!"

"Char—"

"And I hate that I only just now realized that I'm thirty-fuck-ing-years-old and the only thing I want, perhaps more than my job, is my own family—kids and a husband who loves me and—"

He cupped her cheek.

"And I *really* hate that I didn't see through what you were doing, that I internalized it and made you go to a man who I trusted as much as my own father to trick me into making the right decision." A hot tear slid down her cheek, burning a trail from the corner of her eye to her jaw. Annoyed, she brushed it away, shoved hard enough against his hold that he let her go. "And I really hate—"

Her words cut off.

Because she'd wanted to finish that with *you*.

But she couldn't.

She *couldn't* hate this man. Try as she might, she couldn't hate him or what he'd done or even how he'd gone about it.

Sure, she could wish things had gone differently, but also, she knew if the situation were reversed, she would have done something very similar. She wouldn't have let Logan risk his dream for her.

Not ever.

"*That's* why," he whispered, trailing his fingers over her cheek, across her jaw, up to lightly stroke the spot behind her ear. "Because you need some time, sweetheart. To think about us, to sort things out in your head. I'm here to talk through what's going on with your family. I'm here. I really fucking hope to maybe be that person you can build your own family with some-day, but"—he inhaled sharply, released the breath slowly—"I'm also the man who hurt you, who broke your heart, and you need time to process why."

Her heart was pounding.

Anger was a sharp ache in her throat.

Pent-up need a coiled snake in her center.

But . . . he was right.

She needed to allow herself this moment, to not bury everything as she'd done for the last years. Feel. She needed to feel and think and come to terms with all that happened.

Sighing, she rested her forehead against his chest.

"As much as I hate to admit it," she muttered. "You're right."

His laughter—slightly strained—and the hard planes of his body—hard everywhere, heh—relaxed her enough that she could think again. Or at least not feel as though she were going to be swallowed by her emotions.

She glanced up, enjoying the feel of his fingers stroking through her hair, his body pressed to hers, his scent surrounding her.

"Will you at least kiss me before you go?"

A wicked smile, fingers tightening slightly in her hair.

And then he did as she asked, kissing her until her pulse pounded in her veins, until her lips were swollen, until her body was a tangled knot of need.

Eventually, they broke apart, his gaze holding hers, and the need in those beautiful green eyes took her already jagged breath away.

As did his words.

"I plan on kissing you goodnight every day for the rest of my life."

———

It was early East Coast time.

Which meant it was *really* freaking early California time.

But Char had woken just as the sun was beginning to lighten the brown-topped hills in the distance, the summer's heat already turning the green grass dry and brittle. Soon enough fire season would be upon them, smoke choking the air, blocking out the sky, making it impossible for her to see the stars she liked to glance upon with a glass of wine in her hand.

Often, she snuck away for a week or two, recharging at a spa, spending time at a beachfront hotel while doing nothing more than sticking her toes in the sand, or occasionally in the ocean. Last year, she'd skipped the break completely, having spent those weeks dealing with the move and getting her ducks in a row for the season.

She'd swung by her family's house for a weekend, kissed her mom and dad, sat around the kitchen table listening to them cook and bicker in equal measures. But it hadn't been long before she'd felt the vise tighten around her chest, and she'd slipped out, losing herself to emails and work.

She'd left early the next day, had come to San Francisco, and all but lived in her office.

At the time, she'd chalked it up to nerves about her new position, to needing to assure herself that absolutely everything she could control was in order. But now she wondered if seeing her parents so in love and happy and in tune had made her shut down.

And then bolt.

Ugh.

More pondering to do, more thinking to complete.

But for now, she needed to slay the demon that was circling in her mind. Or at least try to cage it and glare it into submission.

Which was why she was back on her deck, a coffee in hand and staring at the lightening sky.

"Just do it already," she muttered.

She hit the button on her phone's screen then put her cell up to her ear.

Ring-ring.

Ring-ring.

Ring—

"Lottie!" Luc's voice boomed loudly through the speaker. "I

was wondering when you'd get a moment to call. How are you? Terrorized any underlings lately?"

God, one call, and she was back in that arena.

Shaking her head, biting back a smile, because seriously this man was like an older brother and father and friend, all in one package. "I was doing better before you decided to use *that* name."

He laughed, and she could imagine him leaning back in his office chair, plunking his feet onto his desk.

"Plus, I don't terrorize anyone."

"Call it unintentional terrorizing then," he said. "You're so damned good at what you do, it's almost impossible to live up to your example."

Her breath caught, an unfamiliar ache sliding through her stomach.

"My mom said that once."

Silence.

The feet would be leaving the desk now, dropping back onto the floor, his brows drawn together. "What's that now?"

"She said the reason I'm single is that I'm so focused on being perfect that I can't accept the imperfections and failings of those around me."

He sucked in a breath, the noise rattling through the speaker.

"That's bullshit."

Char blinked. "What?"

"You know I love you, Lottie girl," he said. "So, I'm not going to mince words. I've waited this entire season for him to make a fucking move, to make things right, but he hasn't, and so now I'm going to do what I should have."

"Do what?" she asked, fingers clenching on her cell.

"You're single for two reasons, and *only* two." His voice was sharp, demanding she pay attention. "One, because you're hung up on Logan Walker and your relationship with him overshadowed every other romantic one you've had since, and two, because none of those dumbasses you've dated since Logan had the balls to drag you down the aisle."

"You—"

"Yes, I knew," he interrupted before she got more than that one word out. "Yes, I also knew what I helped you two give up. Did I hate every fucking minute of it? Yes. Did I still think it was the right thing for both of you? Yes."

Char closed her eyes, was silent as his words washed over her.

Luc sighed. "Look, Lottie," he said, voice gentling. "I know that you were hurt badly by how things went down between you and Logan, and I fucking hated him for getting involved with you in the first place. Hell, I hated you a little bit for wanting to drop everything and take away my best employee." He paused. "Then I realized that you weren't two people looking for a quick fuck, but instead you two were just dumbasses in love at the wrong time in the wrong place, and I hoped you'd eventually find your way back to each other."

"Luc."

"Then when you picked Logan up before the season—which was a bold, fucking move that I'm still pissed you were able to pull off without me—I figured you two would work things out. Would realize this is a different time and place and social climate and get back to remembering that you were two dumbasses in love once." A beat. "Then be able to find your way back there."

"I—"

"And since that seems to not be the case," he said, talking over her, "and since I taught you all you need to know about being a stubborn ass, I figured I might as well give you the shove off the cliff you so obviously need."

That was the thing about her former boss.

He liked to talk.

A lot.

He was never short for words, and while most of the time she could filter through the bullshit and arrow in on the important details, this morning they were talking about her life and her job and—

She sighed.

Her heart.

They were talking about her bruised, damaged, pieced-together heart.

"And—"

"Shut up, Luc," she said, interrupting him for the first time in this conversation. "And let me talk."

Silence. For all of ten seconds. Then, "So talk."

"Logan already told me."

A longer blip of silence. "And you didn't get back together?"

It was impossible to miss the disappointment in his tone. It was also impossible to sum up all she was feeling for Logan, considering it was so fresh in her head. "He just told me last night."

"Waited till the season was over," Luc said, tone approving. "That's a good man. Didn't get between you and your job, even though it had to be killing him."

"What do you mean?"

"He's seen you nearly every day for nine months, Lottie. And he couldn't touch or hold you. The man was thrown into close contact with the woman he's crazy about and didn't want to risk fucking up the good thing she had going." He chuckled. "No wonder he played the best season of his career."

She couldn't deny that Logan had absolutely killed it at the blue line throughout the year.

"He came to me the night we lost," she admitted. "With fucking slippers."

Luc burst out laughing. "Oh man, that slick fucker pays attention. How often did I tell you that you were going to end up with a bum back if you kept wearing those death contraptions, but no, you've got to keep clomping around the arena in them—"

"First, I do *not* clomp. Second, I need them in order to be somewhat the same size as the rest of you giants," she muttered. "I was tired of looking up everyone's nose all the time."

More laughter, but she joined in this time.

Before long, though, she sobered. "Why'd you do it, Luc? Why did you keep me in the dark? Why did you lie? I thought we —" She sighed. "I thought we meant more to each other than that."

"I'm sorry I hurt you," he said, sounding more serious than she'd ever heard him. "I hope you know that."

"I—uh—did you not think I could handle it? Handle being on the same team if we broke up?"

"No, honey," he told her. "No, it wasn't that at all. I thought you were young and needed space to think, needed to figure out what you wanted in your head and heart without anyone else influencing you."

"Except . . . you influenced me."

He inhaled, released it slowly. "Fuck, I never thought about it like that. Shit, Lottie, I—"

She squeezed her eyes shut. "Part of me is really hurt you and Logan had this whole plan about my life without bothering to include me in it. Another part of me understands. Still another is pissed at myself for considering giving up my life for Logan, for thinking that his dreams were bigger and more important than mine." She swallowed hard. "And a final part, one I just realized last night when someone I know announced she was pregnant, is furious for not recognizing that in making my life *only* about my dream after Logan left, I missed out on my family, on making a family of my own."

Char blinked like a madwoman. It was too fucking early in the morning for tears, too early to be a blubbering mess with her former boss, her sort of brother, father, friend.

And it was a good thing that she did all that blinking because when he spoke a few moments later, his words made her eyes sting.

"It's not too late," he said. "Not too late for you, and not too late for you *and* Logan."

She sniffed, and since they were talking about all of the serious shit that morning, she told him the other thing that was bothering her, the deep-seated worry she held because she liked Logan so damned much. "What if I get like before? What if I want to give up everything so I can have a family with Logan?"

"Why are those things mutually exclusive?" he countered. "Why can't you have your family *and* your dream?"

"I—" She stopped, blinked. Because, of course, it was the logical thought, but also . . . "It's not that simple," she said.

"Isn't it?" he replied. "You have a demanding career, but so do plenty of people. You like someone that might put you in a complicated position, but the Gold, as an organization, has weathered that particular storm enough times over that I know there are certain HR and personnel protocols in place. You're in the public eye, but so are plenty of other people."

He was right, the bastard.

"If it's so easy," she grumbled, "why aren't you in a steady relationship?"

"This isn't about me and my almost forty-year-old ass. This is about you and Logan and how the man loved you enough to set you free or some other sappy bullshit."

Her lips curved into a smile. "For all that you accuse him of propagating sappy bullshit, you're the one that helped protect me."

"Meh."

So like him to dismiss his role in anything. Just exactly as he handled his career, never taking credit, even where it was due. It was always the guys, the team, the organization.

She'd modeled herself after him, and often did the same, *felt* the same.

But she knew he'd done more in this case than he'd accept.

He and Logan had risked her hurt and anger to try and do right by her. They'd loved her and protected her, and so maybe she didn't approve of everything they'd done, and yeah, she wished they'd handled it differently, but Char was old enough to know that the tough decisions were rarely ever black and white.

"I can't wait until you find a woman who throws your whole life into disarray, until everything you thought you knew is turned upside down." Like Logan did for her. Like she was starting to recognize was something she craved.

"That's not going to happen," Luc said after a beat. "Hashtag bachelor for life."

Except . . . there was something in his tone that made her pause, made her wonder why there was sad on the edges of his voice. She'd known him for nearly a decade, and she had never seen the same woman on his arm more than a handful of times. A few dates, a few months, but never any longer.

Like her.

And she'd always figured he was like her in that way, that things had ended with the women in his life because he was married to his job and didn't have room for more.

Still, considering she'd just realized that her relationships hadn't failed solely because her career kept her too busy, but also because she'd been hurt and had encased herself in a protective shell that only Logan seemed to be able to penetrate, she figured that Luc might have something happening behind that casual, cavalier shield of his.

"You never got close?"

Silence.

Then, "Yeah, I got close. Once, I got pretty damned close."

Pain in that sentence, so much pain that she'd unwittingly churned up. Damn. She went to apologize, paused. Because Luc was like her, but harder, and he'd shown her a little chink in his armor. He wouldn't want her to poke at it, to draw attention to it.

He'd want to move on and make it about something else.

So, she deliberately lightened her tone and said, "Well, I can't wait until you fall for someone, so I can watch you spew sappy bullshit over her."

"Spew. Such a lovely word." He snorted. "Also, why can't you wait?"

"Because I'm both a nosy bastard and I can't wait to make fun of you."

"Nice," he said. "And here I am, protecting you, being nice. I would never be so mean as to make fun of you."

"Should I circle us back to you saying I was a lovestruck asshole?"

"That's fact," he said. "Also, technically, I said you were a dumbass in love."

She resisted the urge to laugh. Just barely. Instead, saying, "One who needs a man to drag me down the aisle?"

"Man, woman, identifies as neither, or both, or at some other point on that scale, I don't care. But the truth is that you do need someone to drag your ass down that aisle."

"I'm not that—"

"You were burned. You need to know someone won't cut at the first sign of trouble. You need proof that your relationship has staying power. That's not bad or wrong or fucked up," he said. "But with this, you need to not be scared, to realize that the only place you ever really felt safe was Logan's arms."

He was right.

In so many ways.

She'd never needed to have her guard up with Logan. He'd always seen right into her heart, straight down to all of the hidden pieces of her soul. Just as she'd seen the same in his heart, his soul.

That trust had been broken.

But for a very specific reason.

So, the question she needed to ask herself now was whether she had the courage to put it all aside and to move forward.

Because this conversation had answered the other question— whether she wanted to move forward.

She *wanted*. Oh, how she wanted.

"Now's the time for courage, Lottie girl."

If she'd been looking for a sign from the universe that moving forward with Logan was the right decision, then one could certainly consider Luc speaking the same words aloud she had circling in her mind as one.

Was she looking for one?

Yes. No. Maybe.

Yes.

"Yeah, Luc, I think you're right."

"Of course, I am, Lottie Dottie."

She sighed. "You know, you're the only one I've ever let call me Lottie—in any form—right?"

"That's because I'm special."

"It's because you're *something*," she muttered.

He laughed. She laughed.

And then because they had eight years of knowing each other under their belts, of that father/daughter, brother/sister, friend relationship, they didn't need further discussion to move on to talking about something that wasn't sappy bullshit.

And because they both loved their jobs, they moved on to hockey.

As if there were anything else.

TWENTY-THREE

LOGAN

He'd gone slow.
He'd had patience.
And . . . now he had blue balls.

But he'd followed his own advice, and now there was a woman standing on his doorstep for a change. A brown bakery bag in one hand, a bottle of liquor in the other.

His lips curved, and he leaned back against the doorjamb. "What's happening, Starlight?"

She lifted her chin and brushed by him into his house.

Grinning, he closed the door, turned to follow her, only to see that she had stopped all of three feet inside his place. He froze, and maybe he was succumbing to his inner pig, but damn, what a view that was.

Her hair was swept up into a mass of curls. Her skin gleamed in the morning light, set off by the pale blue of her dress—a simple thing that tied at her nape, left the rest of her back exposed. His mouth watered, nearly as much as his fingers itched to touch, because the sweep of that dress, how it teased the tops of her thighs, thighs he wanted to be in between and, fuck, thighs he wanted to stroke, to kiss, to *lick*.

"This is so cliché."

"Me wanting to go down on you?" he asked, slipping his arms around her waist from behind and pressing his front to her back.

Her breathing hitched, hips canting to brush his—

Yes, he was hard.

Hence . . . blue balls.

Char spun in his arms, lifting hers up and resting her hands on his shoulders. She had those fucking tall heels on again, red ones this time that matched her fire engine colored lipstick.

And he wanted to kiss her.

But she was there, and patience seemed to be working, and he needed to keep chugging along, to not fuck this up—

"Logan!" she exclaimed.

"What?" he asked, going for innocent.

Not that it worked, because she glared up at him. "You can't say things like that."

"Why not?"

"Because I'm trying very hard not to jump your bones."

He stilled, held her gaze. "Well, I'm trying very hard to be good," he murmured. "And you talking about bones"—he drew her a little closer, trying to resist the urge to grind his cock against her—"isn't helping my control."

Fingers on his jaw, a smirk on that sexy red-covered mouth. "Yeah?"

"Vixen," he muttered, turning her and cuddling her against his side, keeping that dangerous, tempting body near, while still attempting to maintain his control. Having her curves pressed to him wasn't great for said control, but it was better than finding any excuse to rub his cock against her. Or better yet to lift up the hem of that dress and—

"I thought I was your Starlight?" she asked.

"Yes, to Starlight," he said, leading her farther into the house.

"You've been my guide over the years, my beacon to find my way back to you, to show you—"

He broke off, voice definitely wet, even though he was a big, tough hockey player. Yes, he knew he'd ultimately done the right thing in letting her go, but it had hurt, and part of him worried that he would never find a way to make it up to her, to get her back, to have the opportunity to prove exactly how much she meant to him.

"You've showed me, Log," she murmured, then nudged him lightly. "Sure took your damned time doing it though."

"I had to wait," he said. "You needed that time."

She had, even though it had been painful. Even though, for a time, he'd tried to find happiness without her, same as she seemed to be finding it without him. But no woman had ever come close, and it wasn't fair to them to keep dragging something along that only resulted in hurt feelings and damaged hearts—theirs, not his.

And that wasn't his ego talking.

Because his heart had been damaged long before.

By knowing what he'd given up, what he was missing. He'd known it was special and important and way more than a youthful crush or first love.

It was forever love.

That he'd needed to send to slaughter.

Dramatic much? Probably. But in many ways, that was the best description. He'd sliced away a part of each of them, hoping that one day the pieces might be able to come back together. Maybe not in the same fashion as they'd once been, but in something that had the potential to be more, to be . . . *them*.

She inhaled. "Yeah, I think I needed that time too." Brown eyes on his. "For the record, I really fucking hated it."

He grinned, the painful memories of those years apart slipping away. "For the record, I did, too." Logan turned and drew her into the kitchen. "So, if you weren't talking about your glorious puss—*oof!*" He broke off when she smacked him, and he found he didn't have the strength to resist that glorious mouth any longer. Not when it was lush and red and so damned close.

Not when her eyes flashed at him, but her lips tipped up at the edges.

Not when a shuddering breath slipped from them.

And so, he pressed his lips to hers.

She nipped at his tongue when it slid into her mouth, but then she was kissing him back, her tongue tangling with his, her hands kneading at his shoulders. He slid his palm down, tugged her flush against him, cupping that ass he'd dreamed about for years, the same one he'd stroked himself to over and over that season, seeing her parade around in her heels and slacks.

For the record, he knew she'd kick his ass if she caught wind of him thinking she'd been doing any parading.

He also knew she'd been working her ass off.

It was just his inner pig that enjoyed pretending she was strutting around, the same one that imagined bending her over her desk and—

His fingers brushed bare skin.

Fuck. He hadn't realized he'd been lifting her skirt, hadn't even realized he'd lifted *her* up onto the counter and stepped between her legs.

Patience.

He pulled back.

Hot brown eyes on him, swollen mouth, smeared lipstick, rapid breaths mixing.

"You haven't forgotten how to kiss," she teased, stroking a hand down his T-shirt, making him wish he was wearing a suit of armor, only so he wouldn't be tempted to keep sliding her dress up, to keep touching.

"What were you talking about?" he asked, voice like gravel.

"What?" She pushed her hair out of her face then reached over and rubbed at his mouth, her thumb coming away stained red. "That lipstick is ridiculously expensive."

Logan nipped at her thumb. "Then don't wear it," he said. "Because I really enjoy kissing it off your mouth."

She huffed.

"I promise I'll buy you a new tube once I finish kissing off the first one."

One brow lifted. "You don't know how expensive it is."

"If it means kissing you?" A shrug. "I don't care."

Her lips tipped up, making him want to kiss her all over again, but he resisted because . . . patience.

Fuck, that was going to become his new favorite four-letter word.

Or eight-letter, rather.

Regardless, he got back to the point at hand, which was having a civil conversation with this woman that didn't end with their clothes in a pile on the floor or his mouth on her pussy.

Why? his inner pouty man moaned. *You'd make it good.*

He would. That was irrefutable.

But he needed to make everything else good, too.

Which is why he focused and asked, "When you walked in, you said this was so cliché. What's cliché?"

Her eyes danced, and she waved a hand around his kitchen. "Isn't it obvious?" she asked. "This bachelor pad on steroids. It's the most cliché thing I've ever laid eyes on."

He stared at the kitchen. It was a little spartan, he supposed, but he'd already established his lack of cooking ability. The family room was across the hall, and he had a nice leather couch, a big TV, even some throw pillows his mom had made him buy the last time his parents had been in town.

That had sparked a fight in the middle of Target—his dad saying his mom needed to butt out of Logan's life, and his mom declaring she was "just trying to make sure our son is comfortable. Shouldn't I make sure he's comfortable?"

In the end, Logan had bought eight freaking pillows—which had cost him three hundred dollars *(three hundred!)*—but his mom had been happy, and then after he'd shoved the pillows in the trunk of his SUV, he'd driven them to a local brewery, thus making his dad happy.

Oh, so fun.

His parents were the best.

But aside from the throw pillows, the space was organized, clean, and a pretty decent combination of dark wood, black leather, and stainless steel.

Oh.

Now he got what she meant.

Char dressed nice, did her hair and makeup, but she wasn't what he'd consider high maintenance or a girly-girl. She did what she needed to look professional, and outside of work, she dressed in a way that made her happy.

Her home was like that.

Just as clean and organized as his.

But it bridged the gap between professional and happy, between stark and warm.

She had trinkets on her shelves, brightly patterned kitchen towels draped by the sink, pictures on the walls, throw pillows *and* blankets on her couch. She had all the things, that when put together, made an actual home.

His place was just that.

A place to sleep. A place to watch TV. A place to eat.

There wasn't warmth or happiness or joy.

Joy? For fuck's sake.

He knew he was gone for Char, had been gone for her for years, knew he'd played the sacrificing hero, but fuck, he was also a man.

One who'd played his hand and lived by it.

One who'd seen his opening and made his move.

So what if he didn't have trinkets on his shelves?

And this was a conversation he probably didn't need to be having with himself in this moment, not with the woman he loved at his place, a bag of treats—please dear Lord let it be treats in that bag—in her hand, a sexy dress on her body, and her lipstick smeared across his face.

Frankly, he was finding himself hard-pressed to give a fuck about trinkets or bachelor pads on steroids.

"I'll have you know," he said, "that I have throw pillows. A bachelor pad doesn't have throw pillows."

She snorted. "Is that the rule? Throw pillows mean that you've got a real home?"

"I'm a real boy," he joked, *a la* Pinocchio.

Char giggled, and it made him feel about a hundred feet tall. "Here, you goof," she said, thrusting the bag at him. "I've brought your favorite Cheat Day snack."

"But I don't do Cheat Days anymore."

"The season's over." A beatific smile. "I think you can take a few Cheat Days."

All of his earlier promises and rules about sticking with the diet plan for the foreseeable future flew out the window. Because come hell or high water, he'd find a way back to the plan if it meant that Char would show up with that pretty smile and pride in her eyes. He'd just . . . tie himself to the bike to work off the extra calories.

There. Plan sorted.

He shrugged. "Depends."

Her eyebrows lifted. "On what?"

"On what's in the bag."

Her face fell. "Oh."

Stepping closer, he cupped her cheek. Not smart for his control, but the urge to get close to her, to comfort, was impossible to ignore. "What did I say?"

Instead of answering, she handed him the bag. "Apple cinnamon muffin."

His stomach rumbled, the diet plan all but forgotten now. "From Molly's?"

A smirk. "As if I'd get it from anywhere else?" She nudged him back and unfolded the top of the bag, pulled out a muffin.

Spice and sweet filled the air, and his stomach rumbled again.

Char laughed. "Okay, clearly, you're withering away." She broke off a piece of the top and held it up to his lips. "Eat this."

"You first," he said. "I'm sure you're hung—"

She shoved it into his mouth.

He glared, but it wasn't like he was going to spit out the deliciousness, not with the bite melting on his tongue, cinnamon and apples filling his taste buds. But he *was* going to share.

Snagging the muffin, he broke off a piece then put it up to her lips, trying not to moan when her tongue brushed his finger as she ate the bite.

"Again," she said after chewing for several moments, "you need to work on your bite size, sir. I am a tiny woman with a tiny mouth. I need appropriate-sized bites."

"I notice you didn't say tiny bites."

"I'm not an idiot," she said, grabbing his wrist and nibbling at the muffin. "This *is* from Molly's."

He took a bite, and yeah, he supposed when he compared it to what Char had eaten, one might term it a behemoth. But he was six-four, two hundred and sixteen pounds. He had a big body that needed a lot of fuel.

Behemoth bites were a given.

Didn't mean he couldn't share.

He raised the muffin up to Char's mouth, and they spent the next few minutes devouring the treat, along with two others— one more apple cinnamon and a blueberry—before they spoke again.

"Did you eat an appropriate amount of muffin?" he asked after they'd finished and he'd shoved the wrappers back into the bag.

"Yup."

"Good."

She brushed at his chin, met his eyes when he looked at her in question. "Crumb," she said by way of explanation.

"You thirsty?" he asked, not wanting to step away from her but knowing that the longer he stood between her thighs, the less likely he was to practice his patience plan. "I've got water and orange juice. I can make some coffee or—"

"Just a glass of water would be great."

He stepped back, and she shifted as though she'd slide from the counter, but the move dislodged one of those sexy fucking heels—death traps though they were—and it hit the tile floor with a clatter.

Not thinking, he bent and scooped it up.

Then straightened and nearly bit his tongue.

Because of where he was.

Where he was.

Bare legs, a glimpse of naked thigh. The scent of her lotion in his nose, rose and something tropical wafting up, trailing over him, and musk. She wanted him, and he could smell it.

Fucking hell.

He slipped on her heel, straightened farther, not burying his face where he was desperate to, not lifting her skirt and sliding his fingers through damp heat—

"You could," she murmured. "You could just lift up my skirt and—"

His cock went rock-hard.

His eyes flew to hers . . . and saw that, yes, there was desire there, but it was tempered by the shadows of the past, dimmed by pain.

So, yeah, he *could*, but also, no, he couldn't.

Not if he wanted Char to feel like the most important woman in the universe to him. Not if he wanted to be able to look himself in the mirror and not feel like the worst scumbag on the planet.

He could, however, press his mouth to hers, he could kiss her and hold her tight and put everything he was feeling into that simple embrace.

Then he could step back and help her off the counter.

He could take her hand.

He could ask, "Are those heels for walking?"

And he could feel a hundred feet tall when she rolled her eyes and snorted, even as her body drifted close, and she said, "Yes, Log. They're made for walking."

Twenty-Four

Char

"You know, when you asked if these shoes were for walking," she said, glancing out at the forested trail in front of them, "this isn't exactly what I had in mind."

He'd helped her down from the counter in his kitchen, brushing the fronts of their bodies in one languorous slide, making every nerve in her being prickle and fire and fill with desire.

She'd offered up spending a lazy day bingeing on *Great British Bake-Off*, selling it as him learning how to cook something by proxy.

But he'd seen through her.

Or at least, he'd read that while she'd shown up, while she'd come to terms with a lot of what had happened between them, there was still a part of her that was nervous.

She wanted him and was terrified of what would happen if they went for it.

Physically *and* emotionally.

She loved kissing him, loved touching and how he held her. She loved joking and talking and laughing with him—as they'd done for much of the drive up into the mountains south of San Francisco, twining their way toward Santa Cruz, but turning off before they made it into the sleepy beach town, instead climbing up and up until they'd made their way into Big Basin.

Logan threw his SUV into park and reached into the back seat. He came up with a box that was almost the same size as the one he'd presented her in her office a few days before and plunked it into her lap.

Then he reached back again and came up with a sweatshirt.

"Open it, " he said when she didn't immediately tear the lid off.

"I'm not a puppet," she muttered. "Give a woman a second to process a man who doesn't take appropriate-sized bites and who keeps dropping packages in her lap."

He dropped the sweatshirt on top of the box. "How about sweatshirts *and* boxes?"

A huff. "Really?"

"Really." But he pushed the sweatshirt out of the way and took the lid off for her. "I'd intended on giving these to you in the not-so-distant future, but now seems apropos."

Char had taken one look at the box and frozen.

Now, as she processed the shoes inside, she felt her throat burn, her eyes sting. Silly, romantic, *lovely* man.

"I haven't worn Converse in years," she whispered. "Not since . . ."

She trailed off, heart hurting even though she was happy deep inside.

"I coaxed you into going hiking with me the last time," he finished, running his fingers over the shell of her ear. "I know it's not your favorite, not by a long-shot, but I do think there's something beautiful that you'll really like." He smiled and pointed to a paved path disappearing among the arboreal giants. "And it's not far up the trail."

They'd parked in a lot tucked past the main entrance, and as she'd gotten her ass up at an insane hour, and then had gone over to Logan's at a very impolite hour—so impolite that her mom would have been pissed she'd rung the bell so early—the lot was empty aside from their car. But it was the weekend and it was summer in Northern California. The lot wouldn't be empty for long.

Soon there would be other—she shuddered—hikers and dogs on leashes and families with cute little kids who were either having the best day of their life or their worst.

Her heart pulsed.

She wanted that, and she could admit it—if only to herself, only in her own brain—that she'd always dreamed of having *that* —kids and dogs and tantrums and day trips—only with one person.

This man.

And perhaps that was why she'd focused on work so intently, had tucked that desire down so deeply.

When Logan had gone, she'd buried that longing.

But now that he was back, now that she knew the full story, the craving had made a reappearance.

Either that, or her biological clock was ticking.

She snorted.

"Don't trust me?" he asked innocently, and she narrowed her eyes. Because it was *too* innocent, the scamp.

"When you look at me like that?" She shook her head. "That's a no."

He grinned, unrepentant. "I was going for earnest."

"You succeeded in serial killer."

Laughter filled the interior of the car, bubbling in her veins, making her lips turn up in humor, and then her laughter join in.

"Fuck, I like you, Starlight."

Her breath caught, those emerald eyes holding him captive for long moments until she remembered her suspicions and asked, "What are you going to show me?"

"Something special."

She wrinkled her nose. "Special how?"

He sighed.

She smiled, took his hand, and squeezed lightly to let him know she was teasing. "No bears?"

"No bears," he said then shrugged. "Just on the very rare occasion, a mountain lion."

"*What?*"

His face sobered. "I'm kidding."

"Are you really kidding, or are you just trying to get me out of this car so I can see whatever it is you want to show me?"

"One of those." He tugged a curl lightly, asked before she could press him further, "So, what say you? Will you swap the heels for sneakers and a short, paved path?"

"Do you have a sweatshirt for yourself?" she asked, knowing it would be cold in these hills, especially with the marine layer still visible overhead. Later, the whole area would warm up, a sunny day forecasted, but for now, she snagged the snuggly cotton covering from him and tugged it over her head. The box slid, but she grabbed it as she toed off her heels, plucking the shoes out and thinking that this was probably a bad idea without—

"Socks," came his voice, paired with his hand in front of her face, holding out a brand-new pair.

They were patterned with brightly-colored curly lines—

Or not, she realized with a grin.

Because those curly lines actually formed a hidden pattern of cursive f-bombs.

She grinned up at him. "You didn't forget my favorite curse word."

He cupped her cheek. "I didn't forget *anything*."

"Log," she murmured, her freaking eyes stinging again. "You've got to stop being so sweet."

He snagged the socks from her and tugged off the label and hook at the top, handing them back to her one at a time. She pulled them on, shoved her feet into the pale blue converse that matched exactly the pair she'd worn with him a lifetime before.

The size was perfect.

Not that she'd expected anything less after he'd surprised her with the slippers and the treats and the cooking and—

He was thoughtful.

Very thoughtful.

If this worked, she needed to make sure she was thoughtful right back.

Her heart pulsed and her eyes went stingy again, but as she tied the shoelaces and rolled up the sleeves of the sweatshirt, she blinked any extra moisture away.

"You didn't answer me about the sweatshirt," she said, when she'd finished.

"I've got another in the trunk."

"Good." A nod as she pushed open the door. "Let's go."

She stepped out and felt her breath hitch. Even a non-nature girl like herself could appreciate the sheer size of the trees. Huge redwoods towering over her. A cool dampness to the air that made her shiver. The smell of the earth, a preternatural sort of quiet.

The soft *pop* of Logan's door opening broke that silence, and she watched as he moved around to the back of his SUV and opened the hatch.

A minute later, he had a sweatshirt pulled over his head, the trunk closed, and was walking toward her.

"Okay?" he asked, gaze flicking toward her bare legs. "Not too cold?"

"It's not far, right?"

"Right," he confirmed.

"Then, no," she said. "I'm fine, so long as you promise to cuddle me close when it gets too chilly."

He grinned. "And now you know my nefarious plan."

Char rolled her eyes but didn't protest when Logan laced their fingers together and led her down the path. "Should I be happy that you didn't pair that with a *muhaha*?"

He bopped her on the nose. "Too far, Starlight, too far."

She shook her head, rested it on his shoulder so he wouldn't see her smiling, and walked with him. The trail curved to the right just past the tree line, and she had the immediate feeling of being both dwarfed in size and feeling perfectly sheltered and protected. There were large gaps between the giant trunks, these ancient trees needing plenty of space to grow, but they were so tall, their branches overhead so vast and intertwined that she felt like she'd been transported to another planet.

That was, of course, if she ignored the paved path beneath her sneakers.

In her mind, alien planets didn't have asphalt trails.

Although, it did show that, once again, Logan knew her.

This wasn't a difficult uphill trek, nor a dusty and rocky terrain to traverse. This was flat. This was beautiful. This was . . . short.

Because barely fifteen minutes later, he tugged her to the right, and she found herself in a circular grove of trees.

Of *charred* trees.

She gasped, hand coming to her throat.

"The fires last summer came through here."

She spun in a circle, taking in what remained and what had been destroyed by those rapidly moving flames. And God . . . there was black, so much black.

So much beauty reduced to ash.

"I see that," she said, sad for no other reason than it hurt a part of her deep inside to see what had been lost last summer. Fires were part of California, or at least that was what she'd been told by those she knew who had grown up here, but there was no doubt that the fires had grown in intensity and frequency over time.

That, paired with an increasing population, soaring house prices, years of drought, meant that property and businesses and lives were in ever-magnifying danger.

And places like this one burned.

"This is so sad," she whispered, eyeing the circle, of which only a few trees appeared to have survived. Many others had fallen to the ground, the path of blackened trunks a searing visual amongst the rest of the green forest.

"I didn't bring you here to be sad," he said gently, wrapping an arm around her shoulders and hugging her to his side.

"Well, it is sad," she said. "I remember the news stories. I remember how so many people lost so much, and these trees— God, this clearing must have been absolutely majestic."

He nodded. "It was."

At her questioning look, he smiled. "I found quite a bit of time to explore during my time in L.A." A shrug. "And I discovered that I much preferred this northern part of California to the plastic and fakeness of Hollywood."

"So, it wasn't hard for you to come to San Francisco."

He shook his head. "Though, full disclosure, I would have moved to Siberia to play for your team, Starlight. Not only because of this"—he held her tighter, brushed his lips over hers— "but also because you're very talented and smart, and any player would be lucky to be a part of your organization."

Her heart stuttered, and feeling oddly shy, she found herself dropping her forehead to his chest, not moving when he rested his palm on her nape. "Thank you for saying that."

"I mean it."

"Well, thank you for meaning it," she whispered.

"Anytime, sweetheart."

They stayed like that for a minute before Logan slid his hand down her spine and wrapped it around her hip. "Come this way," he murmured, guiding her over to the far side of the clearing.

A huge, absolutely *huge* tree had fallen over, black charring its side.

She could barely process the breadth of its size, a car could drive on it with plenty of room on either side, and . . . it had collapsed. The strong, seemingly impenetrable giant had been felled by flames.

"Look," he said, pointing and drawing her gaze to what she'd missed on first glance.

She'd been obsessed with what had been, mourning what *might* have been if the flames hadn't torn through this forest, and in focusing on the might have beens and the had beens, she'd nearly overlooked the beauty of the now.

Because, yes, that tree had broken into pieces when it had fallen. Yes, it was less majestic on the ground than it was compared to its brethren growing into the sky. Yes, it might have gone on living and growing and becoming even more breathtaking if only the fire hadn't come.

But . . . fire had come.

But . . . it wasn't less beautiful just because it had been knocked down, because it had collapsed.

And it didn't lose its value.

Because in the ruins of that wonderful fallen giant was new life.

"Did you know that some of these Redwoods need fire in order for their cones to open, for their seeds to be exposed, and ultimately for new trees to grow?"

Carefully, she reached out and ran her fingers over the rough bark coating the trunk in one spot, the ashy, charcoal directly next to it, and then, finally, over the delicate green blades of what would someday—if the conditions were right—be a new giant redwood.

"I didn't know that." She sniffed. "You're making my eyes burn again, dammit."

Logan chuckled and wrapped his arms around her. "We're like these trees, Starlight. We burned hot and bright and furiously. And then . . . we fell."

Another sniff. "I'm not missing the symbolism, baby."

He was grinning. She couldn't see it, not with her head plastered against his chest, the steady thrum of his heart under her ear, but she could feel it nonetheless. "Then you also didn't miss that we have that potential, too. That we can make something beautiful and alive out of the ashes of our past."

Char closed her eyes and let his words, this place wash over her.

They could do that. But, more importantly, she *wanted* to do that. With Logan. She wanted the beauty. She wanted the future. She wanted *him*.

Which was why she held him tight and said, "I didn't miss that either."

TWENTY-FIVE

LOGAN

The next week, he strolled up the front walk of Char's house, confident this time that he wouldn't have to sneak in the back.

They had plans.

They'd spent the weekend together, Char surprising him by taking his hand and leading him on a longer hike in Big Basin. Not far, since neither of them were dressed properly for an all-day adventure—no water, no sunscreen, no—in her case—pants and she wasn't a really outdoorsy person, but they had walked for a little while, stumbling upon a small waterfall that had taken his breath away.

They stood and watched the stream spilling over the outcroppings of rock, covering the bright green moss in mist.

Then they'd driven up to the city, those heels had been slipped on her feet, covering the midnight blue nail polish on toes so adorable Logan was considering developing a foot fetish, and they'd spent the rest of the day together. Eating more food that was definitely not on Rebecca's diet plan then had gone back to her house and watched a movie.

More lingering kisses.

More caressing fingers.

More . . . blue balls.

But it was worth it, because fuck, but he never felt more settled than when he was with Char, as though he could just be himself, just not worry about anything, just . . . *be.*

Thus was the power of his Starlight.

Then Sunday, they'd driven down to Carmel and had picnicked on the beach, the ocean breeze coating her lips with salt when he'd been unable to stop himself from kissing her.

Monday through Thursday, he'd cooled his heels, plotting his next moves because Char had needed to work. Several staff members had requested meetings, and then she'd been looped into a Zoom conference with some of the other GMs. After that, she had been drowning in emails—her words, but based on how hard she worked, he didn't doubt the truth.

So, instead of going to her office and indulging in his bending-her-over-her-desk fantasy, he'd left her to her work and instead had lunch delivered.

And dinner.

Because she was clearing the decks, wanting to go home for a week and visit her family, but she had also promised to go up to his cabin with him. He'd coaxed her into going on a few river walks with him—or rather, had promised her several hours of undisturbed reading in his hot tub if she agreed to the odd walk.

Thankfully, she hadn't asked about bears.

Because Tahoe wasn't known for being particularly bear-free.

Last night, he'd delivered dinner himself when he might have kind-of-sort-of-accidentally driven by and seen her bent over her computer through the windows in her kitchen.

Of course, he *would* have peeked in through her back door, except he'd also gone to the hardware store and bought a lock for her gate that week.

A padlock with letters to form a word or combination that could be used to open it.

He'd chosen *stars*, for obvious reasons.

And when he'd texted her the picture with instructions on how to open it, he'd received a tart reply to *Stop being pushy*. Which had been followed by another text that said simply, *Thank you*, and was paired with a trio of red hearts.

Which made *his* heart squeeze, sap that he was.

Emojis and a thank you. A tart reply, but not holding his need to take care of her against him.

Regardless, the lock meant that any sneaking in would be difficult, so he'd gone to the front door, rang the bell, and kissed the surprised smile off her face, before thrusting the bag of food in her hand.

But when he went to turn away, she'd surprised *him* by snagging his hand and tugging him inside.

She'd shared the food—okay, so maybe he'd brought enough to share, hoping for the invite in—then had coaxed him onto the couch to binge watch some dumbass reality show.

He hadn't bothered to follow the plotline. Instead, he'd followed her—with his eyes, tracking every shake of her head and smile and eye roll. With his ears, committing her laughter to memory. With his nose, soaking in the floral spice. With his mouth, tasting the chocolate cake and coffee they'd had for dessert on her tongue.

And, later, when she fell asleep, with his touch, stroking a finger down the soft silk of her cheek as he'd tucked her into bed.

It had been the best night of his life in years.

Because of Char.

Smiling because he got to see her again tonight, that he might be able to kiss her, and maybe, if she was wearing a dress again, get to kiss her other places and—

His cock twitched.

"Come on, man," he muttered, climbing the three steps that led up to her door. "Focus."

Keep the charm going, the patience in mind. Go slow. Go steady.

With that thought, he pushed everything sexual out of his mind and rang the bell. Footsteps echoed through the door, not loud, and perhaps a sound he might not have ever noticed if he hadn't been so obsessed with all things Char.

But he did hear the pad of her feet.

Just as he heard the lock *click* open.

The door was pulled wide, and . . . his heart thumped, *hard.*

Warm brown eyes, a welcoming smile on lips he wanted to kiss, a dress that had his cock twitching all over again. "Hey," she murmured.

"Hey," he said, too entranced to say anything else.

And . . . silence as they stared at each other.

Him because he couldn't believe he was here, that they were trying this again, that he got another chance with her.

Her because . . . hell, he couldn't begin to read her mind.

All he knew was that she was letting him into her life, and he wasn't going to squander the chance.

"You look beautiful," he said, shaking himself from his Char-stupor.

She grinned, stepped back, smoothing her hands over the amethyst dress. It had a bunch of crisscrossing straps forming a pattern over her chest, making him want to nudge those thin bands out of his way and bury his face between her breasts. The hem was short, flirting at mid-thigh, and she wore another pair of spiked heels—these were black with interlaced bands that matched her dress. "You don't look too bad yourself."

They had reservations at a nice steakhouse nearby that she'd raved about—another meal that would be ruining his diet. Although, he'd eaten fairly well that week, so that was good enough for him at this point.

Salads for breakfast and lunch to get those greens in. Counteract all the unhealthy dinners they were consuming.

She closed the door, touched the corner of his mouth. "Why are you smiling?"

He nipped at her fingertips. "I was thinking if I ate like we have been during the season, that Nutritionist Rebecca would have my ass."

Char grinned. "She would at that." A bump of her shoulder against his. "Let me just grab my coat and we can go." He followed her to the small closet, helped her slip on her jacket.

"It's a crime to cover up this dress," he said, smoothing a hand down her back.

"You like it?" she asked, glancing over her shoulder at him.

He pressed a kiss to the side of her neck. "*Like* is too bland a word."

A trace of wicked in those eyes. "You should see what's under it."

Groaning—because, blue balls—he skimmed his fingers under the edge of her dress. "When are you going to show me?"

Hot eyes on his, white teeth biting into a bottom lip. "Tonight."

One word, but a wealth of meaning. Not just desire or need. Not just something physical. More.

So much more.

The fear had gone, taken anger with it. And hope and affection had replaced them.

"Mmm," he murmured and pressed a kiss to her lips. "I like tonight."

Heat trailing across her expression, her hands coming to rest on his shoulders, to grip tightly as she moved close. "Or we can skip dinner, and I can show you now."

Fucking hell.

He hadn't had this many erections since he'd been a teenager.

And, just like when he was sixteen, he couldn't do anything about them. At the moment, anyway.

"Come on, Trouble," he said, taking her hand and leading her out the front door. "You know you want that loaded baked potato you were waxing poetic about earlier this week."

She groaned and rubbed her stomach. "Cheese. Sour cream. Bacon. Butter. Green onions. Yes, to all."

"Sounds delicious," he said and opened the passenger door for her, buckling her seat belt. "No lipstick tonight?" He'd seen all shades of red and pink over the last year, but he hadn't often seen her lips naked of color, and especially not when she was going out somewhere.

"Nope," she said with a soft *pop* at the end.

Fingers over her cheek, along her jaw, to the corner of that smiling mouth. "Why?"

"Because then I wouldn't be able to do this."

She laid a kiss on him that should have blown his head off.

As it was, it had him thinking about other things blowing, and then not thinking much further than that. Her arms wove around his shoulders, and she pulled him close, nipping at his bottom lip, slipping her tongue past his lips to tangle with his.

Long and deep and wet, she kissed him until his lungs burned.

"That's why," she whispered, her words bursts of damp heat on his mouth.

"I vote for no lipstick ever," he said, voice sounding like he'd swallowed a flamethrower. His hands—one on the console, the other on the seat by her hip, convulsed, wanting to unbuckle her seat belt and carry her back into the house.

But then he wouldn't be taking care of her.

Reluctantly, he pulled back, ducking out of the passenger's side, and starting to close the door.

Her voice chased him as it slammed shut.

"You must really want that baked potato."

He burst out laughing, love for this woman burning down into his soul.

Char was it for him. It was simple as that. Funny, sexy, smart as hell, she was in a whole different league from him, but he'd already given her up once, and there was absolutely no way he was going to lose her again.

No fucking way.

TWENTY-SIX

CHAR

The baked potato was glorious.

The way Logan was eye-fucking her was even more so.

"Dessert?" the waiter asked, coming over to the table.

Log opened his mouth, and she knew he was going to indulge her in a slice of that mountain-tall chocolate cake or a cherry-topped slice of cheesecake. But she'd reached her limit on indulging.

At least in food. And in talking, as she'd dominated the conversation.

"No, thank you," she said, shaking her head at Logan when he would have pushed. "I'm full." She wanted something else. "Did you want something?"

He shook his head, and the waiter left.

"Log?" she asked. "We can just go."

Hot green eyes on hers.

Her lungs froze, her pussy throbbed, and she actually reached for her purse, ready to throw a wad of cash on the table when he asked, "Tell me more about the meeting with Pierre."

"Logan," she warned. She'd already blabbered about her day. Now, she wanted to go.

"We have to wait for the bill anyway," he said, reaching across the table and taking her hand. "Give me all the gory details of the Pierre talk."

"Gory meaning budget talk?" she asked, instead of calling him out. The stubborn glint in his expression was obvious, and she knew he was going to insist she answer, even without dessert.

He shuddered. "Well, obviously." A grin. "Though, feel free to skip to the interesting parts."

Char mock-sighed then smiling, she answered him, telling him about the minor changes the Gold's owner, Pierre Barie, wanted to make for next season. But when she tried to turn the topic back to them leaving the restaurant so she could act on those molten emerald eyes, he asked her about another meeting.

Her lips pursed, but she quickly outlined that interaction. However, when she went again to turn the focus to Logan, he dodged and pointed it back at her, asking another question about one of the Gold's vendors who'd been giving her a hard time and ensuring she'd gotten to say all of what she wanted to say.

She would have to be careful with this one. To make sure he didn't keep giving to the detriment of his own needs.

Because all meal long, he'd been attentive, listening to her rant about her meetings—yes, she loved her job, but, also yes, people were still idiots in a multitude of ways. She'd managed to coax him into sharing what had kept him busy—spoiling her with meals, taking care of her gate that he kept barging through, spending one morning hanging out with Coop and his baby girl while Calle had a spa day. He'd talked about his plans to go home and visit his family during the same week she went to see hers, but aside from deciding to go to the movies the following night—in which Logan again had indulged her by letting her pick the film—she had done more than her fair share of speaking.

Not that he seemed to mind.

And truthfully, she'd been tempted to choose the rom-com

that just released when they'd discussed movies. Instead, she'd gone for action.

He'd watched her show about marrying at first sight without groaning. He'd not uttered a single complaint when she'd picked the historical romance movie earlier that week. Nor that drama the next day.

Accommodating, taking care of her, making sure her needs were met.

Well, she could do some of that in return, and he'd mentioned in passing wanting to see the action flick about a senior citizen assassin—not the premise intended, Char knew, but seriously, why did male action stars always get the cool jobs, even when they were old enough to sign up for the AARP? The female actors just got cast as cranky old ladies and—

Not the point.

The real reason she'd chosen it was because Logan wanted to see it.

And cracks about male action stars aside, she was fully aware that she'd definitely consumed worse movies and TV shows (her recent obsession with reality television a prime example). But, further than that, she could do something for him simply because he deserved it, simply because she wanted to treat him kindly, simply because she wanted to make him happy.

That was how real relationships worked, even though she hadn't spent too much time in one, as of late.

Unless she considered her job to be her boyfriend.

If so, he'd been very demanding and only minimally fulfilling.

Lie. Her job was very fulfilling.

It just wasn't great at giving her orgasms.

Heh.

Anyway, Logan had been very good at giving orgasms, and she wanted to explore how good he was at giving them now. Tonight. Five hours ago. Last week. That night he'd kissed her in her kitchen.

Shifting in her seat, her sensitized thighs rubbing together, she was very aware that she wanted to give some back.

Tonight.

Now.

Five hours ago.

Last week.

He reached across the table and cupped her jaw. "Why are you smiling?"

Char turned her head, pressed a kiss to his palm, and told him the truth. "I'm smiling because I like being with you."

Emerald eyes turning molten, slightly rough fingertips on her cheek. "I l—"

The waiter deposited the bill. He tried to do it slyly, tried to slip it onto the table silently, but it bumped into her wine glass, breaking the moment and drawing her focus.

"Sorry," the college-aged male murmured, slipping away almost as silently as he had arrived.

"I guess I should stop staring adoringly at you." Logan picked up the check.

She shook her head. "Nope. I like it when you stare at me adoringly."

"Yeah?"

"Yup." She snagged the bill from his fingers.

He snatched it back. "Not a chance, Starlight."

"We should split it."

His gaze fixed hers in place. "Are we dating?"

The change in conversation made her frown, mind spinning to understand. "Um, yes?" She felt a sudden thread of uncertainty. "I mean, I *thought* so. I—is this not a—"

"This is a date, Starlight."

"Then why—?"

"I want to date you and be your boyfriend, your lover, *more*," he said, his voice quiet but no less intense for the lack of volume. "Don't insult me by not letting me take care of you."

Uncertainty disappeared, was replaced with *aw* and also annoyance.

"And taking care of me involves paying for things?"

"Yes," he said simply, but when she would have opened her mouth to argue, he added, "When I ask you on a date, I pay. End of story."

She thought of snatching the bill from him and shoving it along with her credit card at the waiter. Instead, she let him throw some cash on the table then take her hand after he'd stood, allowed him to hold it as they walked out of the restaurant.

This was an argument she wanted to have in private.

"And when I invite you out to dinner?" she asked after they'd buckled—well, after he'd buckled them both, something she'd allowed because she felt squishy inside when he did it and liked him close enough to smell his shampoo, his deodorant, to feel the heat from his body—

Focus.

He hit the button to turn on the engine. "Then I pay."

She'd been momentarily lost in LaLa Land, remembering his fingers trailing over her cheek as he'd straightened.

As thus, it took her a moment to process his answer.

"What?" she snapped. "Absolutely not."

"I'm the man. I pay."

"Logan Walker, as I live and breathe, you did *not* just say that."

He shrugged. "What are you going to do about it?"

Her anger spiked, and she went to tell him *exactly* what she was going to do about it, starting with her spiked heel ending up in a very particular location.

Then she saw the edge of his mouth.

It was curved up.

The fucker was playing with her.

She mentally shifted, about to tell him that he'd be out of her life so fast . . . but the words stoppered in her throat.

He was teasing her, just teasing, and she didn't want him to stop teasing or to worry about what he said around her. She could take a joke and dish one back, just as she knew he could take her teasing in that same vein.

But . . . more she didn't want him out of her life, and instinctively, she knew that joking in that way would hurt him.

Probably, because it would hurt her just as much to say it.

So instead, she shrugged and said, "I'll just go down on you until I convince you otherwise."

A blue word.

A curse that blistered even her used-to-profanity ears.

Then the car slid over onto the shoulder, the transmission shifted into park, and suddenly a six-foot, two-hundred-pound alpha athlete was crowding her back into her seat. "And if I say I'd go down on you to convince *you* otherwise?"

She lifted her chin, drifted closer. "Then I'd say we both win."

Hot breath on her cheek, her jaw, her ear. A rough voice whispering, "I think you're right."

And then he kissed her.

Twenty-Seven

LOGAN

The knock came on the door well after the windows had fogged up, long minutes after he'd tugged Char into his lap and kissed and kissed and *kissed* her.

"Fuck," he muttered, wincing against the beam of a flashlight.

Bright lights shone from behind, making what they were doing, and where both of their hands were very obvious to the officer outside the window. Logan smoothed Char's dress down, plunked her into the passenger's seat.

"What—?" she asked, eyes glazed.

"Hang on, Starlight." He pushed the button to roll down the window. "Hello, officer," he said through the window, feeling her stiffen next to him, her soft gasp barely reaching his ears.

Dark hair, deep brown eyes, a smile teasing the corners of his mouth. "Sorry to . . . *interrupt*, but you can't park here."

"Apologies," he said, trying desperately to not think of the fact that his dick was all but poking a hole in his slacks. "We'll head home now."

A nod, before the policeman disappeared back into the night.

Logan watched him get into the patrol car, sucked in a breath, and turned to the woman sitting next to him. "Buckle up."

She did so, and then he drove on.

"I'll have you know that's the politest conversation I've ever had with a police officer," she muttered.

Heart hurting for her, he reached over and squeezed her thigh. "I'm sorry you've had to deal with that bullshit. There shouldn't be a different standard for our interactions with them."

"*Log.*"

His eyes cut to hers before turning back to the road. "What?"

"I like you." A beat. "So much."

More heart action, only this time it was alternating between squeezing and filling up like a balloon. Hurt and hope, who knew they were so closely intertwined?

"I like you, too, Starlight," he murmured, even though it was so much more than just *like*. He loved and adored her. His heart beat steadier when she was near, his skin settled when he held her hand. But . . . he was continuing with slow and steady and patient. And no one in their right mind would declare their love while still rebuilding their partner's trust in them.

Go slow.

On that train of thought, he slowly lifted his hand from her thigh, deliberately gripped the steering wheel. Then because his cock was still threatening to poke a hole in his slacks, he made a joke. "I can say, however, this was the first interaction with the police where I've been sporting a boner like a teenager."

Silence.

Shit.

He turned to look at her, about to apologize.

But then he saw her face, saw that the corner of her mouth was upturned. "How does one sport a boner like a teenager?"

"Namely by frequency and a lack of fulfillment."

She burst out laughing.

He joined in, even though it was at his expense.

"Come on," she said, once she'd gained control of herself.

"Don't tell me you ever had difficulty with girls. I saw you as a twenty-one-year-old, and you had swagger even then."

"That swagger didn't accompany me in high school. I can assure you of that," he muttered. "I hadn't grown into my body, despite my poor attempts at weightlifting. And worse, I had acne."

"Aw, poor baby."

"Somehow your tone doesn't sound sympathetic," he grumbled.

"Well, clearly the awkward stage didn't last long, based on the young man I knew then," she said. "The *older* man I know today."

"Now, you're just being mean," he muttered, turning onto her street. "Cecily likes to remind me that, at thirty, the end of my career, and thus my life, is near."

Char giggled. "I did always like how Cecily teased you."

He pulled into her driveway and tapped her on the nose. "Only because you took notes so you could tease me better."

Another giggle, this one paired with her fingers tracing over his brow. "Only because *I* love seeing you glower at me." She leaned over the console, those straps shifting enough to allow him to look right down her dress. And just like that, he had the teenage boy problem again. Her lips quirked. "Like what you see?" she asked, leaning a little farther toward him, making his hands itch to pull her onto his lap again.

But they were in the driveway of her house.

Much more comfortable surfaces awaited them inside.

"Come on, Trouble," he said, pushing open his door. "Let's go in, and I'll show you exactly how much I like what I see."

He slipped out, closed his door, had just made it to her side of the SUV when hers opened and he got a glimpse of the sexiest pair of legs he'd ever seen.

Click. One high heel on the ground. *Click.* The other.

They weren't inside the house, didn't have any more privacy than they'd had on the side of the road, but Logan didn't care.

He kissed her again.

Lips and teeth and tongue. A lush, softly curved body against his.

Tart and spicy with hints of roses, of sweet.

Char.

All Char.

She wrapped her arms around him, jumped slightly to wrap her legs around his waist, and fuck, it would be so easy to unzip, to push home—

Patience.

A wrenching thought from the sliver of control still present in his brain. It scorched down his spine, burned through his arms, his fingertips, his thighs, his feet. His fingers clenched tighter, arms banding around her. His feet and thighs got into gear, moving them to the front door.

Char broke away when they were there, tearing her mouth from his and turning in his hold in order to punch in the code she had on the keypad.

The lock opened with a *whir.*

He shoved through the door, slammed it behind them, locked it again.

And . . .

Then he paused.

Her fingers wove into his hair, grabbed tight. "Don't you dare ask if I'm sure, Logan Walker." She nipped at his jaw. "I wanted you since the moment I first laid eyes on you."

He started walking toward the stairs, stopped. "You've wanted me for nine months?" he asked, angling his head so he could kiss her temple.

"Nine years," she said. "Since the moment you walked into that arena, I've wanted you. Maybe it's been eight years since we've seen each other, eight years apart, but I will never *ever* forget the way my heart thumped when I first saw you."

"You were standing next to Luc," he said, remembering how earnest she'd been. "You used to carry this giant messenger bag with notebooks, and you had a clipboard in your hand." He nuzzled her throat. "No heels then."

"I didn't mind being shorter then," she admitted. "Not when I was still trying to find my place."

"Didn't take you long."

She grinned. "No, it didn't. And I quickly became addicted to heels."

"You mean foot massages," he accused, remembering all the times she'd come to his hotel room or they'd snuck out in his old truck and he'd rubbed her feet. Hmm. Maybe there *was* something to his quote-unquote foot fetish, or at least when it came to Char's feet.

Her smile didn't dim. In fact, it grew. "Accurate," she said. "You do give excellent foot massages."

He started climbing the stairs. "Want one now?"

"No."

He lifted a brow.

"I'd much rather you massage other places."

He grinned this time. "Yeah?" he asked. *"What* places?"

Narrowed eyes, another nip, this time on his chin. "You think you're so funny, don't you?"

"Funny looking, maybe," he quipped, making it to the top of the stairs and turning to the right. Her bedroom, as he'd discovered earlier that week when he'd tucked her into bed, was the second door on the right. The first was a small closet, and the only door on the left was a home office, one that he thought would be lovely and bright during the day, but also one that he didn't think fit Char at all.

Probably why she always worked in her kitchen.

That was more like her.

Warmth and beauty in the small details. Not grand and over the top. Not that she wasn't outright gorgeous, couldn't glam it up—like she'd done tonight—but rather that her beauty came from the strength inside her. It radiated through the way she carried herself, how she spoke, the expressions on her face.

No one would ever look at her and not think she was completely capable.

But he didn't just see capable.

He saw Char.

Smart and beautiful, but also vulnerable and a little lonely. This was the woman who gasped in outrage on that fiancé show when one of the men was betrayed and laughed when the stars argued about the proper way to grocery shop. This was the woman who'd argued with him about paying the bill, had demanded to share equally or pull her own weight. This was the woman who'd shared the dinner he bought for her, regardless of his refusal. This was the woman who stayed at the arena and spoke with every single player or staff member after they'd lost that game. She'd stayed until consolations were made, until reassurances were given.

This was the woman who'd looked at him with tears in her eyes when he'd broken her heart by leaving.

This was the woman who'd turned that broken heart into something powerful.

This was the woman he loved.

"Where did you go?"

Quiet words pulling him from his mind, soft fingers on his jaw, a warm gaze on his. Logan blinked, realized he'd paused a foot inside her bedroom.

"I'm here," he murmured, shoving the past down and striding over to the bed.

Fingers in his hair again, clenching tight. "That's not what I asked."

Stern words, a commanding tone, and fuck, maybe he was a sick asshole, but he liked that bossy tone, liked it a whole lot. Didn't mean he was going to voice the bullshit in his brain though. "It's nothing," he said and bent to kiss her.

She kissed him back, lips soft, tongue a sleek dart. But then she used her grip on his head to break the contact, to glare up at him. "Nice try," she said. "Now, tell me."

He could either argue, or he could tell her the truth.

And as much as he enjoyed riling her up, he also didn't want to ruin the night with a fight, so he set her on the edge of the bed, sat next to her, then he met her stare and told her the heavy truth sitting on his mind and heart.

"I have so many regrets."

Twenty-Eight

CHAR

Heavy words.

Perhaps she should have been upset the moment had waned, that Logan wasn't tearing her clothes off and attacking her, joining her in her quest for mutual orgasms.

But he was hurting.

And she didn't like it when her people hurt.

And . . . he'd made their time together thus far so much about her. Her needs, her desires. Her, her, *her*. Well, this would only work between them if it started being about him, too. Before, she'd made it only about him. Now, he threatened to do the same only for her.

And that couldn't work.

Long term, they couldn't forget completely about themselves and focus solely on the other person. Both were important, of course, but equally as important was understanding that they were two separate people with two separate hearts and minds and, frankly, with two different sets of needs.

They had to both be equally present.

She might have been grappling with being left out of the decision, with knowing that she would have certainly made a decision she regretted if Logan hadn't intervened. But though Log had said he hadn't regretted his decision, he had to be grappling with being the one who'd hurt her, of spending the last years knowing she thought the worst of him and not being in a position to change her mind.

Old pain. Baggage.

And beneath that, love and affection.

Because even when she'd hated Logan, she'd loved him.

So many other relationships, so many men, so many disappointing, unfulfilling boyfriends. Because of her and the walls she'd erected between herself and the world, more than anything they'd done.

Char knew it had been the same for him.

Never quite being able to fill that empty space inside, always searching for something but not being able to pinpoint what was missing.

Except . . . he'd known what he'd been missing.

Because they'd been great together. Real in a sea of what could be filled with fake hangers-on. True love in a world of first, fallible love.

They'd gone eight years without it.

"Come here," she whispered.

"Char," he began, thrusting a hand through his hair, eyes pained. "I didn't want to do this, to ruin our night. I made the call. I was the one who decided to end things."

"It was the right call," she said, feeling that deep in her soul. "You know that."

A nod. "But . . ." He trailed off, fingers yanking at his hair again.

"What, baby?" she pressed. "But what?"

"I don't want to drop this at your feet."

She took his hand. "Then whose feet will you drop it at?"

He stilled.

She put her hand over his heart, cuddled up to his side. "If we're going to be together, then you *have* to bring it to me. I have to feel needed in that way, have to know you can talk to me about anything, that you'll turn to me when you have problems."

His eyes flicked to hers, held for a long moment. Then he exhaled and said, "I know I made the right call, but I don't know if I can ever forgive myself for hurting you."

Her heart squeezed, her nails dug lightly into his chest. "You *have* to."

A jaw clenching tight, and pain in those emerald eyes. "Why?"

"Because I have."

The truth hit her with the strength of a bullet penetrating skin, quick and piercing, taking breath, followed by a trail of burning agony. She *had* forgiven him, but neither of them had finished mourning what they had lost.

And perhaps, neither of them had completely forgiven themselves.

His breath caught, his jaw relaxing, his eyes widening. "Starlight—"

She clambered into his lap, cupped both of his cheeks in her palms. He needed to understand this.

"I forgive you," she said fiercely. "*I* forgive you."

"Sweetheart." It was a single rough word, one that was paired with his arms wrapping tightly around her, with him burying his face against her curls, with him holding her close for a long, long time.

Eventually, he leaned back, and his emerald eyes collided with hers again. "I love you," he murmured, making her heart thud hard in her chest. "I'm sorry I hurt you, *so* sorry—"

"Enough," she whispered, hands dropping to his shoulders. "Just enough."

A shuddering breath, his arms still around her, still holding her close. "I never stopped, you know? Never stopped loving you."

Her lungs stretched on an inhale, as she held the air deep inside before slowly releasing it. She wanted to give him the words back, her feelings so bright and heady and *big*, but she also knew that she wasn't quite there yet. Yes, she'd forgiven him. Yes, she was ready to move on. But, no, she wasn't quite ready to admit aloud all that was in her heart.

"I know, baby," she said.

His face warmed, and she relaxed, realizing that he wasn't expecting the words just because he'd said them.

Of course, he wouldn't expect that.

Logan wouldn't *ever* demand from her in that way. He'd push her to fulfill her dreams, demand she take care of herself—or let him take care of her, anyway. But he wouldn't ever put pressure on her to bare her heart before she was ready. He might be impulsive and hard-headed and pushy, but he had shown her he would tread lightly and treat kindly.

Which was why, when he just held her, hand shifting to slide up and down her back, she murmured, "Come here."

Amusement danced across his face, his eyes going to the centimeters that separated them. "I *am* here."

"Well, come closer," she grumbled, pressing a kiss to his mouth.

The moment their lips touched, he exploded into a fury of motion.

One hand wove into her hair, his other gripped her hip, tugging her flush against him. He nipped at her bottom lip then slid his tongue inside her mouth, stroking along hers, demanding she meet his intensity. She did. No hesitation . . . and approximately ten seconds later found her back on the mattress, all of Logan's hard, hot gloriousness perched over her.

She reached for the hem of his shirt, wanting—no, *needing* to get her hands on him, needing the steely planes of him beneath her palms.

"Skin," she gasped when he nipped at her jaw, nibbled at her earlobe, laved his tongue down her throat. "I need—" He leaned back, calloused fingers tracing the pattern of the thin straps crisscrossing her breasts. She'd loved how the dress made her feel earlier, how sexy she'd felt with the silk caressing her skin, the strips of fabric hiding but also emphasizing her cleavage. In all honesty, she'd imagined Logan doing exactly what he was doing at that moment.

What she hadn't anticipated was how incredible those little teases of sensation would be.

She wanted the dress out of the way.

She wanted his hands on her.

She wanted *skin*.

He sat back, tugging her up into a seated position. "Skin," he growled, grabbing her hands, which had somehow found their way into his hair, and bringing them to the top button on his dress shirt. "Yes."

Not needing to be told twice, she began working on those tiny discs, slipping one after another through their holes, parting the fabric and revealing golden skin as he kissed his way over her jaw, back behind her ear. His fingers caressed her throat, slipped down to cup one breast through the silk of her dress.

"Mmm," she moaned, her desire ramping to a fever pitch, making her move.

She jerked forward, pressed her mouth to his chest. Fuck, he tasted good. Salty and spicy and driving her to keep tasting him, to continue tracing the hard planes with her tongue, her lips.

A groan that had her thighs attempting to clench together, moisture pooling, but the powerful slack-covered legs between her own prevented the movement.

Logan didn't miss it, however.

He nudged her back, slid his palms down her sides, and gripped the purple silk hem with his fingers. Seeing her dress crumpled in those big hands, so close to where she was desperate for him to touch, sent a wave of heat over her. Head to toe cloaked in desire, nerve endings on fire, fingertips tingling, pussy aching. She wanted her dress off, started to reach for the zipper under her arm, ready to yank it down.

Warm hands covering hers.

"I've got it."

She froze, breath shuddering out when he dipped a finger beneath the fabric, grasped the tag and began to tug it down.

It moved . . . all of four inches.

And she was kicking herself six ways to Sunday.

Because this wasn't one of those easy-on, easy-off dresses.

This was a twist and contort and curse and wiggle dress.

Which Logan seemed to process, at least in some small manner, when his eyes flicked from the open zipper up and down her body.

Then he shrugged, slipped a hand in the opening.

"Oh fuck," she whispered when that rough hand cupped her breast. Arching back, her hips canting up.

"Oh fuck," he groaned, "you're not wearing a bra."

She managed to peel open her lids long enough to see his eyes burning into her, a liquid emerald she could feel down to the marrow of her bones. Then he brushed his thumb over her nipple, and she lost the battle, tossing her head back, arching against him as he rolled that sensitive bud between his fingers, sending piercing bolts of pleasure through her.

He managed to coax and tease her other breast, her other nipple, but slid his hand out when a low tearing sound filled the air.

"Shit, sorry."

Her eyes slid open, and she shook her head. "It's fine." Yes, that was a rasp, her voice so husky with pleasure that she hardly recognized it.

He tugged up at the hem, only succeeded in getting it stuck just above her hips. "How do you get this torture device off?"

"With a fair amount of cursing."

A sharp grin. A quick movement that launched him off her. Another that had her on her feet, wavering from the sudden elevation change. "What—?"

He tugged at the hem again, bunching the dress beneath her arms, just above her breasts.

"Up," he ordered.

She lifted her arms. He tugged it up and over her head.

But the fabric stalled at her elbows when he groaned, bent his head to suck a nipple deep, and Char's legs threatened to buckle under the waves of pleasure. "I—" Warm hands on her breasts, massaging the flesh, his mouth switching sides.

This time she *did* wobble, her knees bending, her body collapsing against his.

He clutched her close, whipping off the dress, tossing it who-knew-where. The next instant she was on the bed, and he was sliding down until he was kneeling between her legs, using those big hands to spread her thighs wide.

A deep inhale, a groan. "Fuck, I've missed this. Missed you."

Hot breath on her skin, his tongue tracing higher and higher, and then . . . his mouth was on her.

Fuck. *She'd* missed this.

The way he devoured her like she was his last meal and he was going to make damn sure it counted. How his strong tongue pressed firmly and deliberately, always knowing the exact spot that made her moan. How—

"Holy hell," she gasped when he pulled out a trick with his tongue she didn't remember him knowing before.

He glanced up at her and grinned. "Should I write and thank the editors of the *Cosmo* blog?" he asked lightly before a curl of jealousy could spiral up and ruin the moment.

She shouldn't be jealous, not when they'd both dated plenty of other people.

But she wanted all his sex secrets and tricks to be about her, to be learned with her. Ridiculous. She knew it. She understood that. So, she was just going to accept the burst of jealousy and move on—

A sharp nip to her thigh.

"Stop thinking," he grumbled.

And then he did the tongue thing again.

And then she forgot about being jealous, forgot about absolutely everything except for Logan's mouth and tongue and fingers and the desire swirling within her.

It tightened.

Had her spine stiffening, moans pouring from her lips.

Heat billowed outward, incinerating her from the inside out.

Her fingers clenched on the sheets.

He pressed the flat of his tongue to her clit, slipped a finger inside, and reached a hand up to cup her breast, pinching her nipple.

One stroke. Two. And . . . she exploded.

Twenty-Nine

She still had her heels on.

They were pressed into his back, sharp bites against over-sensitized skin.

Her eyes were heavy, her lips turned up at the edges. "God, I've missed that," she whispered.

He chuckled, kissed her thigh, and gently dislodged her legs before crawling up her body and taking her into his arms. Fuck, it felt incredible to be able to hold her, even if his cock was threatening to break in half.

The bedroom lights were on, gilding her in golden light. Which meant he didn't miss her frown when he'd gathered her close.

"What are you doing?" she asked.

Fingers in her hair, sweet scent in his nose, warm, lush curves against him. "Holding you."

"I see that."

He waited.

She pushed up on an elbow, glared down at him. "The problem here is that that's *all* you're doing."

"Starlight." Yes, he wanted her. *Of course,* he wanted her. But this was all fairly new, and she needed time, and patience was working so far. "We should pause here. I don't want you to have regrets."

"Regrets?" An annoyed jerk of her head that shook her curls. "*Regrets?*"

"Char—"

"You say you love me," she snapped, poking him in the chest. "You say you've never stopped."

"That's true."

"So, why would I have regrets?" she asked, tossing up her hands. "I'm trying to be with a man who cares about me, who says I own his heart. Why wouldn't I want to—" She stopped. "Or is it you? Do you have regrets? About this *now?* Am I pushing you—?"

"*No.*" He reached up, hauled her down against his chest. "God, no, sweetheart. I just—"

Words cutting off, he shook his head.

How did he begin to explain everything in his mind, his heart? The constant war between his instinct to push, to consume, to devour, and the need to do right by her. The way the past and present were all tangled. How he felt he knew her deep down, even though they'd spent all those years apart.

Tonight, it was as though they'd picked up right from where they'd left off. As if nothing had happened and he'd never hurt her.

It felt . . . like perfection.

And that terrified him because perfection never lasted.

"You're scared."

His eyes flew to hers, mouth falling open. If magic were real, he would have thought she'd cherry-picked the thought from his mind. But it wasn't the paranormal that had Char seeing into his soul, Logan knew. It was just Char.

She knew him like no one else.

"And the stakes feel really high, especially after all this time."

Breath catching, he nodded.

"But the thing is, neither of us can promise the other everything. The world gets in the way. Bad things happen, and nothing is ever really certain." The ghost of a smile. "Why do I feel like I just stated every single cliché saying about things ending?"

Amused instead of terrified and all the more thankful for this woman, he tugged one of her curls. "You squeezed quite a few in there."

Her fingers were gentle on his cheek. "But do you understand why I said them?" she asked. "I want to be with you. If I'm being completely honest, no other man has ever compared. Ugh"—a shake of her head, her eyes narrowing when he felt smug creep into his expression—"don't get cocky now."

He grinned. "You trying to throw softballs my way?"

"I'm *trying* to make you understand that it feels like my heart was on pause for all these years, and now we've hit play."

"*Starlight,*" he murmured.

"We've jabbed the button, the movie's going, and . . . I don't want to stop, Log. I want to see where things go. I want to be with you—in every way."

"Is this you telling me to buck up and stop being scared?" he asked.

Soft brown eyes. "I can say it in those words if you need me to."

He thrust a hand through his hair. "I know I rush into things. I know I push," he said. "I'm just . . . I know it's a lot, that *I'm* a lot, and I'm trying to give you space and time to process everything."

"And if I needed that time, I'd tell you." A nip to his bottom lip before she gripped his chin tightly between thumb and forefinger. "And also, I don't want you to be anyone but you. I like you just as you are. I can handle your pushiness, can easily shove you back if I need to. But"—her hand slid down, smoothed over his bare chest—"I trust you to take care of me, Logan." A shrug. "Plus, if you don't, I'll just steal your skates and dull the edges."

Laughter bubbled up in him. "Devious."

Pride in her gaze. "As needed." A beat. "Let's just focus on now, on building something that's good for both of us."

"God, I love you."

Her shoulders rose and fell on a long inhale, her lips parting. Then she laid back on the mattress, spread her legs and lifted her arms toward him. "Then come here and love *me*."

Which was when Logan forgot about patience and slow and steady.

He shoved the tangled knot of fear aside and just went for it.

His mouth met hers before his next heartbeat, his tongue slipping inside her mouth, coaxing hers out to play. One hand stroked down her side, shaping the heavy globe of her breasts, the slightly rounded plane of her stomach . . . lower.

Her waist, one hip. Her thigh and in between.

She was all liquid heat and swollen folds, and when his thumb brushed her clit, she groaned, hips canting up.

But just as he was touching her, she was all over him.

Her palms running over his chest, nails dragging over his nipples. He hissed out a breath, pleasure shooting down his spine, his cock hardening, throbbing in his slacks, reminding him that while Char was very, very naked—gloriously naked—he had too many damned clothes on.

Thankfully, she seemed to have the same thought.

Her fingers flicked open the button on his jeans, tugged down the zipper.

Before his next breath, those nimble digits slipped beneath the waistband of his boxer briefs and gripped him tightly.

No hesitation. No delay.

Just wrapped her hand around him and began pumping.

Red hazing the edges of his vision, he thrust into that tight grip, lost in how good it felt for her to be touching him. His nerves were on fire, and he felt himself growing in her hand, getting impossibly harder.

Once. Twice. Okay . . . maybe five or ten more.

But then he had to tug her fingers free or else this reunion would be a lot less fulfilling for both of them.

Her mouth pulled into a pout, but she let go, reaching over her head to pull out a condom from the nightstand when he pushed out of bed and stepped out of his pants. "Thanks, Starlight," he murmured, taking it and infinitely glad he didn't have to search through his wallet for the condom he'd stashed there earlier that evening—slow and steady plan, or not, it paid to be prepared.

"What put that gleam in your eyes?" she whispered.

"Only that I'm glad to use your condom because I plan on using mine later," he said, tearing open the wrapper and rolling it on.

Laughter and a shake of her head. Then she crooked her finger at him, placed her lips to his ear. "I have a whole box," she murmured, the heat of her words sending waves of need through him. "How fast do you think we can use them?"

Those waves of desire spiked into a tsunami, tearing through him as images ripped through his mind. Him on top. Her playing cowboy. From behind. Against the wall. In a chair. On the kitchen counter and the lounger on the back deck and the hood of his car—

"Fast," he growled, running his teeth over her throat, tracing the fluttering point of her pulse with his tongue. His hands were shaking. His mind had stopped thinking about the past and the future.

He'd focused on now.

On her beautiful breasts and how they felt in his mouth.

On the way she moaned when he sucked her nipples deep.

The gasp as he nibbled the spot just below her bottom rib.

The slight burn of pain when she tried to grip his hair and pull him up. But he was on the edge. He knew he wouldn't last long. So, he was going to whip out every last skill he possessed in order to have her riding that edge along with him.

He tasted her again, avoiding the sensitive bud of nerves,

licking and stroking her, watching her breaths come more rapidly, feeling the sting of her grip in his hair— only this time it was pushing him more firmly against her pussy instead of tugging him off.

"Log," she groaned, hips bucking against his mouth, seeking more purchase. "That's—" Her head thrashed on the pillow. "I—"

He released her.

"What—?" Eyes flashing open, she glared. "I—"

"I've got you, Starlight," he murmured, wiping his chin on his arm and rising over her, positioning himself between her thighs.

This time, he didn't stop and confirm if she was one hundred percent absolutely sure. He didn't strive for patience, grip tight to ironclad control. Instead, he braced himself over her and let their bodies meld together.

Heaven and hell all at once.

Tight, wet heat. A soft, feminine body surrounding him.

"Now," she whispered. "Please move, baby."

He couldn't resist her, couldn't deny her *anything*.

A slow slide out. A gentle push in until he bottomed out. Feeling her muscles tightening, wrapping around his cock had him groaning and moving faster.

Thankfully, she was with him.

And fuck but she was beautiful.

Perspiration making her skin gleam, her hair a riot of curls in brown and orange and red, all spread out on her pillow. Her breasts bounced with each thrust, tempting him until he found himself unable to stop from bending down and sucking one nipple into his mouth.

Abs burning, back contorted like a pipe cleaner under a toddler's watchful eye, he kept thrusting, continued moving.

There weren't those moments of learning each other, of trying to find a rhythm.

They'd already done that eight years ago.

Tonight was solely about coming together again, about

bringing his woman as much pleasure as possible. He had plans for that box of condoms in her nightstand drawer, nearly a decade of need and fantasies and *wanting* this woman.

But . . . she had plans for *him*.

Plans that unhinged his thoughts of bringing her to the edge so many times it would take the barest touch to catapult her over.

"Fuck!" he groaned.

Her legs had wrapped tightly around him as she did something with her hips that had any hope of drawing this out disappearing like so much smoke. Heat coiled at the base of his spine, every muscle in his body locking tight, and he was suddenly very dangerously at the very edge he wanted to dance with her on.

"More, baby," she said. "I need more."

Fuck slow. He gave her more. He gave her everything.

Teasing her breasts with his free hand as he pounded into her. He slanted his mouth across hers, kissing her in time to his thrusts, ratcheting his own need and desire to dangerous levels, until he was the one at risk of flying over.

But then she stiffened beneath him, mouth torn from his, her legs clenching on his hips, her hands finding their way to his hair again.

They pulled the strands. Hard.

He kept moving.

She groaned, thrust against him.

He didn't stop, just angled himself so he could go deeper, harder, faster.

"Logan!"

And then she was convulsing around him. Not a moment too soon, either, because his own orgasm was upon him, flaring out from his cock, burning through him from head to toe, until he was sucked down into oblivion as they moved and moved and *moved* against each other, wringing every last drop of pleasure from their bodies.

Afterward, he collapsed to the side, unable to hold himself up, finding it impossible to give her any pretty words.

All he could do was hold her tight, press a kiss to the top of her head, and wait for his heart to stop thundering.

Her arms came around him, holding him just as tightly.

And there were no words from her either, just a slowly descending pulse, just gentle fingers tracing circles on his spine, just a head on his chest and warm breath on his skin.

But it was enough.

Because he was here, with Char.

Because they had this moment when he'd hardly dared to hope they would ever get here again.

But they *were* there. Together, they'd found a way back.

So, when sleep came up to embrace him in blackness, he welcomed it with open arms.

THIRTY

CHAR

Fingers in her hair.

Not her own.

Smiling, she watched the hulking hockey player carefully smooth oil into the ends of her hair. It had been a bear that morning, since she'd been too limp last night to bother wrapping her curly locks in the silk scarf she usually wore.

Rookie mistake that.

Her mom had taught her better. She *knew* better.

But they'd dozed off for a little while then Logan had woken her in the most delicious fashion.

The man had the best tongue.

And she hadn't been thinking much about proper hair care when she'd all but passed out.

Four orgasms the night before.

That must be a record.

Or she was pent up. Or . . . that was just *them*.

"Sorry I messed up your hair," he said, pressing a kiss to the side of her neck.

"No, you're not," she teased. "And neither am I." She turned in his arms. "Next time, I just need to summon up enough energy to tame this"—a toss of her head—"wild beast."

"I love your hair." He pushed back the curls she'd spent far too long detangling that morning. "It's the color of fall."

"It can't decide if it wants to be brunette or black," she said with a roll of her eyes. "With a dash of red and gold in there, just to be difficult."

"It's beautiful."

A shrug. "It's me. Plus, I like the hint of my great grandmother. She was a redhead. Did you know that?"

He lifted her up, plunked her on the counter. "No."

"I've only seen black and white pictures of her, but she and my great grandpa lived in England—she was a relocated Scot, and he was a freed slave."

"How did they meet?" he asked, stroking his hand up and down her back.

"Apparently, he saved her from an out of control horse, and she yelled at him for putting himself in danger." She chuckled. "I suppose that might be where some of the women in my family got their fire."

"An ill-tempered redhead." Amusement in his emerald eyes. "That fits."

She punched him lightly. "Rude?"

"What about your parents?" he asked. "How did they meet?"

"In London. My dad was studying abroad. My mom was out celebrating a girlfriend's engagement." Her lips curved. "He tried to buy her a drink, and she sent it back." A beat. "Along with the next three."

Laughter rippled through him. "I'm guessing he eventually won her over?"

"She went over to yell at him, to tell him to stop wasting his money because she was *not* interested in wasting her time with a man, thank her very much." Char giggled. "Six months later, she was getting her master's at the same college he was attending.

They graduated at the same time, were married a year later, and two years after that, Will came along."

"He's five years older than you, right?"

She nodded. "Yup. He's a professor at the college my parents attended, and Amelia just landed her dream job teaching kindergarten."

Her parents were professors, too—her father teaching at a local community college and her mother tenured at a state school not far from home. The teacher gene was strong in her family, though it had clearly skipped right over her.

"Did you ever think about teaching?"

Shivering, since she was still wrapped in just a towel after their shower, and the warmth of the steam had disappeared during their talk, she went to reach for her robe, which was hanging on a hook near the door just to the side of the sink he'd plunked her on top of. But before her fingers grazed the fluffy fabric, Logan was already dropping it around her shoulders.

"You're cold," he murmured, cinching it across her waist. "Sorry, Starlight."

"I'm not complaining." She leaned up to kiss his jaw. "I like talking about this stuff with you. It reminds me of lying in the back of your truck jabbering about nothing." Another kiss. "And for the record, I think despite earning my undergrad degree in business, I would have ended up getting my teaching credentials and in a classroom, anyway." One more kiss. "But then Luc picked me up in that coffee shop and shoved me into the business of hockey."

He helped her down. "I bet your parents were shocked."

"Their scholarly daughter, from a family full of scholars, diving headfirst into sports management?" A grin as she nodded. "Yes."

"Is this where your mom made a fuss about you going into football instead?"

Char laughed, touched that he remembered her mom's obsession with the sport. "Yes," she said. "Although football isn't really a scholarly pastime, is it? So, I really only had her to blame."

"How'd it go when you told her that?"

She lifted a brow. "Do I look like I want to get my ass kicked?"

Laughing, he scooped her up, carrying her through the door and back into the bedroom, plunking them both down onto the mattress. "Your parents love you," he said, holding her close. "There would be minimal ass-kicking."

"Probably." She rested her head on his chest. "But yes, they do."

"What's that in your tone?"

She frowned, sat up. "What?"

"There's sad in your tone, Starlight."

"No, there's not."

"Char."

Rolling her shoulders, she said, "I was thinking about how she's found a new respect of the crazy sport of strapping precariously thin blades to one's feet and adding sticks and regular fights."

"No, you weren't."

"Log—" She paused, considered the thread of emotion weaving through her. "Yes, I am sad. Part of me continues to wonder and worry what I missed out on."

"Because you walled yourself off."

A sigh. A nod.

"Because of me."

She froze then admitted the truth. "Yes."

Pain washed over his face, darkened his emerald eyes to nearly black. He sat up, and an instant later, his arms were around her. She felt rather than saw his hands clench into fists.

Then she told him the rest of it.

"But also because of me, baby. I—" She struggled for a minute, trying to put to words what was in her head. "I've always felt a bit distant, as though I were slightly on the outside, struggling to find where I fit in. With my family, with my friends, with my relationships, as though there was this inner wall I was just too scared to let down." She sighed. "And they respected that barrier, never pushed fully through."

"But I barreled through like a bull in the china shop?"

"No," she whispered. "I let them down with you. You didn't have to push or shove your way into my heart. It was just like you were always there."

A sharp inhale. A clenched jaw. "Starlight—"

Fuck. She was hurting him, and that wasn't what she wanted. "I didn't need the walls with you then," she said. "And I don't need them now. I think that's why it's so easy to be with you, why I missed our closeness so much when you'd gone. I can just be with you, Log. I've never found that with anyone else."

"Char—"

The emotion in the broken off statement had her gaze flying to his, seeing the deep emotion and dampness at the edges.

And she *knew*.

The truth that had always been. The truth that would always be.

This man owned her heart.

He always would.

The terror from before disappeared. She didn't need more time. She just needed . . . Logan.

"I love you," she whispered.

He froze, his body gone ramrod stiff. "What?"

"I love you," she said, placing her hand over his heart, feeling the organ thundering beneath her palm. "Truthfully, I don't think I ever stopped loving you. Even when I tried to hide behind my walls, to pretend to be untouched, you were always there, always *in* me."

"I—" A sharp shake of his head. "I—you *can't*, Char. I need to prove that I—"

"I don't need you to prove anything, baby." When it seemed as though he'd protest, she captured his cheeks between her palms. "I just need you to be *you*—to spend time with me, to let me bitch about my job, and for you to complain about all the lousy parts of yours. I want us to spend time in the kitchen trying to figure out how to cook something more complicated than omelets and to show you all the gloriousness of my myriad reality shows."

"Sweetheart." He swallowed hard.

She kept her hands in place, pressed a firm kiss to his lips. "I don't want us to go back, I want us to move forward. I want us to find what we can be *now*."

His palm dropped her cheek. "I want that, too."

"Good."

He brushed the back of his knuckles down her throat. "You love me?"

Nuzzling into him, safe in the circle of his arms, she said, "You had me at the slippers."

Laughter burst out of him, shaking the bed, vibrating through her. Then his arms tightened, and he lay back onto the bed, hauling her on top of him. "Let's stay in our pajamas and play hooky for the rest of the day. You can show me those reality shows, and I'll make you my world-famous omelet."

Delight trailed through her.

But she didn't miss the tension just hinting at the edges of his expression. Part of him still worried she'd turn away from him. Or maybe he thought he deserved to be punished, that regardless of his words and convictions of having done the right thing that he needed to be put through the wringer.

She was done with that nonsense.

But words weren't going to do it in this case.

He needed to be shown that she'd put the past behind her, had forgiven him, was truly ready to move forward. Just as her heart needed the time to keep learning all the small things about this wonderful man.

Because he'd spent the last *season* showing her that he was good and kind and stable, a great teammate, a proper addition to the organization.

And he'd spent the last weeks showing her he was the type of man who cared and paid attention.

The lock on her gate.

Meals when she worked through lunch.

Breakfast and strong arms and dessert he didn't want but was willing to make time for in case she did.

Reality shows and hair oil.

Omelets.

Those celestial slippers.

Showing love rather than just giving her words.

So really, how could she have *not* fallen in love with the man?

Which is why she leaned down to kiss him, putting every bit of what she felt into that touch. It was heat and sleek darts of tongue. It was lips pressed tight and fingers digging into her hips. It was desire and pleasure and . . . this man.

His hips thrust up against hers, his erection an iron brand of heat. The towel he wore and the robe covering her body were the thinnest barriers.

She wanted him.

But she wanted to put his heart at ease even more.

Pulling back, she smiled down at him, reached for the TV remote on the nightstand. "Okay, now get ready to have your mind blown while I bring you the gloriousness of Britain's bouncers—*ah!*"

He tumbled her over, his towel coming loose. "How about I show you some of *my* gloriousness first?"

Affection for this man swelled within her, right along with desire as he untied her robe and spread his slightly roughened hands on her. "I—*ah*—" Her breath hitched when he cupped one breast. "I'm fine with that."

A laughing kiss.

Gentle palms skating over her body.

Joy in her heart.

Char wrapped her arms tightly around him, met him caress

for caress, touch for touch, stroke for stroke, and let him love her with the same intent focus she then turned onto him.

Because . . . *together*.

That was the only way forward.

"I'm not entirely sure about this," Char said.

"Oh, come on," Brit coaxed. "You're fine."

She was not fine, decidedly *not* fine. She was wearing ice skates in someone's insane idea of a good time.

Sharp metal blades instead of heels. What had she been thinking?

"I've seen those death traps you call shoes," Sara Jetty, Brit's good friend and wife of former Gold player, Mike Stewart said.

As she skated by.

Gracefully.

Not at all like a wobbly deer, a la Char.

"Easy for you to say," she muttered. The other woman had scored a gold medal in figure skating in her younger years. That kind of skill didn't exactly disappear. "Why did I think this was a good idea?"

"It's for charity!" PR-Rebecca shouted.

Shouted because she was on the bench. Pregnancy gave her an out.

Hmm.

Maybe Char could lie and—

"Don't even think about it," Calle said, swooping up next to Char and taking her arm.

The single reason she didn't end up on her ass was because Calle had a solid grip on her, and Char's assistant coach had spent *her* younger years playing for the national team.

Once again, she circled back to: how in the fuck had she allowed this to happen?

But just as she was working up a really big panic, a gaggle of giggling girls swarmed the ice, circling Brit and Calle and Sara.

"Remember," Calle said, releasing Char's arm as the swarm took her away. "Bend your knees and fall forward if you're going to crash—that's where all the padding is."

"Fall forward," Char said, skating tentatively forward. She'd had a few lessons from the guys over the years, but she wasn't what anyone would call skilled.

And that was before she'd been dressed in the bulky hockey gear.

"Knees bent," she whispered, adjusting her helmet and nearly eating shit.

Her eyes went to the stands, and she saw Logan was signing autographs, along with Mike, Coop, Blane, and Stefan. They weren't there for any other reason except to watch their significant others play some hockey with girls from the local teams. The Gold hosted many of these events during the year, drumming up excitement for the sport, especially among those who might otherwise miss out on hockey's awesomeness.

Mandy was on the bench with Rebecca, armed with the pseudo-baby shower gift Char had bought for her—a fancy first aid kit on wheels and emblazoned with snarky statements. She was prepared for any spills. Though, in reality, Char was likely to be the only one in need of its contents.

The girls were skilled enough to skate circles around her, even the younger ones, who were just six or seven.

But Char wasn't the major draw.

She'd been roped in to relieve PR-Rebecca after her pregnancy announcement, but Char would have accepted the request to participate anyway. Empowering girls aside, this was her putting her money where her mouth was when it came to making that family in the Gold.

"Knees bent," she whispered again, tearing her eyes away from Logan and his adoring fans, trying to ignore the way her heart pitter-pattered when she saw him talking to a tiny little girl.

Aw.

Shit!

She almost ate it, remembering at the last minute to bend her knees. "Good grief, Harris," she muttered. "Focus."

"I can help you!"

Char smiled at the girl. "Yes, please."

Without missing a beat, the girl helped Char hold her stick properly and was teaching her how to propel herself across the ice within minutes.

"Hey, Calle," she called, coming close to the coach. "I think you're out of a job!"

Calle grinned, and she ran a passing drill practically with her eyes closed. "I'm fine with that." She blew a kiss to the man who held her heart, who smiled at her and made it clear she held his just as tightly. "I'll just go off and make more babies with Coop then find another team to coach."

"Rude," Char teased.

"Coach us!" one of the girls shouted.

"Yes, Calle! Come to our team."

Another grin from the statuesque blonde. She winked at Char. "Looks like I have plenty of job offers." She passed off another puck. "Sorry, girls. I'll be with the Gold for at least a few more years."

"Boo!" the collective shouted.

But it was short-lived because Calle stopped messing around and got into Coach Mode. A trill of her whistle called them to attention.

Another had the girls separating into different stations.

Then all the moving parts got moving—the girls completed a series of different drills, overseen by far better skaters than Char, though she did her best, and her cheeks actually hurt from smiling.

Full disclosure, her knees hurt from falling, too.

But not as much as her ass did from the one time she'd landed on it.

Calle's advice had been solid.

The hour on the ice ended with a short kids vs. adults game, and the only goal the adults scored was Char's.

On Brit in net.

Her goalie tipped up her helmet and shook her head, eyes narrowed.

The girls cheered.

The men at the glass cracked up.

Calle gave her shit. Sara, graceful, lovely Sara who definitely didn't score on her own goalie, patted her on the arm consolingly and whispered, "She'll get over it."

Brit didn't look like she'd get over it anytime soon.

"I don't think she'll get over it."

Calle giggled. "She'll get over it during Mia's self-defense class."

Remembering Liam talking about being the test dummy getting laid out on his ass, Char murmured, "I think I'll be busy that night."

Sara's tinkling laugh filled the air.

Calle put the puck on her stick. "Make it worth your while at least."

"Char," Brit warned.

"Screw it," Char said and shot the puck hard in Brit's direction. So hard she ended up wiping out and having everyone laugh at her before she declared, "Attack!" and pointed at Brit.

Dozens of pucks began flying in Brit's direction, chaos ensuing. Teasing and laughing echoing across the rink.

She glanced at the boys, saw they were laughing, too.

She looked toward the bench, saw Mandy and Rebecca bent in half as they roared with laughter.

But that was okay. Char would take the crap.

Because teasing and hilarity, because competitive spirit and consoling looks and spending time together. Because . . . family.

And Char was becoming part of the Gold's.

THIRTY-ONE

LOGAN

Oh, the joys of family time.

So. Much. Fun.

Which meant he was wondering again why he'd come home.

Despite his intentions to visit his folks when Char went home to her family, he'd almost blown off the trip, nearly caving to the desire to hide in his cabin and hold on to the bubble of nirvana he and his Starlight had created over the last week.

A weekend spent in bed, watching bad TV and ordering in groceries. They'd trolled the web, had picked several recipes they'd been convinced they could master.

Then they'd nearly set the kitchen on fire because he'd gotten distracted.

By the tiny shorts Char had slipped into that were masquerading as pajamas.

Luckily, she'd surfaced from the haze of desire that had kept Logan in its clutches, realizing they'd turned the bread in the oven into charcoal and the pasta and sauce on the stove into briquettes.

He'd gone out on Monday while she was at work and had bought her a brand-new set of pots and pans.

The other ones had made it as far as the trash.

They'd spent one more night together, not attempting to cook, not watching bad TV shows. Instead, Char had picked him up at his house and coaxed him into her car and driven him to the coast.

Heart swelling because his non-nature woman had taken time out of her busy day to research something for him, he'd kissed her long and deep.

She'd taken him there, just because he would love it.

A narrow slice of land.

A steep staircase winding down and down and *down*.

Moonlight and stars overhead, immune even to the light pollution of the city to the north.

And a blanket spread out over sand. His woman cuddled to his side.

They'd sprawled on that blanket, talking well into the night about nothing and everything, and then he'd taken her home to his house and loved her until the sun came up.

After which he'd handed her the silk scarf to tie around her hair. He'd bought it after the incident with her curls, when she'd been too exhausted to put it on. And after seeing her fight with her hair the next morning, watching her wince as she attempted to put it to rights, he'd promised himself she wouldn't ever go without one again.

He wouldn't do anything to cause her hurt. Not if he could help it.

And in this case, he *could* help it. He now had a stash of her favorite brand of wraps and had watched numerous YouTube videos to learn how to put it on.

If she didn't have one, he now had plenty.

If she was too tired, he would do it.

She hadn't complained about the lack of sleep, even though she'd had to get up in just a few hours in order to make her flight to the East Coast. She'd just shared his bed, cuddled against him, and then fallen asleep in his arms.

Then she'd gone.

And the next day he'd gone, too.

His parents lived in Wisconsin, on a large swathe of property that held a fishing hole for his father—a top priority and must-have that his dad had *needed,* and his mother despised on principle—and a craft room filled with wall-to-wall shelving that his mom had insisted on having custom made that his dad refused to pay for with *his* hard-earned money.

The last had been a major point of contention between his parents over their lives, and one, frankly, he'd lost a lot of respect for his dad over.

His mom might not have worked in an office, but she'd given her job up for them, managed Logan and Cecily and Josh's school and extracurriculars, had cooked and cleaned and *been there.* She'd lived her life for them for many years, and the comments about money had increased tenfold when his mom had gone back to school for her degree without consulting his dad.

Now she worked at the local nursing home, part-time as a receptionist and part-time as the activities coordinator.

His dad, on the other hand, had retired and found himself at loose ends.

Hence, the fishing hole.

But Logan could see he was trying.

He'd spent a lot of time in the garden, particularly concentrating on those spots outside the window of the craft room, trying to make it look lush and green so she would have something pretty to look at. And he made himself lunch when Logan's mother was at *that* job, instead of asking her to—a point that he'd lost any ground on by declaring it far and wide.

But he wasn't going to win any gold stars for his behavior, not when he seemed incapable of understanding how he was hurting Logan's mom.

And on that track, it wasn't like his mom was going to get any either. She just bottled it up, played the martyr, and held on to that anger.

Anger and cluelessness weren't a pretty combination in a thirty-seven-year marriage. Which was how Logan had found himself the referee more and more over the years, how interfering and placating had become his typical standard of dealing with his mom and dad's arguments.

In this case, he'd ensured the fishing hole and the bugs it was drawing toward the house were taken care of—what his mother objected to but seemed unable to give voice to, at least when that person was her husband. Then Logan had hired a custom cabinet-maker to make the craft room everything his mom had hoped it would be. He'd footed the bill because he could afford it, and his mom deserved to have something nice.

But he wished he didn't have to.

Not paying. *That* he was fine with.

It was all the rest of it that had become unbearable. The phone calls and aggravation. The fights and placating. But . . . he'd also learned here was no point in arguing with them or attempting to have them hash out their own issues.

That time had long passed.

In his teenage years, they'd stopped trying to put a happy face on their relationship. Logan wasn't sure if pretending had gotten too difficult or if they just figured he was old enough to deal, but one day the veil had lifted, and he'd seen exactly what was between them.

Tension and resentment.

And then he'd looked back and seen all the other times that had bled through. The sharp comments and hard looks. The anger, the coldness, the distance.

Not healthy. Not fulfilling.

Not *anything* like he had with Char.

But putting the woman he loved aside for the moment, Logan knew if he didn't step into situations like the Craft Room, he had to listen to complaints from both sides, and life was too damned short to deal with that.

His father exalting all the points of how his mother was controlling and demanding. His mother citing every instance over the course of their relationship of how his father didn't care about her feelings.

No, it wasn't healthy to step in.

He knew that.

Still, he also knew that, at this moment in time, stepping in was making his life less drama filled.

So, peacemaker for the moment.

Until he figured out how to get them to see what they were doing was alienating their children. Hell, John had moved miles away. Cecily was in another country. The only thing that had them all returning home at regular intervals was that they were all aware their mom and dad had been excellent parents.

Once.

Now, they were a burden.

One that Logan wished he hadn't decided to shoulder.

He leaned against the doorframe that led into the kitchen, watching his mom aggressively knead a giant pile of dough. She was making cinnamon rolls, both because they were Logan's favorite, but also for the seniors at the center. She had a shift later, and his father was unhappy she hadn't taken the time off to be with Logan.

"They don't need you," his dad was grumbling. "They got on just fine without you for all these years."

"I promised I would be there," she said. "So, I will be there. It's four hours, and then I'll be home. Lacy has already promised to cover for me on Friday."

"She—"

"*Can't* cover for me today, as I told you this morning *and* told Logan when he called to tell us he was coming two days ago," she snapped, punching hard enough into the dough that Log wondered if the rolls would be as hard as rocks or the best ever.

Did violence count in kneading? Because if so, she'd be getting the gold star.

"They—"

Enough.

"It's fine, Mom," he interrupted, crossing over to her and hugging her from behind. He kissed the top of her head, met his dad's eyes, silently telling him to let this go. "My visit is last minute. I can't expect you guys to drop everything."

His father's glare intensified, and Logan prepared himself for his next peacemaking operation.

Read: torture.

"Plus, that will give us time to go fishing."

His dad's face lit up.

His mom stiffened in his arms, knowing that he hated fishing. But as much as he disliked the tension between his parents, he did enjoy spending time with them one-on-one.

He could throw his bobber in the water, pretend to care about fish for an hour or two, especially if it meant he got a glimpse of how his dad used to be.

"I'll go get the gear ready."

Sighing, after his dad left, his mom nudged him back. "You shouldn't keep doing that, you know."

"Doing what?"

She touched his cheek, sadness in her eyes. "I can handle him."

"I know you can." He covered her hand with his. "But you need to *actually* talk to him, Mom. Not just snip and complain."

"I haven't been doing very well, have I?" She winced when he didn't respond, turned back to the rolls, and he felt guilt slide through him. "I'm sorry, Logie Bear. This hasn't been fair to you. I'll do better."

Dammit.

He didn't want her feeling bad.

He didn't want his mom to hurt any more than he wanted Char to.

She was his *mom*. She'd baked cakes and driven to the rink at God knew what hour. She'd held his hand when he broke his arm, flew out and took care of him when he had knee surgery.

He just wanted his parents to get along.

Unfortunately, he wasn't sure how to go about that.

So, instead of belaboring the point, instead of advising as he'd done for far too long, to just sit down with his dad and *talk*, Logan leaned next to his mom on the counter and asked, "Will you teach me how to cook something later?"

Green eyes that mirrored his own widening. "You? Cook?"

"Just one meal. Something a novice like me can accomplish, but something delicious."

Eyes now narrowing. "It's a woman."

He grinned. "It's a woman."

She smiled, wide enough that he felt its impact in his solar plexus. "Oh, Logie Bear, I'm so happy for you," she said, setting down the dough and hugging him tight. "Will you tell me about her?"

"Do I still get to be your taste-tester?"

"Cheeky boy." She kissed his cheek, opened the cookie jar in front of her, and pulled out a chocolate chip cookie the size of his head.

Not on the diet plan.

But his mom was smiling, and he was going to get to talk about his favorite thing in the world—Char.

He could work with that.

By the time the cinnamon rolls were in the oven, he'd confessed all, had planned out a meal his mom was confident he could execute, *and* eaten two more chocolate chip cookies.

Definitely not on the meal plan.

But definitely better than the day had begun.

Of course, he still had to survive fishing.

———

"Hey, Starlight," he said, answering his cell as he pushed out the front door and stepped onto the porch.

"What's wrong?"

He blinked, realized that his parents and their bickering were bleeding over into his interactions with Char, and quickly shoved the dark emotions down. Never would he allow that to happen again. Never would he let his baggage affect what he and Char were building.

Not fucking ever.

"I'm fine," he told her, leaning against the waist-high railing and staring out at the lake. His dad was putzing around at the shed near the pond, would no doubt be waving him down in a couple of minutes.

But for now, he had his woman on the phone, and he wasn't going to waste a moment.

They'd only had one quick chat, her letting him know she'd arrived safely at her parents' house, and then exchanged a few texts. He'd missed her, even though they'd only been apart for two days, but hadn't wanted to intrude on her family time.

She needed this time.

"You're not fine," she accused.

The urge to disagree with her, to push her back and pretend all was good was strong.

Except . . . that wasn't what he wanted to build. That wasn't what Char needed, and she'd been explicit about that fact. He couldn't be the only one who protected and took care. He needed to be open and let her in and not presume to know the best course of action.

Which was why he shoved down the urge to continue with the I'm-Fine-Everything-Is-Fine path and admitted, "My parents are getting to me."

"You—"

She cut herself off, and he got the impression she'd been about to yell at him for not telling her the truth.

Then her voice softened. "Shit, I'm sorry, Log."

"It's nothing more than I expected," he said. "It's just . . ."

"What you expected."

"Yeah." He made a face. "That."

"Is there anything I can do?"

Heart pulsing, he forced himself to not ask her to come up, to rescue him. Even putting aside his urge to be the rescuer, he wasn't going to take her away from her family. "Just call me every once in a while, Starlight," he said. "I've got plenty of experience dealing with them. Plus, I'll be home and in my cabin soon enough."

Silence, and he braced himself, wondering if she'd want more than that.

He'd give it, of course. He loved her, would flay himself to the bone if need be. But just admitting that he was upset felt like he'd given into the bullshit that his parents created.

Drama. Resentment.

God, he just wanted to have a visit where he could sit in a room with them and enjoy himself. No placating. No refereeing.

Just being.

Like it was when he was with Char.

But that wasn't going to happen, and he needed to learn to deal if he was going to keep visiting. To not allow his parents and their drama to derail him, to smother him in their bullshit.

He wanted to be a mountain undergoing an avalanche, its snow sliding off in one large sheet, revealing the steady and unbreakable granite beneath. He wanted to be untouched and unmarred. To be able to love the woman in his heart without baggage.

Ah. Hopes and wishes . . . and then reality.

So, he braced himself and waited for more questions.

"I learned how to make a meal you might like," she murmured, instead of interrogating him. "Barbeque chicken with spicy rice and a bean salad. It's low calorie, tasty, and I nearly cut my thumb off last night when I tried to help my dad cook it."

Now he struggled for words, love for this woman in every cell, wanting to find a way to tell her exactly how much that meant to him.

But he didn't want to weigh down the moment. Instead, he asked lightly, "Is it still attached?"

She didn't miss a beat. "The chicken or the thumb?"

He laughed out loud. "Starlight," he warned.

"It's barely a scratch," she said then her voice went serious. "But . . . thank you, Log. For talking to me. For letting me in."

"I—"

"I know everyone thinks I'm the open book because I'm good at pretending I have my shit together and don't hold back in the media or negotiations," she murmured. "But just like you could see through that mask, I can see through yours, baby."

His pulse raced. "Char."

"I see you underneath all that smooth, carefree charm—"

Throat tightening, he went for a joke. "You think I'm charming?"

A chuckle. "Case in point, right there. But yes, honey, I do. You're very charming—so charming that people don't realize you're hurting inside." She paused. "You're allowed to wish things are different."

Heart pounding, he sucked in a breath. "If only wishes could turn into reality," he said lightly.

A long beat of quiet. "I know you do."

Another breath, releasing the hurt of the morning, the strain since he'd arrived the night before. His jaw ached from clenching it. His shoulders were riddled with knots.

But he was on the phone with Char.

And that was enough.

"I really am okay, Starlight," he said and took the next step, letting her in a little deeper, done with pretending he was an island and nothing affected him—not the tide or a hurricane or an invasive species. "I just . . . sometimes I forget how bad it is. The tension between them is unbearable, and I seem to always want to default back to placating everyone. It just never really works."

"They need to grow up and leave you out of it." Sharp words now, but not directed at him, even though he clearly owned some of that burden by always interceding.

Still, the words were true.

His parents did need to grow up, did need to leave him out of it.

And . . . he needed to not let himself get drawn in.

"Unfortunately, you can't make people grow up," she said, voice gentle. "And they're your parents. You love them, want to see them happy."

"I'm starting to think they're at their happiest when they're the most miserable."

A beat as she considered that. "Somehow that makes sense."

"Logan!" his dad shouted from down by the pond. "Let's go!"

A soft giggle in his ear. "It sounds like you're being summoned."

"Fishing," he muttered.

Another giggle. "I thought you hated fishing."

Hate was too gentle a word. He despised it. But . . . it was time with his dad. Hopefully, *peaceful* time. And the plus was that the yelling would probably scare the fish away, so he'd be unlikely to deal with actually catching a fish. "I do."

"Fuck, I love you," she said.

"Sweet," he murmured.

"What?"

"I'd almost forgotten how damned sweet you are," he said. "Thank you for giving me that."

"I think I'd give you just about anything, Log." A beat. "Because I know you'll give me the same back."

"I love you," he told her.

"Show it to me on the ice next season," she teased then hesitated. "I should let you go."

"Yeah."

Except, he didn't want to hang up.

"I don't want to go," he admitted.

"I don't want to let you go."

"*Logan!*"

"Fuck," he muttered.

Laughter in his ear. "I'll talk to you later. Text me a picture of all the fish you catch."

"That's just mean."

Her voice gentled. "Bye, honey."

"Bye, Starlight."

He hung up, pocketed his phone, and made his way down to the pond.

Fuck.

Now he had to catch a goddamned fish.

————

Fishing was proceeding as expected.

Which basically meant it was proceeding in silence.

They'd picked up their rods, walked to the end of the small pier he'd helped his dad assemble the previous summer. All metal and floating plastic barrels, it was meant for a much larger lake.

But it floated, got them into the middle, and his dad was happy.

Easy enough.

Log had plunked his ass into a rickety chair that didn't look like it had a hope in hell of supporting him and cast his line out into the water after baiting it and tying on a weight and lure.

No small talk.

Nothing biting.

Just sitting in silence as he figured out what had to change.

Funny how he'd spent years living in this exact scenario, but it wasn't until this visit that it felt absolutely stifling. Like his skin was too small. As though he couldn't breathe.

Because of Char.

Because it was so easy with her.

Because he would do anything to make her happy.

His parents, his dad in particular, didn't seem to give a damn either way. He sighed, reeled his line in, cast again.

And maybe sighed again. But, fuck, it just didn't make any sense. How could his dad not care that his mom was unhappy? Why didn't his mom make her wishes known and stand up for herself?

Why did they stay together when they were so fucking miserable?

Another sigh, this one stifled because he was trying to find a conversational topic that wasn't his parents and could bring about some enjoyment.

"What's got your panties in a bunch?" his dad asked.

Suddenly, Logan didn't give a *fuck* about enjoyment.

Suddenly, *he* was the resentful one. Furious that he'd allowed himself to be drawn into this battle between him and his parents.

"You," he said on an exhale. "You and Mom have me all twisted up inside."

A grunt, his dad's eyes on the lake, but no more words or inquiries. Just the requisite question and going back to his own fucking bubble.

"The fighting has taken a toll on everyone," he said, forcing himself to be calm. "I don't know why you and Mom can't just sit down and sort it out. Why you have to bicker and argue all the time. It makes it really not fun to be around you."

His dad reeled in the line, cast again.

But he didn't say *anything*.

And Logan's temper flared. "You don't give a fuck, do you?"

Steady green eyes finally came to his. "Give a fuck about what?"

"That this tension between you and Mom is driving me away, pushing Cecily and Josh away. That you both are fucking miserable and make everyone around you miserable, too."

Silence.

Logan gripped the fishing rod, the fiberglass handle making a cracking sound that had him loosening his fingers and striving for patience. "It's gotten to the point where I don't even want to come home."

A shrug. "Then don't."

He closed his eyes, breathed deeply. "Why are you doing this?"

Maybe it was something more. Dementia or a sudden hormone imbalance that had caused the change. But . . . it wasn't a sudden change, was it? This had been brewing for years, growing progressively worse as the roots of whatever darkness between his parents festered.

"I'm not doing anything," his dad muttered. "Aside from trying to fish."

"And fight with Mom about stupid shit."

"What's between your mother and I isn't any business of yours."

Except, they'd *made* it his business. Over and over and *over* again. Logan reeled in his fishing line, secured the hook, and dropped the rod on the dock. "Do you really believe your own bullshit?" he asked, turning toward his dad.

Who slowly faced him and whose only response was a raised eyebrow.

And Logan lost his shit.

Look, he knew he was impulsive, had to regularly force himself for patience. But that patience wasn't often needed for his temper. He dealt with pain in the ass forwards on the ice, pushing his buttons, slashing his calves with their sticks, cup-checking on an occasional basis—occasional because while he was slow to anger, once he got to that point, it was an implosion of spectacular proportions.

Last time he'd lost it on the ice, he'd ended up kicked out of a game when some fucker had taken a cheap shot at Brit.

Today, it was this fucking stranger in front of him.

This wasn't his dad, wasn't the person he'd respected and had fun with, who'd coached his hockey team and taught him how to ride a bike. This person was a miserable bastard who seemed to be completely lacking in empathy.

"You call me to bitch about her," Logan said. "She calls to bitch about you. I find myself completely stuck in the middle."

"You've got your own life to live." A shrug. "Stop complaining and go out and live it."

Yeah, that was exactly the same conclusion he'd come to.

Because it had taken these last couple of weeks with Char to recognize exactly how fucked up this tangle he'd allowed himself to be ensnared in with his parents was.

And he was done.

"I don't know when you turned from the dad whose opinion I respected more than any other person's to this angry asshole in front of me—"

His dad's fishing rod *clinked* down into the holder. "How dare you call—"

Logan jumped to his feet. "*That's* the only thing that gets a rise out of you? Me calling you an asshole? I don't know what the fuck happened to you, but you're not the man I grew up wanting to emulate, not by a fucking long shot."

"Then go, Log. Go live your fancy life. Go be with your fancy friends and see how happy that makes you."

He sighed. "That's just it, Dad. I don't give a shit about my *fancy* life or friends." The ones he'd made this season he didn't count in that number, but he didn't bother to explain the distinction between them to his father, not when there were so many other important things to tackle. "I haven't been happy. And that's not because of you and Mom," he added, when his dad started to protest. "It was because of me. Because I gave up the woman I loved so she would have a chance at her dream. But now I have her back, and I cannot for the life of me understand how you wouldn't do everything in your power to make the woman *you* love happy."

He shoved a hand through his hair. "Why argue over the craft room or the job or the trip she wants to take to Finland? Even if you don't give a shit about how she stores her fabrics or her dream to see the northern lights or the job, don't you see how working makes her happy, along with piecing together a quilt? Don't you want her dreams to be realized?" Logan waited for his dad to reply, and when he didn't, Log sighed and figured why not say the rest of it? "She gave up her career for yours and didn't complain once. She moved away from her family and support system to advance your career. She gave, Dad, so why couldn't you give back?"

And still . . . nothing.

Beyond fucking done, Logan turned away, started down the dock.

"I would have given her everything," his dad said, and Logan spun back, saw his dad walking toward him. "If she hadn't fallen in love with my best friend."

THIRTY-TWO

CHAR

The smell of peach pie filled the kitchen, and she was sitting full sandwich-style between her sister, Amelia, and her brother, Will.

And having a pile of shit heaped onto her.

Shit of the teasing, sibling variety.

God, it was good to be home.

Her brother and sister had spent most of the last two days at her parents' house, and she was so thankful for her family and their inability to hold the fact that she'd been beyond distant over the last few years against her.

Even when she'd been too wrapped up in work to appreciate them, they'd still reached out, and being here with them, finally being aware of how she'd felt and acted over the years—closed down and separate and probably a bit cold—made her realize how much she'd been missing out on.

Amelia bumped her shoulder against Char's. "You look happy, Char-Char. I'd thought we'd be consoling a defeated barrier-breaker who'd been denied her ultimate prize."

"I was considering holding a Chubby Bunny contest, just so Lo-Lo can win something."

She narrowed her eyes even as her lips quirked. "I may be defeated in my search for the Cup, but I'll never lose another Chubby Bunny contest."

A bag of marshmallows landed on the counter in front of her. "Prove it."

She glanced up to see her dad grinning at them, a laughing expression softening the planes of his face.

And that was how she found herself defending her title of Chubby Bunny champion.

"Twenty-three!" she exclaimed—or rather attempted to exclaim.

She moved to the trash can, spat out the clump of gelatin and sugar in a very unladylike gesture—sometimes sacrifices to beauty and elegance had to be made—and turned back to her siblings, who had stopped at ten and fourteen respectively.

Will shook his head at their mom, who had come in mid-competition. "Isn't the middle child supposed to be the peacemaker?"

"Not our Charlotte," her mom said, kissing their father on the cheek. "She's fire and steel and determination."

"Makes all the rest of us look bad," Amelia grumbled, her eyes sparkling with humor as she wrapped her arm around Char's waist. "Always got to excel at everything."

Will snorted, since Amelia had recently returned for her master's degree and had just finished explaining how excited she was that her bid for a spot on a new committee to develop curriculum with the school district had been accepted. Not that Will was one to talk—earlier he'd shared that his research paper was going to be published in a well-known scientific journal. He'd also just been tenured at the University, not an easy feat in this day and age of adjunct professors.

"My little gig of playing with athletes can't compare with corralling elementary school students"—she squeezed Amelia's hand—"or, for that matter, college students"—a nod at her brother—"I just get to be the face of a group of people who are more family than workplace." She picked up the bag of marshmallows, began rolling down the plastic.

When silence greeted her, she looked up into the surprised faces of her siblings and parents.

"What?" she asked.

Her mom's eyes were damp. "I'm so glad you're back," she whispered. "I've missed you, honey."

Char blinked, opening her mouth to say she'd always been there.

But that would have been a lie.

She hadn't been there, hadn't been present, and her family had clearly seen that, even if they hadn't called her on it.

"What's his name?" her grandmother asked. Char had almost forgotten she was there, sitting on her usual stool pulled up to the island, silently playing solitaire as they'd all caused chaos in the kitchen while her father cooked dinner.

The room fell quiet.

"What?" she asked, though she had a sneaking suspicion she knew the *him* her grandma was referencing.

"Or her," her grandmother pressed.

Char attempted to play dumb. "Him or her who?"

Steady brown eyes fixing her in place. "The one who brought you back."

She wanted to say she'd brought *herself* back, but that would be a lie. And not only would her family call her on that lie, but she knew they wouldn't stop pestering her until she admitted the truth.

But that was what family did.

What she'd failed to appreciate until she'd seen it with the Gold.

They were nosy and when it came to the important things, they didn't cut each other slack. They pushed and expected more and dammit, they made it known that they wanted to be privy to all the little details.

Because they mattered.

Because *she* mattered.

Which was how she came to spill the whole story of Logan and her relationship to her entire family. Their clandestine start, the breakup, his present of slippers and lunches and cooking for her. How he'd fixed her gate and filled her fridge with groceries. How he took care of her in a hundred small ways—ways she'd never begun to think of and ways that touched deeply.

And how—most importantly—she wanted to take care of him right back.

"I thought that he'd broken something inside me, that he'd taken away my ability to love a man in that way," she finished, "but the truth was that no other man has ever understood me like Logan. I'm with him, and a part of my soul just relaxes. I don't have to worry about being Char the GM or Char the role model for black women or Char the kickass businesswoman who doesn't get pushed around." Her eyes stung, voice dropping to a whisper. "I can just be Starlight."

Amelia sniffed. "Char-Char, you really love him."

Char made a face. "I do." A beat as the room filled with laughter. "As much as I hate that it ruins my tough as nails exterior."

Will tugged her back against him. "I still want to kick his ass for hurting you."

"He was trying to help me," she argued. "But"—her lips curved—"I already threatened him with dull skate blades if he presumed to make a decision about me without me again."

"That's my girl." Her dad kissed the top of her head. "You sure about him? It makes the work situation tricky, and I know you love your job."

Char was already nodding, lips parting, when her mother spoke.

"Meh," her mom said. "Those Gold players have made the

news for far bigger scandals than this. I bet it'll barely make a blip on the radar."

That was to be determined, Char knew, but she wasn't going to give Logan up regardless of the press or that they both were important to the Gold. "Plus, the HR department with the team is well-versed with this type of relationship."

"And it can't be any more of a conflict than Pierre Barie being the GM for the team his son played on."

"Or his son's wife. Or my coach Calle dating my player Coop."

"It's like a soap opera," Amelia said on a giggle.

"They're a family," Char said. "They're messy and intertwined, friendships and lovers and business all tangled together, but . . . beneath all that is love." She smiled. "And I'm happy to be just beginning to find my place in all of that messy."

"With Loooogan," Will teased.

"Shut up, you," she muttered, smacking him lightly across the chest. "But yes. With Logan."

"I'm happy for you, baby," her mom said, "but make sure he knows that he needs to get his ass here in order to pass inspection."

"Exactly," her grandmother said.

Char laughed. "I'll pass that along."

The timer went off, and even though they were all grownups, each of them still moved to do their assigned job. Her dad headed to the oven. Amelia sprang to her feet, Char joining her. It was time for Amelia to set the table, for Char to gather drinks and condiments. Will would be on dishes, her mother on lighting the candles her dad required for ambiance.

And her grandma . . . well, her only job was getting her tush to the table and sitting down.

Perks came with age.

As they moved, the conversation turned to other things. To Amelia's rundown of her class and how she was going to miss them in the fall. To the underfunded educational district she taught in. To Char's mind sparking with an idea of how to get her players involved with San Franciscan schools and her whole family helping her refine and perfect the notion.

For the first time in years, she didn't feel distant.

And she knew that was because Logan had filled her up, given her the strength to look into her heart, and helped her recognize what she was missing.

She'd done the hard work.

But he'd had her back.

As she ate some of her father's delicious cooking, she thought back to the phone call, to the way Logan's voice had gone sad, the pain radiating through the airwaves, and she promised herself she would have his back in return.

They'd both spent too long alone.

Now was the time for them to move forward.

Together.

————

But by the next evening, she wasn't sure if together was what Logan wanted.

She'd called.

She'd texted.

She'd called again.

She'd even sent an email.

"Maybe I should send a carrier pigeon," she muttered.

"What's that, honey?" her mom asked, glancing up from the thick book in French she was reading quote, "just for fun."

She made a face, shoved her phone in her pocket. "Nothing," she said, half to convince herself and half to focus on the time with her family. She only had a couple more days with them before she needed to get back to the Bay Area. She wanted to enjoy this time in Baltimore.

"She said she wanted to send a carrier pigeon," her dad chimed in.

"A carrier pigeon?" The book hit her mom's lap. "Why?"

"Mom—"

"No," her mom snapped, and the sharp tone was so different from what she usually used that Char blinked and stopped talking. "Tell me," she demanded.

"I can't get ahold of Logan."

"Was everything you told me about him bullshit?"

Another blink, Char's mouth opening and closing like a guppy. "Um, no?"

"Is that a question or an answer?" More stern.

More blinking, but enough that Char finally pulled herself together. "An answer, Mom. He's always been available, or at the very least, called me back as soon as he could."

"How long has it been since you talked to him?"

"Yesterday morning."

"That's not so long—"

Her dad shut up when her mom's sharp gaze transferred to him.

"You told me this man adores you," she said. "So, is that part bullshit, or is something else going on?"

That was what she was worried about. He'd been upset and now not to hear from him after he'd been so careful to rebuild her trust in him. But at the same time, she didn't want to make something out of nothing. Maybe he was just busy. She certainly hadn't been glued to her phone. Or maybe he dropped his phone in the lake while he was fishing and couldn't call her—

"Char."

She nibbled at her lip. "It's weird to hear you curse."

A sigh. "Charlotte."

"Damn," she muttered. "I haven't heard that tone from you in about fifteen years."

"I haven't had much cause to use it with you, honey. Tell me why I'm feeling the need to now."

"I don't want to make this a big deal, to start letting our relationship dominate my every waking thought. What if it becomes more important than everything else, and I suddenly—" She cut herself off.

"Suddenly want to quit your job and become Suzy Homemaker."

Char sighed. "Yeah." A pause. "Not that there's anything wrong with that. I think it's amazing that you stayed home with us when we were little, am so thankful that grandma was there, too. I just worry that there's something inside me that will make me forget everything important."

"Maybe what you think is important isn't really."

Soft words that had her spinning toward her dad.

"Your job can't love you back, baby. It can fulfill you in many ways, but it can't fill that hole inside your heart."

No, it couldn't.

"And," her mom said. "You're my smart, talented, lovely, stubborn daughter. You're not one to repeat your mistakes."

There was that.

"What if I decide that work is less important than Logan?" she asked.

"Isn't that how it should be with the man you love?" her mom asked, gaze full of warmth when it met her father's.

The question was both terrifying and also . . . right.

Because would it be the end of the world if her priorities were something *other* than work, if they shifted to the family she hoped to build with the man who held her heart?

No.

That seemed to be the only way forward.

Logan hadn't hesitated to put her first over the last weeks.

Now, it was her turn.

Thirty-Three

To say the last twenty-four hours had been tense was the understatement of the century.

The bombshell revelation.

Him walking away from his father, totally unbelieving.

And then his mom coming home from work, taking one look at his face, her face falling, words tumbling from her lips.

"He told you."

Then she'd begun crying, and he'd gone through a spectrum of emotions—disbelief, fury, horror, sadness, disappointment—before he'd crossed through the kitchen and taken her in his arms.

Tears.

God, he'd never seen her cry like that.

Wrenching sobs that shuddered through her, dripping down her cheeks, soaking into his shirt.

So much pain.

Her knees had eventually given way, and he'd picked her up, carried her to the couch and held her.

Such a strange experience, holding the woman who'd cared for him his whole life, who'd kissed his hurts and comforted him when he'd had a bad dream. Seeing her so broken, the tearing sobs coursing through her when the most he'd ever seen was her upset at a movie or book, a few tears here or there.

She hadn't even cried this hard when Logan's grandmother had died.

And all the while his father hadn't come in.

Through the night, when eventually the tears stopped coming.

All through the next morning, when his mom had finally fallen asleep and Logan had covered her up on the couch.

Through the rest of the day, even when Log had gone out to search for him.

Gone.

The fishing poles stowed away and his truck not on the property.

Now Logan was on the porch, his mom having retired to her bedroom and a long bath, and him trying to figure out what to do.

He had no details, wasn't sure he wanted any more, frankly.

In fact, he just wanted to GTFO and lock himself up in his cabin, or maybe track down Char's parents' address in Baltimore and pretend this whole damned thing hadn't happened.

He'd thought he had it all figured out.

His mom was upset about her job, resentful of years spent living her life for everyone else. She could be encouraged to speak up and advocate for her needs and things would improve. On the flip side, his dad was being an ass for the most part but could be forced to see that he needed to change and treat her differently. They both just needed to sit down and hash it out, to figure out their differences and stay together, or to decide the chasm between them was too large and to divorce.

But now . . . what?

This revelation about his mom had changed *everything*.

Or had it?

Fuck. He didn't know.

What he did know was that he wanted to talk to Char. He missed her, *fuck* he missed her. But did he want to lay this burden on her shoulders?

I need you to need me.

The memory of her words sat heavy on his heart.

He didn't want to burden her, and yet, how could he not?

He wasn't that solitary mountain in the middle of nowhere. He was a man who missed the woman he loved and had all he'd thought he knew shredded to pieces.

His mom a cheater?

What in the actual fuck?

His finger lifted, readying to press the button to call her—

The door creaked open, drawing his gaze to the front of the house, to his mom wrapped snuggly in a robe. "Hey," she croaked. "Come inside, I made dinner."

And because he loved her, he pushed off the railing and went into the house, waiting patiently while she served up bowls of a hearty soup, all the while noticing that the table had been set for three, even though his dad wasn't there.

How long had it been like this?

How long had he missed what was really going on?

"Middle school," she murmured.

His eyes flew from the bowl of soup up to hers.

"You were in middle school when it happened. I was . . . stupid. I was feeling unappreciated and lonely, and what I did was unforgivable." She set the spoon down. "I—I probably shouldn't have told your father, should have just ended things and moved on, but as time went on, I couldn't hide it any longer."

"Mom."

"I'll not tell you anything further, as that is something between your father and I, but you need to know I was in the wrong. He was nothing but faithful, and I'm the one wh-who betrayed—" A deep breath. "I betrayed our vows."

Her gaze drifted to the table.

"Why stay, Mom?"

"I love your father," she said. "It's a twisted, wrong love now, but I-I keep hoping that I can make it up to him, that if I just keep moving forward, we'll be able to make each other happy again."

"That's a lot of years, Mom."

"Yeah," she whispered. "I think recently I've realized that probably won't happen."

"That's why you're working?"

"I do love being there, but yes, I need to be able to support myself."

"I—"

"Don't you dare, Logan," she said. "I've relied on you in a way that I shouldn't have for too many years, and I am so sorry for that." Her chin came up. "But damn if I'll keep doing it."

"Mom," he began.

"Eat your stew, Logie Bear," she murmured. "Then we'll give you some cooking lessons. You only need a few solid recipes, and pretty soon you'll have swept your Charlotte off her feet."

Her tone was familiar, one that told him he wouldn't get any further by pushing her.

He reached across the table, squeezed her hand.

"I love you, Mom."

Her eyes misted again, but she just blinked rapidly, told him she loved him too, and then they dug into the stew.

THIRTY-FOUR

CHAR

She'd been concerned she had the wrong place, but then she'd nearly mowed down a man who was the spitting image of Logan, only a few decades older

"Shit!" She slammed on the brakes, skidding to a stop far too close for comfort.

Her hand clamped over her heart, and she took a deep breath, making sure to set the rental car in park. "Go to Wisconsin, they said," she muttered. "It will be fun, they said."

Okay, no one had promised her fun.

But she also hadn't planned on running over Logan's father.

Knock. Knock.

Char jumped, gaze flying to the window.

The man indicated she should roll down the pane of glass. It was nearly one in the morning, the area surrounding Logan's parents' house was pitch black—though light blazed from the windows of the home itself—and she suddenly wondered if coming here was a really bad idea.

"Are you lost?" the voice echoed through the glass.

He even sounded like Logan. She hadn't recognized that

when she'd met them at Parents' Day, probably because she'd been too closed down at that point to process anything about Logan, least of which were the similarities between him and his father.

Taking a breath, she shut off the ignition, grabbed her purse, and opened the door.

"John," she said, forcing her voice to be steady as she extended her hand.

He was silent, and from the little she could see of his face, there was no recognition there.

"It's Charlotte Harris," she said. "From the Gold."

A flash of white as his eyes widened. "You're here for Logan."

In more ways than he could probably anticipate, but all she said was, "Yes."

"Come on, then."

He led her toward the house, extracting a set of keys as he jogged up the steps and then unlocked the door.

What they walked into was . . .

Unexpected.

Logan and his mom were in the kitchen, the radio blasting with oldies, both wearing aprons, both . . . covered head-to-toe with flour and collapsed on the floor laughing hysterically.

Her heart pulsed with equal parts relief and worry.

She'd flown up here expecting something tragic had happened.

Instead, he was having the time of his life.

Anger bubbled up, furious words filling the back of her throat, threatening to explode into the space.

But Logan's dad beat her to it.

"What the fuck is going on here?" he bellowed.

Two sets of eyes flew up in shock, going first to John then to Charlotte.

Logan scrambled to his feet, closed the distance between them. "Starlight, I—are you all right?" he asked, gripping her arms lightly. "Why are you here?"

The radio switched off.

She glanced between him and his parents. "I thought something was wrong," she whispered. "I thought . . ." Her voice went even quieter. "I thought you needed me."

His hands convulsed. "Starlight," he rasped, and she saw the pain now. It clouded at the edges of his vision, hung to his frame.

"What happened?" she asked, cupping his jaw.

"It's—"

"You *have* to be fucking kidding me," his dad yelled, and they both jumped, stares darting in his direction. "Your son finds out that you fucked around on me, and you two are *baking?*"

Char's lungs froze.

Logan went stiff, spun to face him fully. "Don't, Dad," he said. "Don't say something you're going to regret."

Hostile green eyes in their direction. "You heard me when I said she fucked my best friend, right? And yet, here you are, taking her side." Furious words. "Did she lie? Did she tell you she didn't—"

Logan opened his mouth.

"No."

The word was fierce enough to have all of them looking at Logan's mom, Hallie. "I didn't lie, John. I cheated on you. It was a horrible mistake. I promised to never do it again." She shook her head. "I've spent a long time trying to make up for it, but I see now nothing I do will ever make it right."

Char's eyes darted to Logan, and she saw the pain intensify there, knew this wasn't an old hurt. This was new and fresh and why he'd been out of touch.

She leaned against his side, wrapped one arm around his, and held him tight.

"So," Hallie continued. "I can only offer two choices. One, we go to therapy. We stop ignoring this giant elephant in the room and try to work through it. Two, we divorce. I'll move out, leave you to your life. I'll explain to Cecily and Josh that it's my fault, and we both do our best to repair the damage our unhappiness over the years has done to our kids." She sucked in a breath. "I was too scared to leave before. Too worried about ruining what we once had, terrified to hurt our kids." She looked at Logan. "But I see now by not doing anything, by not taking ownership of what I've done, that I've hurt them more than divorce ever could."

Char wanted to retreat, realizing too late that she shouldn't be hearing this, but when she actually went to step back and out of this conversation, Logan wrapped his arms around her shoulder and whispered, "Please, Starlight."

As if she could deny him anything.

She stayed.

Stayed still and silent and on tenterhooks.

Until she saw the fury replace the shock on John's face.

"Don't," Char blurted before she could stop herself. "Don't say it. Go to therapy."

That fury turned in her direction, but Char had always had courage. She didn't let it fail her now. "You obviously love her, even though part of you hates what's she did. Otherwise you wouldn't have stayed. Otherwise you wouldn't be so mad now." She swallowed. "Don't give up on that love. Just . . . try. For yourself, for the woman you love, and if for nothing else, then try for your kids. They deserve to have parents who are happy."

A long moment of taut silence.

"I think you should be careful who you give advice to, little girl," he said coldly.

"John!" Hallie exclaimed.

"Dad," Logan warned.

Char didn't flinch. She was well-used to dealing with big personalities, didn't shy away from cranky men.

She could handle Logan's dad.

Of that she was sure.

"You either find the balls to do this," she said. "Or you'll regret it for the rest of your miserable life. And it will be a miserable life. If Hallie is half the person Logan is, you'll hate being without her, even though she did something terrible."

Green eyes narrowed. "You—"

"Not a word, Dad," Logan growled. He shifted, snagged Char's hand and tugged her down the hall, not stopping until they were at the end of it and through a door.

It slammed shut, and she found herself spun and pressed to the plank of wood a moment letter.

Another set of furious green eyes met hers.

And suddenly, she had the feeling that she might have seriously fucked up.

THIRTY-FIVE

LOGAN

His heart was pounding.
Fury was in every cell.
He bent close.
"You were magnificent."

Char's mouth fell open, breath shuddering out to coat his lips, and Logan gave in to the urge that had gripped him from the moment she'd stepped into the situation. He pressed his body to hers and kissed her with every bit of love he felt for her.

Only when his lungs were screaming did he pull away.

"Thank you," he whispered, so fucking touched that she'd stood up for him. "Thank you for saying that—"

Fuck, his voice cracked, and his eyes were burning.

But, damn, he could barely comprehend how much that had meant to him. First, she'd come to him, even though he hadn't asked. Then she'd stayed by his side. Then she'd intervened . . . for him.

With barely any context, wading into an emotional minefield of a situation.

"I love you," he said. "Starlight—"

His voice broke again, but it was okay. Because this time, she wrapped her arms around him and kissed *him*. This time, she held him close and grounded until he felt steadiness return.

This time . . . he wasn't alone.

The rock sitting on his heart was gone. He wasn't facing the world by himself.

He had Char.

And that made all the difference in the world.

"I think I didn't make a very good impression on your parents," she murmured when they broke apart a second time.

He'd just reached up to cup her cheek, and her words had him bursting into laughter. "I don't give a shit what my parents think of you," he told her. "You made a fucking incredible impression on me, sweetheart. You're here. You had my back. That means *everything*."

He froze.

"Wait. Why are you here? Your family—"

"Reminded me that sometimes the most important person in your life is the one who keeps your heart safe."

"Char."

"I love you, baby."

He tugged her close, held her tight, and for a long time they just stayed in place, arms around each other. Then Char nodded, and he remembered exactly how late it was. One smooth move had her in his arms. The next had him walking toward the bed, sitting her on the edge, and tugging off her shoes.

"Log—"

"Let me take care of you now, okay?" The need was strong.

She frowned. "This isn't some tit-for-tat I take care of you, you take care of me thing."

"I know," he said. "But you're here, and I've missed you, and you've just pulled some superwoman wonderfulness that has taken me almost thirty years to get the guts up to consider saying." He ran the backs of his fingers over her cheek. "And twenty-nine years in, I hadn't even gotten my head wrapped around verbalizing it. But you . . . you swept in there and took that weight off my shoulders."

"Log."

"Thank you."

"It was probably overstepping."

"Then consider yourself warned that I might overstep one day for you."

Her eyes narrowed. "Not for breaking up."

A grin curved the corners of his mouth. "No, Starlight, not for breaking up. Not ever again."

"Okay," she said, nodding regally. "Then I'll allow you to take care of me." He started to straighten, but she laced her fingers into his hair and held him close. "But you be forewarned that I'll be taking care of you right back, Log."

"I can live with that."

"Good."

"Good," he repeated, pressing a firm kiss to her mouth before standing up and heading to his luggage. She probably had things in her car, but honestly, he wasn't up for traversing the gauntlet of his parents anymore that night—or morning, anyway.

He just wanted to be with Char.

After tugging out a T-shirt and one of the spare scarfs he'd tossed in when his imagination had taken him to Baltimore instead of Wisconsin, he crossed back over to find her glancing down at her clothes.

Logan winced at the state of her shirt and pants.

Streaks of flour marred the black slacks and a dribble of chocolate was streaked across her right breast—well, the turquoise fabric covering that glorious right breast. Because if it had been on her skin, he might have been tempted to clean it off with his tongue. Cliché, yes, but this woman did it for him. He wasn't ashamed, but he was also completely aware that she was tired, had traveled to him, and then waded through some emotion B.S.

Which was why he kept his tongue to himself and helped her undress . . . and then *re*dress.

Or at least, helped her tug on his T-shirt, handed over the scarf for her to tie up her hair, and resisted the urge to trace every inch of her beautiful skin with said tongue.

A minute later, he'd stripped out of everything except his boxer briefs.

A moment after that, the light overhead was off, and he was in bed next to her, pulling her into his arms, tugging the covers up and over them both.

"How did *your* family visit go?" he asked lightly.

Tinkling laughter coated his skin.

Then she told him about the Chubby Bunny contest and her sister gaining a position on a committee she was excited about. She told him about her brother's paper getting published and her dad's peach pie.

She told him about her mom's advice to follow her heart.

"For the record," she said, cuddling into his chest. "She's summoned you to Baltimore at the earliest convenience, and if that convenience doesn't meet her convenience, expect a visit to San Francisco."

He grinned. That wasn't an order he had the least bit of issue following. "I guess I'd better brush up on my Chubby Bunny skills."

A kiss to his throat. "I won't give up my Chubby Bunny title easily."

"Prepare to go down," he teased, pressing a kiss to the top of her head. Movement on his chest that had him glancing down in question. The room was dark, though his eyes had adjusted enough to see the outline of her body. "What are you doing?" he asked when the movement continued.

"I'm waggling my brows," she said. "You said prepare to go down"—a nip to his pectoral—"don't give me that look."

"It's pitch black, what look could I possibly be giving you?"

"The Char-is-cray-cray look," she said, snuggling closer. "I was making a joke." A beat. "And don't tell me it's a bad joke, I know that already."

He snorted. "I love you, Starlight."

"Well, *I* love you, Moonlight."

His chest vibrated with laughter. "What is that?"

"My attempt at a nickname. I have to up my game beyond *baby* and honey."

"Moonlight isn't going to cut it." He ran his hand up and down her back.

"Cupcake?"

"Nope."

"Comet?"

Another snort. "No way."

"Candlelight?"

"Are you sticking with the letter C?"

"Not intentionally." She yawned. "Speedy?"

"Are you trying to insult me?"

Her chuckle slid over his skin. "No," she said, "and you're right. Speedy definitely won't work. How about Lamb Chop?"

"Starlight," he growled.

"I love you," she whispered. "Thank you for needing me, for inviting me into your life. And thank you for giving me these last eight years." She pressed her palm onto his chest. "I feel so lucky to have had the opportunity and a man who'd give up everything for me."

He covered her hand with his own, throat tight. "I want to have all the fancy, romantic words, sweetheart, but none of them come remotely close to being good enough. Just know you're in my blood, my soul. You're burned into my DNA, the marrow of my bones." He held her tightly, stroked a hand down her spine. "You're my heart, Starlight."

"You did fine with the romantic words, baby."

"I like baby," he murmured, and yawned, the last twenty-four hours plus catching up with him.

"I like *you*," she said softly before ordering, "Now sleep."

He let his eyes slide closed on another order he didn't mind following, happy in the knowledge that these were probably the first of many orders from the Harris women in his life and not giving a damn in the least.

Starlight had filled him from the inside out.

———

A week later, after he and Char had flown back to California, after they'd woken up to find the house empty, his mother at work, his father who knew where, Logan got a text.

The first two words made his heart sink.

Your mother . . .

Fuck.

He hadn't heard a word from his parents since that blow-up, and now it appeared that nothing had changed.

Tossing the phone onto the counter in disgust, he went back to meal prepping.

Char was going to a self-defense class that night, but the next day they were finally going up to his cabin. He was endeavoring to pull together enough palatable food that she would want to come back.

"Hey, baby."

Arms wrapped around him from behind, lush breasts pressing to his spine, sending heat arrowing to his groin.

"Hi, Starlight."

"You're slaving away in the kitchen while I go to work?" She pressed a kiss to his back. "Just as it should be."

He spun and took her in his arms. "Just for that, more river walks for you."

"Oh, the horror," she teased. "I have to spend time with the man I love."

"In nature," he said. "You have to spend time in nature with the man you love."

A shrug. "I'm starting to see that *some* nature is okay."

"Oh?"

"I like the big . . ." Her lips curved. "Trees."

He snorted, nuzzled a kiss to her throat . . . just as his phone buzzed again.

"Oh, that's your cell," Char said, slipping out of his arms. "Let me grab it for you."

"I—"

But she'd already picked it up, her eyes widening when she caught a glimpse of the screen.

"Log—"

"It's okay," he said, turning back to the food. "I can't control them. They'll make their own decisions." But his gut had sunk at those words, at the notion that nothing would ever change.

Nothing except him.

Because he wasn't going to be drawn in again.

"Baby."

"I'm fine, Starlight."

"*Baby.*"

The urgency in her tone had him spinning back around. "What?"

"Look."

"I don't need—"

She stepped close and shoved the phone in his face. "Look."

Your mother found a therapist. We're going next week.

The second message was the buzz that Char had heard, and it said, quite simply:

I'm sorry.

His lungs froze just as another message came through. This one was from his mother, and the words made the organs unstick, his heart squeeze hard. Because it didn't start with *Your father is.*

Instead, it read,

I love you. I'm sorry. I'll do better.

"Progress," Char murmured.

"Yes," he said, slipping an arm around her shoulders. "Honestly, I'm a little shocked they've decided to go to therapy."

"I'm not."

He lifted a brow.

"They love you."

He lifted the other.

"You're worth someone making the effort, Logan," she said. "They can see they're hurting you, and both know it needs to stop." Her fingers traced his jaw. "But more than that, I think—I *hope* they're finally understanding that their relationship is worth just as much." She kissed him. "Otherwise, what's the point?"

"The more important point is that I love you."

Her lips curved. "Yeah?"

He kissed her. "Yeah."

"Good"—she nodded at the food laid out on the counter—"then get back to cooking, wench."

Logan burst out laughing, and because he couldn't resist, he kissed the woman who held his heart again, kissed the mischief off her lips, swallowed her giggles, tasted the love on her tongue.

And then he got back into the kitchen while she went to work.

As one did.

Epilogue
Part One

Char, Three Months Later

She closed her laptop in disgust and glared over at her family, who were gathered around the island in her kitchen.

Which had never smelled so good.

Definitely not when she and Logan had begun expanding their cooking repertoire. Speaking of which, they were up to three whole recipes they could consistently make without threatening her smoke detectors.

But that wasn't what had her filled with disgust.

"That blog post is absolutely ridiculous." The sports blog had sounded more gossip site than real sports news reporting—detailing every moment of their "romantic night out" and how besotted she and Logan were.

Yes, they'd actually used the word *besotted.*

Ugh.

Will poked her in the arm when she fell silent, pondering her ability to learn some hacking skills in order to take the drivel down. "You upset because the title is *BAMF Harris tags Walker*?"

She shuddered. "No, I don't mind being called a badass mfer," she said, slanting a look at her grandmother, who was apparently enthralled by her solitaire game.

But Char knew from personal experience that her grandma had big ears.

"Then what, Starlight?" Logan asked, running his fingers down her arm.

"They're saying I tagged you, but *you're* the one who came after me."

"I had to," he said. "I know my stubborn Harris women—"

"Hey!" Amelia and her mom said at once, though both of their faces softened when Logan turned his charming smile on them.

Double ugh.

Mostly because that charming smile worked on her, too.

She glanced back at Logan, wrinkled her nose, and . . . pressed a kiss to his mouth. "I love you," she murmured against his lips, "even if you're a pain in my ass."

He just grinned and then went back to the counter where her mom had set him to shucking corn for the vegetable salad he was learning how to make. God, he was pretty, especially all ready for the season, his diet plan locked in and his body . . . her thighs clenched because there were definite perks to him getting into tip-top shape.

Six-packs and strong thighs. Hip bones and biceps she wanted to lick like a popsicle.

She was drooling over him so intently that she didn't realize the room had gone quiet at first.

Not until her grandmother said, "Well, are you going to open it or not?"

Blinking, she tore her gaze from Log and glanced over at her grandma. "Open what?"

Amelia nudged her, nodded at the counter. "Char-Char."

A box.

There was a box in front of her. A box with a card that had

her name on the envelope. A name that was written in Logan's handwriting.

She looked at him, but he was still deliberately shucking corn.

So, she reached for the envelope.

Will groaned. "Why? Open the big box in front of you!"

Char smiled even though her heart was pounding. "This is my box, and I say I'm going to open the envelope first." She tore open the flap, lips curving at the short note.

For keeping you on even footing during the season.

-L

Amelia snagged it from her before she'd barely processed the words, passing it to Will and then her dad. Char hardly noticed.

Because she was working on the box.

Slitting open one side.

Tearing the paper off.

Opening the white cardboard lid.

Her mom whistled long and low.

Char was feeling the same upon looking at the contents of the box. Sexy, red heels with just the faintest hint of glitter in their fabric, small twinkling stars that both took her breath away and threatened to have her heart pounding out of her chest.

Her eyes flew to Logan's, and he winked.

"Love you, Starlight."

Another nudge from Amelia, and annoyed at her for intruding on the moment, she glared at her sister. "What?"

"There's another box," Amelia said.

Her heart went well beyond pounding. Now, it was stampeding in her chest, threatening to burst free.

Because there was another box.

A small box.

Her fingers shook as she reached for it, but Logan beat her to the punch, snagging it from where it had been nestled between the gorgeous heels and opening it as he knelt in front of her.

It sparkled.

Just like his eyes.

"What do you say, Starlight?" he asked softly. "Will you keep me around even though I currently hold the Chubby Bunny championship title?"

"Because you cheated!" she exclaimed, jumping up.

He stood and caught her around the waist, lips twitching. "We'll have a rematch," he promised, "so long as you answer the question."

"I didn't hear a question."

Lips on her cheek, near her ear. "Technically, there were two in that. But not the most important one." He straightened, cupped her jaw. "I love you to the stars and back, and you're in my heart until it stops beating." Soft fingers on her cheek, wiping a tear she hadn't realized had fallen. "Will you marry me?"

"Will you admit you cheated at Chubby Bun—"

"Char!" her family yelled in unison.

She threw her arms around Logan's neck and kissed him until her lungs burned. "Yes, baby," she whispered when they pulled away. "I'll marry you."

"Thank God for that," her grandma said.

The room filled with laughter. Love and laughter and happiness that was *all* tangled up. It was complicated and messy and reported about on sports blogs . . . and Char couldn't care less.

Because she was building her family.

———

DANI

Shy.

She was painfully shy.

Great with tech. Horrible with people.

But that was okay, because her job *was* tech. As video coach for the Gold, her livelihood depended on how well she could interact with the tech around her.

That tech currently consisted of multiple monitors on her

office wall, a desktop, a laptop, and a trio of tablets. She actually had a dozen tablets at her disposal, but the rest were currently being used by the coaching staff.

The Gold had just finished their third game of the season, and though she wouldn't say her job got lighter as the season progressed, this time in particular was dizzying.

There were new players to get up to speed.

Changes to the system that needed to be addressed.

Specific plays the coaches wanted highlighted.

And she was down her assistant, who was out with the stomach flu, and an intern, who'd lied on his resume and couldn't actually isolate and/or edit video.

Video. Coach.

Both of those were important—okay, both were *critical* to her job.

But, crying over spilled milk and all that. Dani didn't have time for, not when she had enough work for three people and only one person to do it.

She focused on the screen in front of her and began transferring the video.

Then turned and focused on the next one, repeating the process.

Once the third one was complete, she gathered the tablets, pushed out of her chair and hurried into the hall.

Unfortunately, she hurried without looking.

Unfortunately, because the tablets she'd been holding tumbled from her hands, hitting the ground with a sickening *crunch*. Yes, they had protective covers. No, she didn't normally launch them at concrete floors.

Also *unfortunately,* because she crashed into a giant muscled mass of a sweaty man. He was tall and blond and too fucking pretty for her mental well-being, especially with gentle gray eyes sliding to hers.

A sliver of heat slid through her stomach.

Oh, no.

That would not do.

Tearing her eyes away, she dropped to her knees and picked up the first tablet she could reach, running her finger over the screen and checking for damage.

"Do you stroke everything so carefully?"

Desire coated her spine in honey, filled her throat with cotton.

She glanced up, saw that he'd crouched next to her, and in an instant, was lost again in his eyes, the pale gray of the sky hinting at a thunderstorm.

Storm.

Well, that was fitting, considering the storm that had awakened in her the first time she'd seen this man. Through her monitor, just after he'd joined the team. Tall and big and yet somehow still graceful, even despite the beard and the tattoo peeking out of the collar of his jersey. He'd reminded her of a giant grizzly bear, something any smart human had to fight the urge to not cuddle with.

Fluffy, but would tear a woman to shreds with those razor-sharp claws.

"No," she said simply and reached for the next tablet, doing a visual scan this time instead of any *stroking*. When it looked okay, she thrust it at him, at Ethan Rogers, at the sexiest man she'd ever laid eyes on. "Here. This is the one Calle wanted you to have."

"No stroking?" he said, almost lazily, taking the tablet from her with a slow brush of his fingers.

More heat—sparking up her arms, sliding down her torso, pooling in her stomach.

Her words stoppered up in the back of her throat.

She shook her head.

"Dani?" he asked, still crouching next to her. The smell of spice and male should have been off-putting. Instead, it was tempting, drawing her in like catnip, but she couldn't look up at him, not even when he stayed still, stayed near, clearly waiting for her to speak or meet his gaze.

One rough finger brushed the back of her hand.

Gasping, her eyes flew up, collided with his. Her heart absolutely pounded, but other than that single touch, he didn't make any other moves to close the distance between them.

"Why don't you like me?"

Her jaw dropped open. Why didn't *she* like *him?* Dani drooled after Ethan on a regular basis, she had dreams about him, had named her favorite vibrator after him.

See? Good with tech.

People—including the gorgeous man all of two feet away—horrible.

But what could she say? It wasn't like she was going to share the name of her vibrator. Hell, she might as well be honest, she wasn't going to share *anything.* This is what she did.

She got shy. She got quiet. She came off as a royal bitch.

"Y-you're fine," she finally managed, reaching for the last tablet, intending to find a way to bolt, to end her misery and GTFO.

But he stood when she did, those gray irises dancing with mirth. "Fine?"

"I—uh—" Her cheeks burned, and worse, she felt tears prickle at the backs of her eyes.

Ugh. She hated that she did this, too.

Pushing past him, she tried to bolt.

"Hey," he said, catching her arm. "*Hey.* I'm just teasing."

She shrugged, stepped away. "Okay."

A soft chuckle. "I actually came to find you."

Her heart pounded. *He'd* come to find *her?* What universe was she currently living in?

"I wanted to ask you a question—"

Ah. This was how all of these conversations began. They came. They needed help with their TV or laptop or cell phone. Ethan, she guessed, would need laptop help. He looked like he could handle a cell or a television.

And no, don't ask her how she knew what he needed help with, okay? She'd been to this rodeo many a time before. Dani's tech guru-ness was a gift that had been bestowed upon her at birth . . . okay, *fine*, it had been honed by many lonely preteen and teenage years.

"I can fix your computer," she said, trying to pretend that she wasn't miserable at the prospect, that she didn't want someone to come to her for once for some other reason.

She wouldn't know what to do with them if they did.

"What?"

Perhaps, her guru skills were out of practice. She hadn't been hit up too often since she'd joined the Gold.

"You need help with your phone?"

He frowned, shook his head. "No."

"Your TV?"

"No, Dani," Ethan said on a husky laugh, and she ignored the prickles of desire trailing over her skin.

"Okay." She turned away.

"Are you seeing anyone?"

Slowly, she spun back, eyes wide.

"That was my question," he said when she just stared at him in shock.

A slow shake of her head.

He smiled.

And she actually felt her brain cells collide and fizzle into smoke. That smile was dangerous, could without a doubt, turn her stupid. *Really* stupid.

"Good," he murmured. Swallowing hard, she nodded, turned away again.

"Will you go out with me?"

Her fingers went limp. The tablets hit the ground.

This time the *crunch* sounded much more ominous.

Or maybe that was just her heart.

———

Thank you for reading! I hope you loved meeting Char and Logan! The next book in the Gold Hockey series is CAGED. **She'd thought he was going to ask her to fix his computer. Instead, he'd asked her *out*.**
CLICK HERE TO READ CAGED NOW>

And if you enjoyed CHARGING, you'll love the sexy, sweet, and close-knit Breakers Hockey crew. The first book in the series, BROKEN, is now live!

———

EXCERPT FROM BROKEN
Breakers Hockey, Book 1
Available now!
READ BROKEN HERE NOW>

LUC

He was forty years old.

He was single.

He was happy that way.

Sighing, he lifted his beer to his lips and internally shook his head at himself. He wasn't happy. He was miserable and lonely. Oh, and he might as well add fucking pathetic to that tally.

Because the woman he was in love with was married.

To a perfectly nice man who loved her and cared for her and treated her like the fucking queen she was.

But that didn't help Luc or his loneliness problem.

So, he was drinking a beer, trying to forget the woman he'd fallen for two years before, only to find out she was married two weeks later. Lexi was with the legal team for the Baltimore Breakers, the NHL team he was the GM for. He'd fallen hard over her skills at contract negotiations, fallen harder when she'd proven to be whip-smart and hilarious in equal parts.

Then he'd run into her and her husband while grabbing a cup of coffee.

"*Luc,*" she'd said, smiling up at him, its intensity punching him right in the gut, "*this is my husband, Caleb.*"

Caleb?

What kind of name was that?

"Fucking hell," Luc muttered, taking another sip, hating the other man, and yet respecting him, because there was love there.

Deeply rooted love that spoke of a happy relationship.

He hated it.

Cue lonely, pathetic asshole.

Sighing, he stood up and turned toward his front door, reaching for the handle when he heard the screech of tires.

Spinning, he watched the car pull to a stop, the driver's door open, and Lexi tumble out.

He was running before he realized he'd moved, reaching her in seconds.

"What's the matter?" he asked, noting the tears, the reddened eyes, the mascara blackening the skin beneath her eyes. "Lexi, are you hurt?"

She nodded, threw herself into his arms.

"Where, honey?" he asked. "Where?"

Lexi tore herself away, and the pain in her gaze shredded his insides. "It's Caleb."

<u>READ BROKEN HERE NOW></u>

———

Her life was a disaster...Don't miss the hilarious Life Sucks series, starting with TRAIN WRECK. Derek Cashette was determined to salvage the train wreck of her life...and she was just as determined *not* to let him be the hero.

DOWNLOAD TRAIN WRECK FOR FREE at www.elisefaber.com/train-wreck

I so appreciate your help in spreading the word about my books, including sharing with friends! Please leave a review on your favorite book site!

You can also join my Facebook group, the Fabinators, for exclusive giveaways and sneak peeks of future books.

SIGN UP FOR ELISE FABER'S NEWSLETTER HERE: https://www.elisefaber.com/newsletter

Wanna find out about that date? ;)
Caged available now!
Get your copy at https://www.elisefaber.com/caged

———

Want to know what's up with Caleb?
Broken, Book 1 of the Baltimore Breakers series.
https://www.elisefaber.com/broken

———

Want a free bonus story? Hate missing Elise's new releases? Love contests, exclusive excerpts and giveaways?
Then signup for Elise's newsletter here!
https://www.elisefaber.com/newsletter

———

And join Elise's fan group, the Fabinators https://www.facebook.com/groups/fabinators for insider information, sneak peaks at new releases, and fun freebies! Hope to see you there!

GOLD HOCKEY SERIES

Gold Hockey

Did you miss any of the Gold Hockey books?
Find information about the full series here.
Or keep reading for a sneak peek into each of the books below!

Blocked
Gold Hockey Book #1
Get your copy at https://www.elisefaber.com/blocked

BRIT

The first question Brit always got when people found out she played ice hockey was *"Do you have all of your teeth?"* The second was *"Do you, you know, look at the guys in the locker room?"*

The first she could deal with easily—flash a smile of her full set of chompers, no gaps in sight. The second was more problematic. Especially since it was typically accompanied by a smug smile or a coy wink.

Of course she looked. *Everybody* looked once. Everyone snuck a glance, made a judgment that was quickly filed away and shoved deep down into the recesses of their mind.

And she meant *way* down.

Because, dammit, she was there to play hockey, not assess her teammates' six packs. If she wanted to get her man candy fix, she could just go on social media. There were shirtless guys for days filling her feed.

But that wasn't the answer the media wanted.

Who cared about locker room dynamics? Who gave a damn whether or not she, as a typical heterosexual woman, found her fellow players attractive?

Yet for some inane reason, it *did* matter to people.

Brit wasn't stupid. The press wanted a story. A scandal. They were desperate for her to fall for one of her teammates—or better yet the captain from their rival team—and have an affair that was worthy of a romantic comedy.

She'd just gotten very good at keeping her love life—as nonexistent as it was—to herself, gotten very good at not reacting in any perceptible way to the insinuations.

So when the reporter asked her the same set of questions for the thousandth time in her twenty-six years, she grinned—showing off those teeth—and commented with a sweetly innocent "Could've sworn you were going to ask me about the coed showers." She waited for the room-at-large to laugh then said, "Next question, please."

–Get your copy at https://www.elisefaber.com/blocked

Backhand
Gold Hockey Book #2
Get your copy at https://www.elisefaber.com/backhand

SARA

"Sorry I messed up your sketch," he rumbled.

She nibbled on the side of her mouth, biting back a smile. "Sorry I stole your hand for so long."

He shrugged. "My mom's an artist. I get it."

Well, there went her battle with the smile. Her lips twitched and her teeth came out of hiding. If there was one thing that Sara had, it was her smile. It had been her trademark in her competition days.

Which were long over.

Her mouth flattened out, the grin slipping away. Time to go, time to forget, to move on, to rebuild. "Thanks," she said and extended a hand.

Then winced and dropped it when her ribs cried out in protest.

"You okay?" he asked, head tilting, eyes studying her.

"Fine." And out popped her new smile. The fake one. Careful of her aching side, she shrugged into her backpack. "I've got to go." She turned, ponytail flapping through the hair to land on her opposite shoulder.

"That—" He touched her arm. "Wait. I *know* I know you."

She froze. That was the second time he'd said that, and now they were getting into dangerous territory. Recognition meant . . . no. She couldn't.

There had been a time when *everyone* had known her. Her face on Wheaties boxes, her smile promoting toothpaste and credit cards alike.

That wasn't her life any longer.

"Thanks again. Bye." She started to hurry away.

"Wait." A hand dropped on to her shoulder, thwarting her escape, and she hissed in pain.

"Sorry," he said, but he didn't release her. Instead, he shifted his grip from her aching shoulder down to her elbow and when she didn't protest, he exerted gentle pressure until Sara was facing him again. "It's just that know I *know* you."

No. This wasn't happening.

"You're Sara Jetty."

Her body went tense.

Oh God. This was *so* happening.

"It's me." He touched his chest like she didn't know he was talking about himself, and even as she was finally recognizing the color of his eyes, the familiar curve of his lips and line of his jaw, he said the worst thing ever, "Mike Stewart."

Oh *shit*.

—Get your copy at https://www.elisefaber.com/backhand

Boarding
Gold Hockey Book #3
Get your copy at https://www.elisefaber.com/boarding

MANDY

Hockey players had the *best* asses.

No pancake bottoms, these men—and *women*—could fill out a pair of jeans. She wanted to squeeze it, to nibble it, bounce a dime—

Mandy dropped her chin to her chest, losing sight of the Sorting Hat cupcakes she'd been pondering.

Blane with his yummy ass had a unique way of distracting her.

No, it wasn't even distraction, per se. He had *always* been able to get under her skin.

And that was very, very bad for her.

"Ugh," she said, tossing her phone onto her desk and standing, knowing that she wouldn't be able to sit still now.

Nope, she needed about forty laps in the pool and a good hard fu—

Run, her mind blurted, almost yelling at the mental voice of her inner devil. *A good hard run.*

Unfortunately, the cajoling tone wasn't completely drowned out. *Some sexy horizontal time with Blane would be more fun—*

But the rest of the enticing words were lost as the roar of the crowd suddenly penetrated through the layers of concrete. Her stomach twisted. Mandy could tell, even before her eyes made it to the television, that it wasn't in celebration of a goal or a good hit either.

This was fury, a collective of outrage.

She was on her feet the moment she saw the prone form lying so still face down on the ice.

Her gut twisted when she spotted the curving line of a numeral two on the back of the player's jersey.

"Not him," she said and the words were familiar, a sentiment she had whispered, had *prayed* a thousand times before. She needed the camera angle to shift, for her to be able to see more clearly *who* was hurt. "Not him."

Then Dr. Carter was on the ice and the player moved slightly, rolling away from the camera, giving a full shot of his back and the matching twos adorning his jersey.

Fuck. Not him. Not Blane.

And that was when she saw the pool of blood.

—Get your copy at https://www.elisefaber.com/boarding

Benched
Gold Hockey Book #4
Get your copy at https://www.elisefaber.com/benched

MAX

He started up the car, listening and chiming in at the right places as Brayden talked all things video game.

But his mind was unfortunately stuck on the fact that women were not to be trusted.

He snorted. Brit—the Gold's goalie and the first female in the NHL—and Mandy—the team's head trainer—would smack him around for that sentiment, so he silently amended it to: *most* women were not to be trusted.

There. Better, see?

Somehow, he didn't think they'd see.

He parked in the school's lot, walked Brayden in, and received the appropriate amount of scorn from the secretary for being thirty minutes late to school, then bent to hug Brayden.

"I'll pick you up today," he said.

Brayden smiled and hugged him tightly. Then he whispered something in his ear that hit Max harder than a two-by-four to the temple.

"If you got me a new mom, we wouldn't be late for school."

"Wh-what?" Max stammered.

"Please, Dad? Can you?"

And with that mind fuck of an ask, Brayden gave him one more squeeze and pushed through the door to the playground, calling, "Love you!" over his shoulder.

Then he was gone, and Max was standing in the office of his son's school struggling to comprehend if he had actually just heard what he'd heard.

A new mom?

Fuck his life.

—Get your copy at https://www.elisefaber com/benched

Breakaway
Gold Hockey Book #5
Get your copy at https://www.elisefaber.com/breakaway

BLUE

"Thanks for the ride."

"Try not to go out and get a fresh bimbo to ride tonight. I hear STIs on are the rise in the city."

Blue sighed, turned back to face her. "Really?"

She shrugged, smirk teasing the edges of her mouth, drawing his focus to the lushness of her lips. "Just watching out for Max's teammate."

He rolled his eyes. "Not hardly."

"Okay, how about I'm trying to prevent you from spreading STIs to the female populace."

"I'm clean, and I'm smart," he told her. "Condoms all the way."

"Ew."

Except there was something about the way she said it that made Blue stiffen and take notice. Because . . . he stared into her eyes, watched as the pale blue darkened to royal, saw her lips part, and her suck in a breath.

Holy shit.

"You're attracted to me."

Her jaw dropped. "No fucking way," she said, too quickly, pink dancing on the edges of her cheekbones. "You're delusional."

Blue got close.

Real close.

Anna licked her lips.

And fuck it all, he kissed that luscious mouth.

—Breakaway, https://www.elisefaber.com/breakaway

Breakout
Gold Hockey Book #6
Get your copy at https://www.elisefaber.com/breakout

PR-Rebecca

A fucking perfect hockey fairy tale.

Shaking her head, because she knew firsthand that fairy tales didn't exist outside of rom-coms and occasionally between alpha sports heroes and their chosen mates, Rebecca slipped through the corridor and stepped onto the Gold's bench.

Lots of dudes in suits—of both the boardroom *and* the hockey variety—were hugging.

On the ice. Near the goals. On the bench.

It was a proverbial hug-fest.

And she was the cynical bitch who couldn't enjoy the fact

that the team she was with had just won the biggest hockey prize of them all.

"I knew you'd be like this."

Rebecca turned her focus from Brit, who was skating with the huge silver cup, to the man—no, to the *boy* because no matter how pretty and yummy he was, Kevin was still a decade younger than her—leaning oh so casually against the boards.

"Nice goal," she told him.

A shrug. "Blue made a nice pass."

And dammit, the fact that he wasn't an arrogant son of a bitch made her like him more.

She nodded at the cup. "You should go have your turn."

"I'll get mine," he said with another shrug.

She frowned, honestly confused. "You don't want—"

Suddenly he was in front of her on the bench, towering over her even though she was wearing her four-inch power heels. "You know what I want?"

Rebecca couldn't speak. Her breath had whooshed out of her in the presence of all that sweaty, hockey god-ness. Fuck he was pretty and gorgeous and . . . so fucking masculine that her thighs actually clenched together.

She wanted to climb him like a stripper pole.

"Do you?" he asked again when her words wouldn't come. "Want to know what I want?"

She nodded.

He bent, lips to her ear. "You, babe," he whispered. "I. Want. You."

Then he straightened and jumped back onto the ice, leaving her gaping after him like she had less than two brain cells in her skull.

The worst part?

She wanted him, too.

Had wanted him since the moment she'd laid eyes on the sexy as sin hockey god.

"Trouble," she murmured. "I'm in *so* much fucking trouble."

—Breakout, https://www.elisefaber.com/breakout

Checked

Gold Hockey Book #7
Get your copy at https://www.elisefaber.com/checked

"Rebecca."

She kept walking.

She might work with Gabe, but she sure as heck wasn't on speaking terms with him. He'd dismissed her work, ignored her contribution to the team. He'd made her feel small and unimportant and—

She kept walking.

"*Rebecca.*"

Not happening. Her car was in sight, thank fuck. She beeped the locks, reached for the handle.

He caught her arm.

"Baby—"

"I am *not* your baby, and you don't get to touch me." She ripped herself free, started muttering as she reached for the handle of her car again. "You don't even like me."

He stepped close, real close. Not touching her, not pushing the boundary she'd set, and yet he still got really freaking close. Her breath caught, her chin lifted, her pulse picked up. "That. Is. Where. You're. Wrong."

She froze.

"What?"

His mouth dropped to her ear, still not touching, but near enough that she could feel his hot breath.

"I like you, Rebecca. Too fucking much."

Then he turned and strode away.

—Checked, https://www.elisefaber.com/checked

Coasting
Gold Hockey Book #8
Get your copy at https://www.elisefaber.com/coasting

COOP

Without thinking, he caught her arm.

"You're not okay."

She shuddered to a stop when he touched her, not fighting the grip, chin dropping to her chest. "No," she said, "you're right. I'm not okay."

"Who was on the phone?" he asked gently.

Her jaw went tight. "My ex."

Fury blazed through him. "Did he hurt you?" he growled.

A shake of her head. "Not like you're thinking." She sucked in a breath. "He broke my heart."

Coop's own heart gave a twinge. "I'm sorry, Calle. That's—"

"Fucking stupid." Another tear joined the first, dripping down the pale skin of her cheek.

"It's not stupid to have loved someone," he said gently.

Her eyes went fierce. "It's incredibly stupid when the person who supposedly loves you right back doesn't give a damn that you're pregnant."

His jaw fell open. He knew it did.

But Calle? Even, gentle *Calle* had gotten knocked up and—

"Yup," she said, brushing by him. "See? Really *fucking* stupid."

And without another word, she disappeared into the rink.

—Coasting, https://www.elisefaber.com/coasting

Centered
Gold Hockey Book #9
Get your copy at https://www.elisefaber.com/centered

"Watch out!"

The warning came a second too late.

He'd already stepped off the curb, already put himself in range of the car that was blowing through the red light, tearing through the intersection, not giving a shit that there were pedestrians walking—

Well, of all the ways to go, at least this would be quick.

But just as the car came within an inch of him, Liam found himself jerked back onto the curb, his one-hundred-and-eighty-pound frame becoming unwieldy and clumsy.

Kind of like on the ice over the last few years.

That was his last thought before he found himself sprawled, ass first, on the San Franciscan sidewalk.

Gross.

"What. The. *Fuck?*" a female voice snapped.

The same female voice that had warned him.

"Do you have a fucking death wish?" she yelled, causing his eyes to snap open, making him look up at an angel . . . a foot tapping, arms crossed, seriously pissed, and seemingly way too small to have been able to haul his ass back onto the curb female.

Liam thought he just might have that death wish.

Especially if it meant he got to be rescued by a woman who looked like an angel. He opened his mouth to reply.

But apparently didn't work fast enough.

Because the woman, the beautiful, curvy female, made a disgusted noise and strode away from him.

He watched her go, watched that gorgeous ass stride down the sidewalk, and stop outside a storefront.

And suddenly, he thought that, hockey or not, he might just want to stay in San Francisco after all.

—Centered, https://www.elisefaber.com/centered

ALSO BY ELISE FABER

Billionaire's Club (all stand alone)

Bad Night Stand

Bad Breakup

Bad Husband

Bad Hookup

Bad Divorce

Bad Fiancé

Bad Boyfriend

Bad Blind Date

Bad Wedding

Bad Engagement

Bad Bridesmaid

Bad Swipe

Bad Girlfriend

Bad Best Friend

Bad Billionaire's Quickies

Gold Hockey (all stand alone)

Blocked

Backhand

Boarding

Benched

Breakaway

Breakout

Checked

Coasting

Centered

Charging

Caged

Crashed

A Gold Christmas

Cycled

Caught

Cap

Breakers Hockey (all stand alone)

<u>Broken</u>

<u>Boldly</u>

<u>Breathless</u>

<u>Ballsy</u>

<u>Bewitched</u>

Love, Action, Camera (all stand alone)

Dotted Line

Action Shot

Close-Up

End Scene

Meet Cute

Love After Midnight **(all stand alone)**

Rum And Notes

Virgin Daiquiri

On The Rocks

Sex On The Seats

Life Sucks Series (all stand alone)

Train Wreck

Hot Mess

Dumpster Fire

Clusterf*@k

FUBAR (March 29,2022)

Roosevelt Ranch Series (all stand alone, series complete)

Disaster at Roosevelt Ranch

Heartbreak at Roosevelt Ranch

Collision at Roosevelt Ranch

Regret at Roosevelt Ranch

Desire at Roosevelt Ranch

Phoenix Series (read in order)

Phoenix Rising

Dark Phoenix

Phoenix Freed

Phoenix: LexTal Chronicles (rereleasing soon, stand alone, Phoenix world)

From Ashes

In Flames

To Smoke

KTS Series

Riding The Edge

Crossing The Line

Leveling The Field

Scorching The Earth

Cocky Heroes World

Tattooed Troublemaker

ABOUT THE AUTHOR

USA Today bestselling author, Elise Faber, loves chocolate, Star Wars, Harry Potter, and hockey (the order depending on the day and how well her team -- the Sharks! -- are playing). She and her husband also play as much hockey as they can squeeze into their schedules, so much so that their typical date night is spent on the ice. Elise changes her hair color more often than some people change their socks, loves sparkly things, and is the mom to two exuberant boys. She lives in Northern California. Connect with her in her Facebook group, the Fabinators or find more information about her books at www.elisefaber.com.

f facebook.com/elisefaberauthor

a amazon.com/author/elisefaber

BB bookbub.com/profile/elise-faber

O instagram.com/elisefaber

g goodreads.com/elisefaber

P pinterest.com/elisefaberwrite

www.ingramcontent.com/pod-product-compliance
Lightning Source LLC
Chambersburg PA
CBHW071547110726
47908CB00007B/2019